I0630995

THE QUEST

FOR

ARANWA

DONNY HUNT

This is a work of fiction. Names, characters, places, and incidents are products of the author's imagination or are used fictitiously and are not to be construed as real. Any resemblance to actual events, locations, organizations, or persons, living or dead, is entirely coincidental.

World Castle Publishing, LLC
Pensacola, Florida
Copyright © Donny Hunt 2017
Paperback ISBN: 9781629896533
eBook ISBN: 9781629896540
First Edition World Castle Publishing, LLC, March 20, 2017
http://www.worldcastlepublishing.com

Licensing Notes

All rights reserved. No part of this book may be used or reproduced in any manner whatsoever without written permission, except in the case of brief quotations embodied in articles and reviews.
Cover: Melissa Davis
Editor: Maxine Bringenberg

PROLOGUE

It wasn't supposed to be like this. The future of mankind was supposed to be one of leisure and convenience. It was supposed to be filled with flying vehicles and cities in the sky and glorious technology.

It didn't happen that way. Complacency, selfishness, and laziness were mankind's downfall, and they were nearly its extinction. By the time man realized that their time was running out and Earth was dying, it was nearly too late.

The threat of impending doom finally motivated mankind to put aside their differences to work together. Harnessing the best attributes of man — imagination, ingenuity, and hard work — man looked again to the stars for their salvation.

By either luck, fate, or divine providence, they found it; a distant planet that was nearly identical to Earth, devoid of sentient life but full of natural resources. It was a planet that could sustain humanity for countless millennia. They just had to get there.

While the scientists and engineers raced to build crafts that would take mankind to its new home, the rich and powerful jockeyed to secure positions aboard them. If Earth was doomed, it was in the best interests of humanity to save its best and brightest first. The battle to secure one of the first seats was intensely fought.

It was late in the process before some finally posed the questions: How would a group of politicians and millionaires settle an untamed world? Did they really want to be the guinea pigs on an untested rocket?

So The Powers That Be changed course. Instead, one thousand families were carefully chosen to be the first. They were chosen based on skills and genetics. Each family had to have at least one child, and multiple children had to be mixed gender. They carefully screened for genetic defects. No one with a strong religious belief was accepted, because no one wanted a holy war erupting in the middle of the cosmos. They chose farmers and ranchers, doctors and nurses, architects and construction workers, hunters and survival experts. These pioneers would, in turn, begin to lay the foundation for those to follow.

These thousand families boarded three identical deep space transports at three different locations, each carrying the hope of an entire planet on their shoulders. They knew they would never see land again, as the trip would take hundreds of years to complete. A world-wide audience watched with bated breath as the ships prepared to launch.

The first problem occurred almost immediately. A shoddy weld doomed the third transport, which came apart and exploded in a massive fireball in the skies over Germany just after takeoff. Had that transport been the first to launch, the others might have been aborted. However, the German transport went last, and the other two ships streaked into the heavens, their passengers unaware of the tragedy behind them.

Once free of Earth's orbit, the remaining transports set their courses for a truly New World, and the passengers settled into their new lives aboard the metal craft. Along the way, a critical computer error doomed the second transport in flight. The navigation systems shut down and the ship drifted helplessly off course, stranding its passengers in the heavens.

Finally, the third ship reached the destination, a planet simply labeled T-1883. Only three hundred of the original thousand families reached their destination. During the flight, children had grown, married, and reproduced, and the races mixed until the settlers who emerged on Eden were one race. Old bigotries were lost to the stars.

These new settlers immediately began to make a home for their brothers and sisters to follow. They had limited supplies and learned quickly to live off the land. Though life on this new world was difficult, the settlers comforted themselves in the knowledge that additional people and supplies were sure to follow.

That never happened. The failures of the second and third transports rattled the project leaders, who scratched any additional launches until they could deem the massive transports safe. Earth's clock ran out before that happened, leaving those three hundred families as the sole remains of mankind. They would have to make it on their own, without all the conveniences and technology that they had left behind. Man, would have to start from scratch.

As time passed, the settlers scattered. They learned about their new land. They created towns and roads, and their society began to resemble that of Earth's past. The lure of freedom and adventure drew some to push into undiscovered lands, while some settled comfortably and built cities.

In time, two nations emerged. In the West was the nation of Iridia. Iridia was a rugged land, a place of extremes, where green prairies gave way to rocky mountains and arid deserts. The Iridians were a determined and humble people. They learned to make the best out of what little they had and developed a communal attitude. Their settlements were often far apart, and each became self-sufficient communities in and of themselves. This often led to conflicts with other settlements and led to an often fractured nation.

In the East, the land of Cadoa was a land of lush valleys and thick forests. The weather was mild and wet, and natural bodies of water were plentiful. It was a land great for farming and hunting and timber. The people of Cadoa became noted for their willingness to push the boundaries. They were a people who craved exploration and adventure, and their stubborn determination allowed them to overcome almost any obstacle.

They were also a rowdy people, possessive of what they had and distrustful of the machinations of government. So as civilization grew behind them, those on the Cadoan frontier continued to press onward, interested more in their own success than that of the group.

The nations bordered each other at a gently flowing river that flowed into the foothills of a massive mountain range. Decades of fierce fighting broke out between the two nations as each pushed to absorb the other. Eventually, with neither side proving capable of overcoming the other, a fragile peace was struck.

In the interior life became easier, but on the border the fighting never completely stopped. Both governments agreed to let the populace settle their differences locally. As a result, life on the border was one of constant struggle, and the people of both nations continued to be distrustful of the other.

Beyond the borders and in the mountains, the river split into two forks, one that flowed southeast and one southwest. Over the mountains and between the rivers lay a land of unparalleled beauty; one that encompassed almost every climate within it. There was fertile farmland, rich vegetation, plentiful game, thick woods, plenty of water and, at its southern terminus, an expansive sea. It was a glorious, untouched paradise, and both nations hungered to possess it. It was named Aranwa.

Obtaining Aranwa was no easy task. The rivers were fast flowing, rocky, and treacherous, making crossing massive amounts of men and supplies impossible. The mountains were massive and its weather harsh. No explorer had ever successfully crossed its peaks. The sea coast was protected by jagged rocks and fierce predators.

The Cadoans wanted Aranwa, but the government was gridlocked and lacked the cohesion and resources to put together a proper expedition. The Iridians, being a less ambitious people, gazed on Aranwa with a mixture of wonder and fear while a military coup against their king threw the nation into chaos. Colonization was put on hold as civil war erupted.

In the meantime, Aranwa sat there; a gleaming treasure waiting for whoever chose to take it.

CHAPTER 1

Aribeth Fuller stood on the wood plank walkway across from her childhood home and took a long look around. It had only been two years since Father had sent her away to school, and the little community had grown so much. It was becoming an actual town now, with defined roads and oil lanterns posted on every other corner to provide light for night travel.

Aribeth was a slight girl with a light complexion and chestnut hair that hung in a single, heavy braid down the center of her back. One wild strand had broken loose and hung in front of her right eye, causing her to swat it away every so often, though she knew it would snap right back into place. She wore her school uniform, which consisted of tight black pants with the legs tucked into high black boots, and a white shirt under a thick black coat.

It seemed so much longer that she'd been gone, and she realized immediately that she had become spoiled to the trappings of life up north, where progress came much faster. She had to fight the urge to look down her nose at the muddy streets and the poorly constructed wooden homes that made up Bretonville. She'd spent too much time around the well-to-do and their finely constructed homes. She'd forgotten that here on the frontier, everything was built to be serviceable and simple. The people here had no want for elegance.

She glanced overhead. Echonos, the Eternal Moon, kept his

constant vigil directly overhead, shining in all its pale glory. With dusk approaching rapidly, soon Akil, the Traveling Moon, would begin its nightly stroll across the sky, bathing everything in her soft purple glow. She thought back on the many nights she had scampered up the natural mounds outside of town to greet Akil's nightly appearance like the return of a long lost friend.

Aribeth sighed heavily and stepped down off the platform into the soggy street. A fine mist hung in the air, glazing everything and everyone with a sheen of moisture. She stepped quickly across, darting between villagers pushing carts of produce home after a long day trading at market. Judging from the loads she saw on the carts, the fields were producing nicely, just as Father had predicted they would when he chose to settle here.

She stepped up on the platform on the other side of the street and took a moment to scrape the bottom of her boots on the edge to remove the mud. If she had been thinking about it, she would have worn more appropriate attire than her uniform, but she had hardly been concerned about her clothing when she received her mother's desperate cry.

The Fuller residence was a modest one, surprising considering that this town wouldn't exist were it not for the vision of Breton Fuller. The town bore his name, an honor bestowed by the townspeople, not by him. Breton Fuller was, in his way, an egotistical man, but he took great pains not to show it outwardly.

She entered without knocking, a custom that ran counter to the manners they had tried so desperately to impart at Houland Academy. This was her home, no matter how long she had been away, and manners could be damned. She had little use for them. With each passing moment, the girl she had been came flooding back, undoing all of that fancy schooling Father had paid for. She was the girl that her classmates had derisively called Prairie Flower. She never let on that she found the nickname to be an honor, not an insult. It kept her from becoming one of them.

Mother was sitting in her chair, rocking nervously back and forth and watching the door when Aribeth walked in. The heavy winter drapes were still hung, blocking all light from outside, while two small lanterns tried and failed to beat back the shadows. Mother was up and on her in an instant, sweeping Aribeth up in an embrace that was more bitter than sweet. "Oh, my sweet girl," Mother whimpered in her ear. "I've missed you so much."

"I missed you too, Momma," Aribeth responded, almost losing her composure as the words slipped out of her mouth. She fought to hold on, and once she was sure she had reined her emotions in, she gently pushed out of her mother's arms. "Where is he?" Mother looked over her shoulder at their closed bedroom door. Aribeth nodded. "Do you mind?"

"No child. He has been waiting." Mother was bringing herself back under control as well, that old Fuller reserve kicking into high gear for them both. Aribeth pulled away and began walking across the floor, her footfalls heavy against the wood floors. The sound took her back again as she remembered the same sound announcing her father's return at the end of a hard day.

She paused briefly at the door with her hand on the door handle. She was reluctant to go in, to see what awaited her on the other side. Aribeth took a moment to recall all those old memories and hold them close to remember her father as what he was, not whatever shell of a man was laying on the other side of the door. She took just a moment to do this because Aribeth knew that Father was running short on moments.

Aribeth did her best to prepare herself as she pushed the door open and stepped quickly inside, pulling the door closed behind her quietly. Father was lying in the bed she had watched him carve with his own hands. The massive bed swallowed him now. He was thin and gaunt, sickly pale, his mouth open slightly and his breaths coming in jagged, uneven gasps. His hair was a wiry wisp on top of his head.

There was a single chair at his bedside, and Aribeth pulled it as close as she could before settling in. She was certain that Mother had not left his side until now. How long had he been this way? How long had he been sick and they had never told her? Aribeth steadied herself, driving her anger away. This was not the time for selfishness. He would not have wanted her to worry or give her an excuse to leave school.

Aribeth reached out gingerly, taking one of Father's hands in hers. His eyes opened slowly. With a great effort, he turned his head, but there was no stopping the smile that spread across his weary face when he saw her. "My Aribeth," he whispered. "Come home at last."

I never wanted to leave, she thought. She scolded herself internally. "I would have come sooner."

"I know," he rasped again. "I know. I've missed...you. Regretted...sending you away." It was difficult for him to talk, the effort taking air he just couldn't pull into his lungs anymore.

"Well, I made it and that is what matters. I will not leave you again."

Father chuckled, and it triggered a coughing fit that made his entire body quiver. "Not long...for you to stay."

Aribeth knew that he wanted to say more so she gently rubbed his hand. "You don't need to talk, Father. I am here and I will not leave you."

Father nodded in understanding and turned his head away. They sat in silence as Father stared at the ceiling, Aribeth listening to his labored breathing for several minutes. When he had finally gathered enough air to speak again, Father whispered without looking at her. "I never...loved...on you enough, girl. Never told you...."

"I never doubted your feelings for me, Father," she answered him. Her voice sounded much stronger and self-assured in her ears than she felt in her heart. "You didn't need to tell me."

Again, he nodded that he understood and went silent. To see him like this was tearing Aribeth apart, but she knew that she couldn't show it. She had to stay strong. She bit into her bottom lip to stop tears from forming in her soft brown eyes.

After several more minutes passed, Father spoke again. "I have…something…for you. Something…I need done. Something only…you…can do." He slowly turned toward her again. His body may have been weak, but his eyes still held his strength and they focused on her now. "Promise me."

"Whatever you need," Aribeth answered, though her mind raced. What could he possibly have for her to do? Knowing Father, it wouldn't be easy. Nothing was ever easy with him.

"I need you…to repeat…what I've done…here. In Aranwa."

"What?" Aribeth jerked her hand away from his and darted up out of the chair, tipping it over.

"Is everything all right in there?" Mother asked through the door, her voice filled with worry.

"Yes, Mother," Aribeth called, feeling slightly embarrassed. Realizing that there was no better way of asking, she finally blurted out. "Are you mad? Has the sickness gotten to your head?" It was a legitimate question.

"No child," he wheezed. "I…have been there. It is…glorious land. Ripe…for the taking. I was going…to do it…myself. But…."

"You are dreaming, Father. Aranwa—"

With a grunt, Breton Fuller pushed himself up and leaned towards his daughter. "Is your legacy," he hissed. For that one moment, he was himself again, strong and unwavering. Then his momentary surge expired and Father collapsed back onto the bed. Aribeth hurried to his side to rearrange him.

13

"Father," she said with reprimand in her voice. "You must not act like that. You don't have the energy. And I am not interested in a legacy. I'm only sixteen."

"Old enough," he struggled to say. "You're the only one... who...can do it."

Aribeth fixed the chair and sat back down, taking his hand in hers once more. "What about the boys? They are big and strong and much better suited —"

"The boys...," he grunted again, "are...big and strong. But not...leaders. They don't have...vision. You...are...the one."

She sat and stewed and thought it over. Father himself had not been much older than she was now when he had started his first enterprise. Age, as she well knew, meant very little out here. You grew up fast or you didn't grow up at all. After a minute, another question came to her. Aribeth licked her lips and leaned forward to whisper in Father's ear. She was afraid to ask the question out loud.

"Did the Ministry ask you to do this?"

Father coughed/laughed again, his whole body racking. "The Ministry...waits...for others...to do...the work...then... takes...the credit. They...are...nothing."

"But Father, I would hate for you to get in trouble." He smiled again and twisted his head slightly. It took a moment for Aribeth to realize what she had said. "Of course that doesn't matter to you, but would you want me to get in trouble with the Ministry?"

"The Ministry...has no say...in Aranwa. It is not...their land. Yet." He swallowed and the act was difficult for him. She could almost see the life draining out of him. His gazed fixed on the ceiling but she doubted that he was seeing it any longer. "Promise me, child," he said again, his voice stronger than it had been.

Aribeth knew what he needed to hear in order to be at peace. She also knew that if she said it, then she would be bound to follow through with it. Father had deeply instilled in her the meaning of one's word. Could she make this promise to him? Did she have a choice? Finally, Aribeth bowed her head. "I will, Father. For you."

"Good," he whispered. "In my bag...is all...you'll need."

"I know the bag," she said softly, patting his hand again. "Rest now, Father. You have earned it."

Father did not acknowledge her. He had what he wanted. Aribeth sat and watched him as he breathed ever more slowly. Time ceased to exist for them in that tiny room. She marked it not in minutes but in breaths. Fatigue and sorrow threatened to overtake her repeatedly, but she resisted them, forcing her eyes to remain open. Aribeth would not allow herself to fall asleep as long as Father still lived. Sometime long after Akil had finished her nightly jaunt across the sky, his hand went slack and his skin turned cold. Only then, when she was certain that he had gone, did she allow herself to cry.

Once the tears stopped flowing, Aribeth wiped the last lingering wetness from her cheeks and began to think. His bag. Aribeth searched the bedroom and found what she was looking for in the bottom of his closet. She brought it back to the chair and held it in her lap, running her hands over the soft material.

Aribeth knew well the story of this bag; Father had told her often. It had been made for him by Mother as a wedding present. Mother had even killed and skinned the narshoba herself. It had taken weeks for her to age and tan the hide so that it was both malleable and durable. She had refused to marry him until the bag was done. It was, according to Father, the most tantalizing few weeks of his life.

Aribeth held the bag now and ran her fingers over the hand stitching. This was love, she thought. The fancy people in the civilized places up north could just buy their loved ones gifts, but store bought gifts would never have the deep meaning this simple bag did.

She opened the flap and felt around until she found Father's journal and pulled it free. The cover was badly aged and the pages yellowed. Aribeth flipped through it, stopping occasionally to read an entry, but the act threatened to bring the tears cascading back down.

She flipped to the end and found what she was looking for. He had made detailed notes, all in his exquisite handwriting, along with carefully drawn maps. This wasn't the work of madness. She held in her hands a roadmap to a new world. Aribeth snapped the book closed and stared down at Father.

"You really think that I can do this?" She went to Father's side and sat on the bed, laying her head on his chest. "I can't. You are wrong. This is too much. I am just a child." Aribeth looked up, hoping that somehow his eyes would be open and he would have something wise or encouraging to say, but he was gone. She was alone.

It would be easy to just forget about the whole thing. No one else knew of this crazy plan or of his research. She could go back to Houland Academy and finish her schooling and leave settling the last frontier for someone more adventurous and brave.

Aribeth growled and forced herself up off the bed. She had made a promise, now she owed it to Father to try. "You are not a child," she said to herself. "You are a Fuller, and you can do this. You have to do this."

Aribeth walked back over to the chair and picked the journal up again, thumbing through it more carefully this time. There were two names written on the pages about Aranwa. Aribeth recognized the name of Thom Berens, a longtime business partner of Father's. The second name was a mystery. Leland Jax. His name was underlined three times. Father only did that for people that he considered especially important. "Mr. Jax," she whispered. "Who are you?"

CHAPTER 2

He had been tracking the issi through the woods all day and had only managed to catch a few tantalizing glimpses of the animal. However, what he saw made his heart fill with joy. It was the biggest, most magnificent issi he had seen in these woods in ages. His hoof prints alone hinted at the heft of the creature, and it had a magnificent crown of horns around its huge head.

Now Leland Jax, stepping lightly through the brush, had the creature in his sights. He had great respect for this animal. He knew that for the animal to have achieved this level of maturity, it had to be an intelligent creature with razor sharp senses. He was a worthy adversary.

In better times, Leland would have let it go. Such a beast deserved to live out his life, but these were not better times. His family had been living on rodents and small game for months, subsisting but not really living. Leland himself had been going days at a time with no meat at all so that the others could have some. This creature would feed them all for weeks.

Leland slowly positioned himself behind the animal as it munched on the colorful leaves of a polona bush. The sound wasn't loud, but it was enough to cover Leland's soft and sure steps. He had finally managed to get himself downwind of the beast, and was now in prime position to take it down.

Moving with the slowness that only a practiced and patient

hunter could, Leland lifted his long rifle and gently thumbed the hammer. Steadily, Leland brought the rifle up to his shoulder and, looking out over the barrel, sighted the creature. He didn't use a scope, like most hunters did; he trusted his own vision implicitly.

The issi raised its head, stopping his dinner to listen. Had it heard Leland? He was losing light quickly, and if the animal bolted into the woods he would have to admit defeat. This far back in the forest, the canopy was too thick for Echonos to shine his eternal light through. It had to be now.

Again, most hunters would have taken the shot right then, when the back of the animal's skull was clearly visible, but Leland waited. He wanted the animal to bend back down, when the hump of its neck would be in his sights. Leland remembered when he had killed his first issi and he had taken the head shot. He remembered how, though dead, the creature had quivered and kicked and bucked for what seemed like forever, the body not knowing that it was dead yet. It had been heartbreaking for young Leland to have to sit there and watch and wait. It made him sick.

He didn't understand how the animal worked…that was for people much smarter than he. What he had discovered, though, was that a shot through the neck hump would kill the animal just as quickly without all the death rails of a head shot. It took much more skill to make that shot, but Leland wasn't lacking in skill.

The issi, satisfied that he was safe, turned his attention back to the bush, the head dropping and the neck coming up. Leland focused his pale blue eyes on his target and sighted the animal again. He adjusted his right hand reflexively, looking for that exact grip, when it would feel just right. This was hunting to him, blending into the environment, feeling it, breathing it. He was a part of nature, not just a person inserted into it

He set his grip, his trigger finger resting lightly on the trigger.

He breathed once, twice, three times, his mind calculating every factor — the wind, the light, the possibility that the animal could move — his eyes watching for any slight indication that the animal was alerted to his presence, any quick twitch movement. Confident that he had everything right, he let out one last, slow breath, made one last mental check, and slowly began to tighten his finger.

"Hey, hey, hey!"

The issi didn't look up or hesitate in the slightest. In a blink the magnificent animal bound away, disappearing into the darkening woods. Leland took his finger off the trigger and let the barrel drop. He looked to the sky with frustration. He heard the stranger behind him and to his right, tromping through the woods with an incredible racket.

"Hey, you, what do you think you're doing?"

Leland used one hand to lift and stow his custom made long gun in a sling on his back. He reminded himself to be nice, and turned to face the stranger with a forced smile on his face.

The stranger came crashing through the trees, wagging an angry finger. He was a farmer, Leland noted with a hint of disgust. He could tell by the dirty clothes; or to be precise, how his clothes were dirty. He could just tell…there was a way they all looked. Leland didn't respect farmers.

"I was just trying to bring in some dinner, sir," Leland answered. "That's the best issi I've seen in ages."

"Well, tough for you. You can't hunt back here. This is my land. You can't be here." The man now stood, gasping for breath. He was chubby, out of shape. He sloppily held a rifle of his own, but Leland could tell by how he handled it that he wasn't experienced.

Leland chuckled. "These are the woods, sir. Nobody owns the woods."

"The Ministry says different. I got a deed says I own this land all the way back to Arge's Creek. You're on my land and I want you off, now." To drive home his point, the farmer cocked his rifle.

Leland had to work hard to force his temper down. It was one thing to scare off his game or to order him off the land, but to cock his gun was a threat of violence that Leland didn't take lightly. Leland was a survivor, an outdoorsman, and to be threatened by a farmer just wasn't right.

"Sir, I mean no disrespect, but my family has been hunting these woods for generations...."

"Not any more. You got a Ministry deed to these lands?"

"Never had a need for any deed, sir." Leland had even less use for the machinations of government than he did for farmers.

"I thought not. I catch you or any of your kind back here again and I'll pop you good and I won't give you a warning. Understand me?"

Leland didn't answer right off. He sized up the man, his rifle, and his own hunger, and wondered for a fleeting moment what farmer tasted like. Then he drove the thought out of his head. "Yes, sir. You won't be seeing me this side of Arge's Creek again. My apologies."

The farmer could have been polite and let him go on his way, but instead decided to drive home his point by thrusting the barrel of the rifle towards Leland. "Get out."

That was a step too far. Leland felt the handle of his knife where it was tied down to his thigh. With the speed of a man used to hunting quick game, he pulled the knife and flicked it at the farmer. It struck him in the left shoulder, its razor point piercing skin and meat. His hand came away and the gun barrel dropped. Too late the farmer fired, his blast blowing up dirt and twigs at his feet, and then Leland was on top of him, knocking the gun from his hands and driving him back until he slammed the man into the trunk of an old tree.

Leland, a large and powerful man, was in a barely controlled rage now, his teeth gritted and his lips turned up in a snarl. He twisted the blade of the knife deeper into the man's shoulder. "Now I was nice to you, even when you scared off my dinner, but you ever point a gun at somebody in these woods, you better be prepared to use it. I don't care about any Ministry or any damn deeds. These woods are for the people to use. You damn farmers are ruining the land, and then you wave some stupid paper in our face and you think we're going to like it?"

He ripped the blade from the man's shoulder and wiped the blood off on his pants before holstering the blade. "Now, you won't see me back here again, but it's not because you pointed a gun at me. It's because if I see you again I'll kill you and use you to bait my traps."

Keeping his left hand pushed against the writhing man, he reached up with his right and broke off a branch thick with leaves. He peeled the leaves and wadded them up in his palm, then shoved them into the man's wound. "This will help staunch the bleeding until you get home."

Leland let go and the man slid to the ground, clutching the leaves to his bleeding shoulder. Leland walked back and picked up the man's gun, ejected the remaining bullets, and threw the rifle at his feet. "Have a nice evening," he said as he started the long, lonely walk back towards home. Empty handed again.

He worked his way back across Arge's Creek onto what he assumed was Jax family land, unless the Ministry had sold it to someone else. If they had, good luck to them staking that claim. He worked his way out of the thickest part of the woods, and now the pale light of Echonos shone down from directly overhead, lighting his way home.

He came to the banks of another creek and decided to camp for the night. He quickly built a small fire, then crouched by the edge of the water. The water was shallow and clear, and by the light of the fire he spied a nunni fish gliding through the water, feasting on the tiny bugs that dipped into the water. Leland tracked it and when it came around, speared it out of the water with his hands. The nunni wasn't the tastiest thing in the world, but it would help combat the hunger that he'd been fighting for days.

As the nunni roasted over the fire, Leland thought back on the confrontation with the farmer. He shouldn't have lost his temper with the man; after all, he was just trying to protect what was his. When Leland's great-grandfather had built their family home here, they had been far away from anyone else and they had free run over all the land. Now, civilization was catching up to them and Leland was feeling claustrophobic.

If it wasn't for his brothers and sisters at home, Leland would just pack up what few belongings he had and push on. He'd find some other secluded wilderness and live out his life. He didn't need the company of others, and he certainly didn't want the trappings of society.

His oldest brother was almost ten, which was how old Leland had been when Daddy had died and he had been forced to become the family provider. Rey was already a talented hunter…maybe it was time to turn the responsibility over to him. But game had been more plentiful then, before the farmers began clearing all of the timber. Even as good a hunter as Leland was, he was having a hard time providing for everyone. How could he expect Rey to handle it?

Then there was the issue of the Ministry and their damn land deeds. This land had been Jax land for more than a hundred years and no one had ever dared challenge it, but they had no deed to make it legal, and worse, no money to get one. How long would it be before someone showed up and demanded for them to move? He had to do something.

The next morning, weary after a sleepless night, Leland doused his fire and started home. Along the way he tagged a handful of brita birds with a homemade slingshot and put them in his bag. At least he would be bringing something home for the family, but he still felt like a failure.

He arrived at the family cabin and walked in to the hungry and expectant faces of his six siblings. He knew what they were thinking. They were expecting Leland The Great to come home bringing enough meat for a month or more, and here he was with nothing but a bag full of tiny birds. They couldn't hide their disappointment.

He cooked up the birds and portioned them out to the six, along with some wild berries that he had picked during his hunting trip. It was hardly sufficient for growing children, but they devoured it anyway. He sat and watched them eat and felt guilty for even thinking of leaving them behind. There was no way he could leave them to fend for themselves, no matter how badly he wanted to go. They needed him too much.

He spent the day catching up with his siblings. He played games with the smaller ones and taught the older ones the necessities. He made the decision to step up Rey's training so that in a year, he could go on an extended hunting trip and leave Rey in charge. If it worked out, then Leland could go, confident that the family would be in good hands.

That night they sat around the fire and Leland told them stories of his hunting adventures, though he always made sure to embellish the details. He wasn't against encouraging a little hero worship in his siblings.

Leland was ready to put them all to bed when a heavy knock

on the front door startled them. They had come. Leland had dreaded the day, but he hadn't expected it this soon. He grabbed his pistol and, ordering his siblings to take shelter, crept up to the door. He would fight the Ministry to his last breath if he had to. He positioned himself to the side of the door, took a breath, and threw it open.

Ready to meet whatever fate awaited him, he threw himself into the doorway, pistol ready to fire. There were no Ministry strongmen on the other side at all. Instead there was a girl. A pretty, pale, brown eyed girl who found herself on the wrong end of his gun. The girl gasped and took a step back, but other than that she did not waver.

Leland, embarrassed, put the gun down and gave her a sheepish grin. "Sorry, ma'am. We...uh, don't get many visitors here. Especially this time of night."

The girl relaxed and began to breathe again. Then she gave him a warm smile, and Leland discovered in one fleeting moment what it was that caused men to give up their wandering ways. "I'm sorry," she answered, her voice soft like the spring breeze. "I knew I should've waited for morning, but the men in town said that you might be gone again if I waited."

"The men in town?"

"Yes. I've come a long way looking for you." She held out her hand. "My name is Aribeth Fuller. You took my father to Aranwa. I need you to take me back."

Leland took her hand, amazed at the feel of her skin. He couldn't think of anything that he had ever touched that was so soft. "I remember," Leland answered. In that moment, his brain screamed at him to kick her off his doorstep and be done with her. There was no way he should ever return to Aranwa. Yet he knew that, no matter how foolish, he would never tell her no. In one moment, the brave and fearless hunter had been tamed. "I can take you there."

CHAPTER 3

Leland let Aribeth in and she took a seat by the fireplace, holding out her hands to the fire. Slowly, the rest of the Jax clan showed their faces, curious to meet the stranger. Leland took the time to introduce his siblings. He watched her as she patiently listened to the childish ramblings of his smallest siblings. He watched the smile on her face and he couldn't help but think about what a good mother she would be someday. He had never thought that way about a woman before.

Once the others fell asleep, he motioned for Aribeth to follow him outside. The night was cool, though for an experienced outdoorsman like Leland it was tolerable. Aribeth, on the other hand, pulled her brown jacket around her tightly. Leland leaned against the outside of the cabin and looked skyward. Akil was at the peak of her nightly orbit, right next to Echonos, the light of the two bright enough to illuminate dark woods.

"Ms. Fuller. I can take you to Aranwa if you want, but can I ask why? Weren't you going to school?"

"I was," she said, trying hard to keep from shivering. "Father called me home. He had this idea about settling Aranwa. He wanted to build a new nation there, and when he fell ill he asked me to take over. I made him a promise on his deathbed."

"He died?" Leland dropped his head in a moment of silence. "I'm sorry for your loss. I've lost both parents, I know how hard it is. To be honest though, he shouldn't have made you promise that."

"He didn't make me. I made the promise on my own."

"Did you really? Or did you do it because you felt you had to? Like you owed him something?"

Aribeth shrugged and tucked her hands deeper into the pockets of her jacket. "Does it matter? I made a promise and I intend to keep it. My father always stressed how important it was to keep your word. It would be a disrespect to his memory if I didn't follow through."

Leland looked deep into her eyes, then glanced away, surveying the surrounding woods. "He's dead. The dead don't feel disrespect. You're talking about the guilt of the living. Do yourself a favor and give this up. You're not cut out for this sort of thing."

Shock played across Aribeth's face for a moment, quickly replaced by a quiet rage. She stepped towards him and crossed her arms in defiance. "Who are you to make that judgement? You don't know me. You can't tell me what I'm cut out for."

Leland put his hands up and backed away. "You're right," he said. He admired the way she pushed back against him. She had spirit. "I don't know you. If you're anything like your dad, then you've got a chance."

Aribeth's stance eased and the quick flash of anger died down.

"But," Leland began again. "Aranwa is…different. I've lived outdoors my whole life. I know the land. But Aranwa is scary. It's wild. It won't be easily tamed. It's gonna take blood and sacrifice. Are you prepared for that? Can you watch people die and know that you're the one who led them to that death?"

Aribeth let her breath out in a slow hiss between clenched teeth as she thought about it. Then she paced, looking at the twin moons overhead, whispering something under her breath. Leland watched her with curiosity. Finally, she stopped pacing and looked back at him with the same determination he had seen in her father.

"Yes, I can. Because I can lead people away from here, from under the thumb of the Ministry and all of their silly laws. I have had a taste of civilized living, and I don't care for it. I may not be a survivalist like yourself, but I have grown up on the frontier. I know struggle and sacrifice and hard work. It doesn't scare me."

Leland smiled warmly at her and nodded as she spoke. "You're tough. I can see that." He walked a slow, deliberate circle around her. "These woods are tough. The animals, the ones that are left, are vicious. The winters are cold; the summers are brutal. I can handle that. Aranwa, though, has more." His circle was getting tighter and he was slowly closing in around her. "Aranwa has predators unlike anything I've ever seen. Storms that blow in out of nowhere. And…."

Aribeth was hanging on his every word now, and as she tried to keep up with him, she drifted even closer. "And?"

Leland stopped, held her gaze for two heartbeats, then looked away, as if embarrassed to say. "There are stories of a tribe of cannibals that live in Aranwa."

Aribeth gasped. "Are you talking about the lost tribe? The so-called First Family that drifted away?" He nodded slightly and she laughed. "That is nothing but a myth. A story to scare children at night. I would think that someone like you would know better."

Her flippant attitude rubbed him the wrong way. "I've been there, Ms. Fuller." He put a little edge in his voice. "I never saw them, but I know that they're there. I saw signs. Someone was tracking us during your father's little expedition. Strange things walk in the night in Aranwa. It's no place for a schoolgirl with fantasies."

"A schoolgirl with fantasies? I know all about your suspicions. My father wrote all about it in his journal. He didn't fear the night and neither will I. I know full well how treacherous the trip will be. He left me everything I need to know. But I will not be scared off by some silly tall tales."

Leland chewed on his bottom lip as he thought about it. He knew that she was staring holes into him. He looked to the cabin, a thin tendril of gray smoke escaping from the chimney. "If I do this for you," he said without looking at her. "I'm gonna need some things."

"What do you need?"

"Well, those little ones in there are gonna need food. I won't be here to hunt for them. I want...say, six months' worth of supplies. Good stuff, not that garbage the Ministry hands out. Meats, fruits, veggies, grains. I want a good supply."

"I can do that. I'll need to talk to Mr. Behrens when we get to Norales. I don't think it will be a problem."

"That's not all." He was rolling now, seeing a chance to give his family the comfort that he had never been able to give them. "Not just food. Clothing, oil, ammunition. I can get you a full list tomorrow. We'll also need gear for the trip."

"Get me a list," she answered. "I will make all the arrangements in Norales. Is that all?"

"No." He turned slowly, almost embarrassed to ask, but he knew that he had to. His family needed it. "I need a deed."

"A deed?"

"Yes. To this land. As much as you can get. The Ministry has been selling land around here. My family's lived here for generations, but we've got no paper. I have nightmares sometimes, thinking of the day when some sorry farmer and his sorry family come and run us off of our own land. I can't—"

"That's a big thing," Aribeth responded coolly. "I can't promise that. Getting a Ministry deed isn't cheap. I'm not made of money."

"But," Leland said, slowly approaching her. "You can deliver Aranwa. That's going to mean something to your investors. Make them understand. Use it."

"As leverage, you mean?" He nodded. "I don't know. Aranwa is a huge risk. I'm not sure—"

"Make it happen. This isn't negotiable. I need that deed. My family needs the deed. I can't go without that deed. It means too much for my family."

Aribeth thought it over for a long time. Leland watched patiently as she turned a tiny circle and chewed on her thumbnail, apparently deep in thought.

Leland, sensing her reluctance, decided to go for the kill. "I'm the best there is, Ms. Fuller. You might find a cheaper guide, but you won't find a better one. I can get you to Aranwa, help you find yourself a good spot to lay out your town. I can protect you. If you want this to succeed, you need me."

"Fine," she answered. "I'll see what I can do. I cannot make a promise. Get me your list of supplies and I will take them with me to Norales. You can make your final arrangements here while I talk to Mr. Behrens. He has some...influence. Maybe I can make this work."

Leland felt the weight of the world lifting off his shoulders. "Good. I'll get you the list." He looked up into the night sky. Akil had moved on past Echonos and would soon begin descending. "It's getting late. You should probably get some sleep."

Aribeth sighed and surveyed her surroundings. "It's a long way back to town."

"That's why you can't go to town. Even I would think twice about travelling these woods at this time of night. I've got an extra bag inside, and there's plenty of floor to go around."

Aribeth chuckled. "You're offering me your floor?"

"Yes ma'am. It's the finest floor for several miles around."

"It's the only floor for miles around." She smiled softly. "But I appreciate the offer. Truth is, I'm exhausted and the floor sounds great. I trust that you will be a gentleman?"

"I'm no gentleman," Leland said. "But you have nothing to fear from me. I wouldn't think of hurting you."

"I hope so," she said, studying him in the moonlight. "Let's get some sleep."

CHAPTER 4

Norales was by far the biggest city in Southern Cadoa. A thriving port town, Norales straddled the gently running Aramor River. In Norales, the streets were covered with fine rocks, not the sloppy mud of Aribeth's hometown, and the lanterns came on automatically at dusk.

Aribeth's coach pulled into Norales just before sunset and dropped her off at a nice but not luxurious boarding home a short walk from Thom Behrens' office. Aribeth checked in hurriedly, glad to be off the rugged trails and back in civilization. It had taken nearly three full days of travel to make it to Norales from Leland's tiny village, and she was weary from the trek.

Aribeth dropped her bags just inside the door and sat heavily on the edge of a bed that was just big enough for her. The springs groaned under her weight, and she briefly wondered how many bodies had laid on this bed prior to hers.

She sighed and pulled her hair out of the heavy braid, letting it run loose over her tiny shoulders. Aribeth caught her reflection in the mirror on the opposite wall. She was ragged, her face dirty, with dark circles forming under her eyes. It had been forever since she had a decent meal and it was beginning to show.

Aribeth looked hard at the reflection, amazed that she was looking at herself. "How are you going to do this? Look at the toll this has taken already. I haven't even started for Aranwa yet." The self-doubt was flooding into her mind, threatening to overwhelm her wavering resolve.

Aribeth ran both hands over her face and through her long hair. "You'll do it," she said again, stronger now, "because Father asked you to do it. Because you owe it to him. Quit being a baby." Then she began to chuckle. "Listen to me talking to myself. I'm already going crazy."

Aribeth pulled off her tall black boots and tossed them aside, then quickly stripped the rest of her clothes away. There was a small bathroom off her room and she ran the water in the tub just as hot as she could stand. When the tub was full, she slowly slid in, the water burning at first, but soon it felt perfect. She could almost picture all the knots in her muscles relaxing in the heat.

Aribeth leaned her head on the edge of the tub and closed her eyes, running through a mental checklist of things to talk to Mr. Behrens about. She had only met the man on a couple of occasions when Father had dragged her along on business. There was no reason for Mr. Behrens to honor any agreements that he might have made with Father. Aribeth would have to convince him that she was the right person to lead the expedition.

First Aribeth would have to find a way to silence the doubts that were raging inside her. She had to be the picture of confidence if she was to win over Mr. Behrens and secure the funds and supplies that she would need.

Aribeth let her mind drift, and only the creeping cold of the bath water snapped her out of it. Aribeth finished up quickly, but the cold had overtaken her, and she shivered as she wrapped herself in one of the thin towels that were provided. She hurried to her bags and dug out a thick nightgown for the night. As Aribeth waited for her hair to dry, she stood at the window and overlooked Norales. The sun was gone, but a sliver of fiery orange still played across the horizon as the fancy automated lanterns begin to click on in succession.

The city was a sight. People continued to scurry about, appearing to be in no real hurry to go home. On the frontier, only the bravest of souls journeyed out at night, but there was nothing to fear here. The settlers had long since beaten back the predators and made the city safe. "Are you really ready to give all of this up?" she muttered.

She didn't have an answer for herself.

#

Thom Behrens was a dignified gentleman in fine gray clothes and a cleanly shaven face. He looked much better than he should have, given his advancing years, but a life of privilege could do that for you. Mr. Behrens had never been on the frontier, had never chopped down a tree or built a cabin or slept under the moons. All of his life had been in lived in Norales, and before that in the even more advanced cities to the north.

It was curious that he should be Father's best friend. The gentleman banker and the rugged outdoorsman must have made a curious pair on their nights about town. Aribeth had long known of Father's taste for drink and female companionship when he went on one of his adventures. Mother had known it too, but never said anything. Whatever he did on his journeys was his business, but he never brought it home to the family.

Now Mr. Behrens sat behind a ridiculously oversized desk and peered intently at Aribeth through thick rimmed glasses. "Ms. Fuller," he finally said after a long deliberation. "I am very sorry for your father's passing, and even more sorry that you are allowing him to draw you into his foolish adventures."

Aribeth sat on the other side of his desk, sitting ramrod straight with her hands folded in her lap. She was wearing her finest dress, and dripped of the manners that private school had somehow engrained in her. She needed all of those manners now, because she wanted to jump across the desk and strangle the pretentious old geezer on the other side. "I hardly consider it foolish."

"You wouldn't," he laughed. "You are just like your father. He used to tell me all of the time. You have a wandering spirit and you crave the thrill of the unknown. It killed your father…it will kill you. So I'm going to do you a favor and reject this silly notion of yours outright."

Aribeth breathed deeply and collected her thoughts. "Did you reject it when my father brought it to you?" She met his eyes with a steely glare. She was challenging him to lie to her.

"No," he said reluctantly. "I did not. But I tried to. I tried everything I could to dissuade him. You know your father," he half chuckled, half wheezed. "Impossible to turn that man down." Behrens pushed himself out of his overly plump chair and straightened his custom-tailored jacket. "He sat right there, sick already, a walking dead man, and somehow convinced me that he could settle an untamable land." He shook his head sadly. "I was a bigger fool than he."

"There is no such thing as an untamable land," Aribeth answered. "All it takes is will."

Behrens hobbled to a window and looked out over Norales in the early morning light. "You would say that." He turned and sat gingerly on the window sill. "And you would be wrong. Aranwa is a farce. A fairy tale. You can't even get there."

"My father got there. And I have his guide."

"Good for you," Behrens answered solemnly. "The two of you can make it, just as they did. Two of you. How will you get an entire caravan across that raging river? There are no bridges, no shallows. The rapids will crush whatever craft you try to build. The winds will destroy whatever bridge you try to build."

"Then we cross two at a time, like Leland and Father did. It will take time, but we can do it."

"And all of the supplies? How will you get them across?"

Aribeth realized that she was grinding her teeth and forced herself to stop. She had known that he would resist. "We'll find a way. I will find a way. Do you think the original families had it easy here? Pioneers always find a way."

"But you are no pioneer, my dear," he said sharply. "You are a private school girl who should be learning about courting rituals and homemaking. You have no business traipsing across some unknown wilderness."

Aribeth stood slowly and measured her words carefully before speaking. "I grew up on the frontier, Mr. Behrens. I followed my father and my brothers to every stop. I have seen how you create a town out of nothing. How you clear the wilderness and lay out the grid and bring in the families. I have watched the master do it."

"But Aranwa is different," Behrens pleaded.

"No, it's not," she snapped. Behrens faced showed his shock at her outburst. Aribeth winced and took a moment to regain her composure. "Aranwa is just a place. That's all. I do not buy into all of the wild rumors and baseless stories." She walked up to him slowly, trying to project confidence. "Mr. Behrens. If you give me the funds, I will settle Aranwa. Failure is not in my blood."

Behrens looked up at her with his watery blue eyes as if she were a petulant child. "You are a bigger fool that I thought. You want to know why you will fail, Ms. Fuller? Two words. Talon Volpe."

"Talon Volpe?" Aribeth was caught off guard by the name.

"Yes, Talon Volpe. He is an outlaw who has been preying on every settlement between here and Aranwa. He and his gang are ruthless and absolutely deranged. If you try to settle Aranwa they will kill you, in a most brutal way, but only after they ravage you first. The Volpe Gang is not a wild rumor; they are the cold truth. You would need an army to protect you."

"Then give me an army. Outlaws are just thugs who haven't met a bigger thug yet. I'm not afraid." She sat down on the window sill next to him. "I can do this."

"I know that you believe that you can," he said as he laid a wrinkled hand on top of hers. "But I simply cannot approve this. The money is there. There are plenty of investors willing to bank on Aranwa, and if I had an experienced guide—a proven commodity, like your father—then I could sell it. But if I go to the investors and give them…this," he said, gesturing at Aribeth in her fancy school dress, "I will be laughed out of town. I'm sorry."

Aribeth pushed herself up off of the sill and stormed across the room. For a moment, she was glad. He was giving her an excuse, an out. She could honestly say that she had given it her best shot and failed. Then she could go back north. She could go back to civilization, far away from raging rivers and bloodthirsty pirates.

And do what? Study to be some rich man's plaything? Learn how to be a society woman? She had never wanted that life to begin with. She had fought against Father sending her. She had grown up with her hands dirty.

She stopped her pacing, then tore down her hair and began tearing away at her dress, shredding the fine material in her hands until she was down to her underwear, then she turned quickly. "How about now, Mr. Behrens? Am I still nothing but a private school girl now?" She stormed over to him and stood over him. "Am I still just some pretty girl who should be studying homemaking? Look close, Mr. Behrens."

Behrens tried to stand and Aribeth took a half step back. He got to his feet and removed his coat. With a shake of his head, Mr. Behrens wrapped the coat around Aribeth's shoulders. "You're

37

as impertinent as your father."

"And just as tough, Mr. Behrens. I can do this. I have the best outdoorsman in the territory to guide me. I will not fail. Just give me a chance."

Behrens slowly circled his desk, chewing on a thumbnail and occasionally glancing up at her. After an unbearable silence, he sat down behind his desk with a heavy sigh. "I can try to convince the investors. I will leave it up to them. But," he pointed a stern finger at her. "You must take a security force with you. I have some contacts. If I get approval, I will put your team together. I will not send you off into that wilderness alone."

"That's all I can ask for. Thank you," Aribeth answered. "Just promise me that you will fight hard for me. Oh, and my guide, Mr. Jax, he has some demands I will need met."

Behrens shook his head in disgust. "You are lucky that I am even considering this idea…you definitely shouldn't be giving me demands."

"They're not for me, they are for my guide, and I need him. He's the best that there is."

"I will talk to the investors. Then we will talk again."

CHAPTER 5

The auditorium was packed with students, each in their gray uniforms, impeccably starched and creased, their black boots shined to perfection. They sat in groups of threes or fours, whispering quietly among themselves, tiny giggles occasionally escaping.

Parrie Barrows sat in the back row and stared down at them all, silently hating them. She was keenly aware that she was the only woman in the group, one of only a handful enrolled at Plenwaite Military Academy. She looked down at the boys as they joked with each other. They had it so easy, she thought. They could half ass their way through classes, take seminars like this one as a joke, and it wouldn't matter. They were here because they had been chosen. They were here because they were big and strong or smart or came from the best families. Many of them were legacies. Their places had been reserved the moment they emerged from the womb. The nation needed an army, a strong army, and they need soldiers, and more importantly, they needed officers. The boys here were the best of the best.

Parrie had forced her way in by working harder than all of them. She had stayed up late nights studying, then emerged early the next morning to work out to make herself stronger and faster. She existed on rushed meals that could be eaten on the run and sleeping in fifteen minute increments.

Yet Parrie still struggled.

Her dedication was unquestioned, as was her love of country. Her grandfather had died in battle decades before, when the nation of Cadoa was more of a dream than a reality. He had died in a muddy swamp to salvage that dream. Her father had been a prisoner of the Iridians during a bloody border war when she was a baby. He had been emotionally shattered by the experience, and Parrie had never shaken the sight of him crying like a baby at the slightest provocation.

Parrie was determined to carry on that proud legacy, and would give her life for her country if need be. She lived and breathed military history and tactics. Parrie knew in her heart that she could be the finest officer in the Academy, if only she could get the chance.

Everyone agreed that war with the Iridians was inevitable. A new leader was emerging in Iridia, uniting the fractured people and selling them on the vision of one nation. He would win the civil war and then he would turn his sights on Cadoa. They had to be ready.

She had to be ready. Parrie wanted Iridian blood. She hungered for it.

But she was a woman and women didn't fight. They were pushed off into support roles…glorified secretaries, sorting intelligence, coordinating messages. It was an important job and all armies needed good support. She knew that, but that wasn't the life she wanted. She was too good for it.

"Hey, wake up."

Parrie shook herself out of her daydream and turned to find her friend Temple Goodwin sitting beside her, two steaming cups of bala in his hands. He handed one over to her, then followed her gaze down to the students below.

"Are we loathing our classmates again? Don't get me wrong,

it's fun and all, but it gets a little old after a while."

Temple wasn't like them, which was why they had become such friends. He was an intellectual, a planner, and an ideologue. For him, military service was just a rung on a ladder that would lead him to a much higher calling someday.

Parrie and Temple had grown up not far from each other, exploring the woods and hunting for the family supper. They excelled in school but often found themselves in trouble because neither was afraid to stand up to those in power. That rebellious streak that ran through them both made the structured life of a military cadet difficult.

Temple was a good-looking kid with sandy colored hair and deep brown eyes. He had an impish smile, and unnaturally white teeth that had helped him charm many young ladies out of their virtue. He had thought that he could do the same to her, but she had proven him wrong.

Parrie was tall and lean, but muscular everywhere, with white blonde hair and piercing blue eyes and a constant scowl on an otherwise pretty face. Parrie almost never smiled, never cracked a joke. Humor was not something that had existed in her world. She had no use for it.

"Hey, did you hear about our good friend Bethel?" Temple asked.

"What about him?"

"He got kicked out."

"What?" Parrie heard her voice shoot up in surprise and could feel the eyes of her classmates all turning towards her. She could just imagine the things that they would be saying to each other. "What happened?"

Temple took a cautious drink of his bala and shrugged. "You know Bethel. He's brave and tough, but dumb as all get out. No one could figure out how he was passing all the classwork. Then they found out. He was cheating." Temple made a jerking motion with his thumb. "Gone. Had his stripes ripped off in front of his whole barracks."

Parrie whistled. "Wow. I never would have thought. I mean, I knew that he was cheating." Temple gave her a warning look. "Okay, I suspected that he was cheating. But still, with his pedigree and how well he did in the physical challenges? I wonder what he'll do?"

"Don't worry about Bethel. His family will pull some strings, get him a job, and wait. He'll never be an officer, but once war breaks out, he'll be a perfect soldier. He'll earn his way up or die trying."

Parrie whistled and shook her head, her gaze drifting over the crowd below. "Bethel Hough, gone. Wow."

Temple leaned in closer. "They're going to be looking for whoever was supplying him with answers."

Parrie recoiled from him, shock on her face. "Not me. I wouldn't—"

"I know you wouldn't. But they are going to be looking for someone. Bethel's family will probably insist on it. Just…." He looked around nervously, then dropped his voice another notch. "Just watch yourself."

She understood where he was going. "I will."

Down on the floor, a heavy door clanged open and Commandant Miley marched in, hat tucked under his arm, posture arrow straight, every short gray hair in perfect place. Behind him, another man trailed. This man was unusually tall and muscular, strikingly good looking, his raven hair unprofessionally long over the high collar of his navy blue uniform jacket. A jacket that almost glittered with medals. Even from the back row, Parrie picked out the two most noticeable things about him: his piercing gray eyes and his limp.

The commandant stepped to a lectern in the center of the floor, and with a loud click of his boots brought the room to attention. "Attention gentleman," he called, his voice ringing like a bell through the lecture hall. "Today, it is my privilege to present to you one of the true heroes of our day. The hero of Sebastian Ridge. I expect you will give him the utmost respect men, because he has seen and done things that would make the toughest soldier cower in fear. I give you Colonel Stockton Bays."

The tall man nodded slightly as the commandant stepped aside, then strode confidently to the lectern. "Gentlemen," he said. His voice was deep and commanding. He probed the audience with his stern gaze. Parrie leaned forward, her focus entirely devoted to the war hero below.

"You probably don't want to be here today. I don't blame you. I wouldn't want to be here today either." There was a mild wave of chuckling through the ranks. He continued, unabated. "When I entered the army, I entered in a time of war. I didn't have to sit in boring classrooms and listen to mind numbing lectures." More laughter, a little louder now.

Colonel Bays smiled, but it was a menacing smile. "No. I learned by holding my commanding officer's guts in my hands while he bled to death in the snow." The laughter stopped as Bays' voice took on an edge. "I learned by getting gunned down on a foolhardy charge at an encamped position. I learned by crying through the night, begging to die, gripped by fever. I learned by finding myself covered in the blood of my enemies, by watching the light go out of another man's eyes and knowing that I was the reason. That is how I learned about war, gentlemen."

Parrie was on the edge of her seat, hanging on every word. She could see the images in her head. Parrie pictured herself on the battlefield, gunfire everywhere, bodies flying. She saw herself charging into the battle, an Iridian devil on the tip of her sword.

"This is war, men," Bays continued. "The next time you want to complain about taking a test, remember that." The contempt was clear in his voice. "You spoiled, snot nosed little brats. I see you." He focused his gaze on one particular student. "Your fine upbringing." He pointed at another. "Your impeccable manners." His eyes drifted up the crowd until they found Parrie, who thought she was invisible to him at the back of the room. "You charity cases. You disgust me. The mark of a true warrior doesn't come in some classroom. It comes in the moment you have to make a decision, and someone is going to die. Will you kill or be killed? Ask yourselves, can you do it? Can you make that split-second decision? If not, you need to leave here, right now. You have no place in the army."

Parrie didn't find his words insulting in the least. In fact, she felt honored just knowing that he had noticed her. She was sure that to him, she looked like a charity case. She was happy drifting along on his words.

"They bring me here because they want me to inspire you." Beside him, Commandant Miley was looking increasingly uncomfortable. Bays had a reputation for being unpredictable. "They want me to tell you how I saved the day at Sebastian Ridge. How I nearly died in the assault on Fulton Hollow, and how I managed to somehow get back up and make it in time for the final victory at Arnaud Hill. They want me to do this, because figureheads like Commandant Miley here think that it will make you better soldiers. It's a lie."

At this point, the class was noticeably nervous. Many students looked around, picking out the exits. Parrie grinned down at them with derision. Bay was many things, but he spoke the truth. If they couldn't handle it, then they should get out.

"It takes heart and courage to be a great soldier. It takes discipline and commitment. You can't learn these things. You either have them, or...." He took a long glance at Commandant Miley. "You don't." He turned his attention back to the students. "You are either a warrior or you're not. Listening to me isn't going to make you a soldier. This entire thing is a waste of my time, and yours." He turned sharply and strode out of the room without looking back.

The students watched in silence while Miley struggled to gain his composure. "Barracks, men," he finally called. "Barracks inspection, ten minutes. Move! Move!"

The students scrambled up and out of their seats, hastily gathering their books as they went. Parrie leaned back and laughed, aware that Temple was looking at her like she was crazy. "That was brilliant," she exclaimed. "What a performance."

"A performance? The man is certifiable."

"No, he's not. Think about it," she started, turning in her seat. "How would you feel if you did all of this, suffered and killed and watched people die, and when it was all over, the government rolled you out like some trained animal to impress a bunch of nothings like us? Of course he's pissed. Wouldn't you be? He's not some show pony, he's a war hero."

Temple sighed and gathered his things. "He's an ass. I don't know why you admire him so. It doesn't take a brilliant man to charge into gunfire. He was lucky."

Parrie looked up at Temple and shook her head sadly. "It doesn't hurt to be lucky."

"I'd rather be smart," Temple said dismissively. "Catch you at dinner, Parrie."

Parrie watched him duck out the door, then slowly stood. Commandant Miley stood on the floor, glaring up at her. "Did you hear me Barrows? Barracks inspection."

She held her books over her chest. "I heard, Commandant. I'm on my way."

"You'd better be," he threatened. "I think I'll check yours first."

"Please do, Commandant. Please do." She turned and started for the door, smirking as she went. Let them check her barracks. They wouldn't find a thing. She knew how to keep her barracks straight, and she made sure that her bunkmates did as well. The women at Plenwaite didn't take risks with something as easy, or silly, as a sloppy barracks.

Parrie made her way briskly across the campus, which was beautiful in the early spring. The breezes were warm and light and the trees and shrubs were coming back to life, bathing the campus in a sea of lush green.

All around, the Academy pulsed with life. In the fields she could hear the sounds of cadets chanting as they ran or grunting as they tackled the obstacle course. As she crossed the courtyard, Parrie watched as her fellow cadets made their way across campus, all in their crisp gray uniforms, books either held tightly to their chests or on their right side, never on the left. She heard the groundskeepers hard at work on keeping the campus pristine, and the metal hooks banging against the flagpole in the breeze.

Parrie loved this, the structure and discipline. When times got tough and quitting seemed so much easier, she would come and sit on the steps of Main Hall and just watch. Spring was the best time, before summer dropped intense heat and unbearable humidity, and after the barren depression of winter.

Given an unexpected early release, Parrie would have loved to have found a place to sit and appreciate it all, but she didn't have the luxury. The commandant was upset and looking to take it out on someone. She chuckled at how thoroughly Stockton Bays had humiliated the commandant. She had picked up the hint of a personal rivalry between the two.

Parrie was still reliving the rush of Bays' address when she entered the barracks, but the smile quickly faded from her face. Colonel Amarylis was already there, accompanied by two of his staff. Her bunkmates, the ones who weren't already in class or on the fields, each stood arrow straight in front of their bunks, most in some state of undress.

The surprise inspection had served its purpose, and several of her mates had yet to straighten their beds or properly stash their toiletries. Parrie sighed in advance of the countless sprints they would all incur for this.

Yet, Amarylis stood in front of her bed as his two privates combed through her locker and tossed her bed. Amarylis, his dull brown eyes dripping disgust, turned to her. "Barrows."

Parrie snapped to attention and executed a perfect salute. "Colonel. I think that you'll find everything in perfect order, as always." She added that last part for a reason. Amarylis had been after her from the beginning, and random barracks checks were common. He had never managed to catch her before.

He just grunted and turned his attention to the search at hand. Parrie took her appropriate stance in front of her bunk, back straight, eyes ahead, resisting the urge to turn and watch.

To her right, she heard the door hiss open and the commandant strode in with all the weight that decades of distinguished service afforded him. He strode into the room and stood in front of Parrie without acknowledging her, and addressed Amarylis. "Have you found it?"

"Not yet, sir," Amarylis snapped back.

Parrie stood unflinching but her mind raced. What could they possibly be looking for? The thought occurred to her a half second before one of the privates, the one who was going through her locker, yelled out "sir" and pulled out a journal with a battered red cover.

Amarylis's eyes slid to Parrie's, and he grunted and took two quick steps towards the private and took the journal from him. He flipped the pages, and he sounded like he was purring as he did. "Commandant," he finally said.

Amarylis marched up to his commander and offered the journal to him. The commandant took it and quickly flipped through as well. Finally, he handed the book back and turned to face Parrie.

"Cadet Burrows. You are hereby and immediately expelled from Plenwaite Academy for breaking Section One of the Honor Code. Cheating is one of the most despicable acts a cadet can commit, and as I'm sure you are aware, we have a zero tolerance for cheating. Your belongings will be packed up for you." His eyes moved quickly to the two privates. "Please escort Ms. Burrows to the platform."

The commandant's cold stare came back to Parrie. "You are a disgrace to this Academy and a shame to your country." In a swift, violent motion, he tore the black and gold stripes from the shoulders of her jacket. "When you get to the platform you will remove this uniform and leave it folded neatly for pickup. You will then wait for transport back to Norales. From there it will be up to your family to provide your way home, if they'll even have you."

Parrie did not cry; instead, she forced down a boiling rage. She felt it bubbling up from deep inside. They had set her up. She'd been doomed before Stockton Bays had even walked into the auditorium that morning. The two privates took her by the arms and began leading her away. Her bunkmates said nothing. Parrie knew that they couldn't, or would risk joining her. They led her out of the door and down the steps, where a large crowd of students had gathered. She caught sight of Temple, books at his side and a stunned expression on his face.

"Temple! I didn't do this. You know me." The privates led

her on past, but Parrie turned and shouted over her shoulder. "You know that I didn't do this!"

Then they led her past. As they led her to the landing platform and the rail that would take her away from her dreams, from everything she had hung her future on, she thought of Bethel. Had he named her? Had they made him? They had always had an adversarial relationship, but she never thought the fool would take her down with him.

She would find him and she would make him tell her.

Chapter 6

Thom Behrens entered the dimly lit café with a heavy heart. It had been a tough day for him. Despite his best attempts, the investors that Brenton Fuller had lined up continued to pledge their support for the Aranwa endeavor, even with a teen girl leading the mission. Their determination had surprised Behrens, a man not easily caught off-guard. As he took his last, unexpected meeting of the day, carts were being loaded with enough supplies to keep Leland Jax's family in comfort for a year, maybe more if they were careful.

Stockton Bays sat at a window side table, a tall glass of amber liquid over ice in front of him. He was wearing his uniform, a fact that instantly had Behrens on high alert. Bays was staring out the window at the pedestrians milling about outside in the dying light of day.

He took a seat opposite of Bays silently, quickly placing his napkin in his lap.

"The Fuller girl came to see you," Bays said, eyes still locked on the goings on outside. It was not a question. "That was faster than expected."

Behrens cleared his throat politely before speaking. "She has many of her father's less redeeming qualities; a foolish willingness to throw her life away seeming to be among them. She does have his journal."

Bays finally brought his attention back into the restaurant. "I trust that you had no trouble with the investors?"

"Curiously, no," Behrens answered.

Bays chuckled and took a long drink from his glass. He closed his eyes and seemed to savor the burning sensation from the drink. Behrens had heard many tales of his taste for drink. A similar drink would have put himself on the floor.

"You find it curious that people want to invest in new, untouched land? I would have thought you to be a wiser man than that. Land is the ultimate intoxicant, Mr. Behrens. Men will die for it; they will kill for it."

Behrens had suddenly lost his appetite and he ordered their waiter away. "I find it curious that no one has a problem with a little girl leading this expedition. That such successful men would invest their wares to someone —"

Bays cut him off with a hearty laugh. "You think that she'll be leading?" He took another long drink, finishing the glass and whistling for the waiter to bring him another. "You're right. No one with a lick of sense would trust a silly girl with such an important mission. But she won't be leading. She'll think that she will, but she won't. I'll have men of my own choosing in her security detail. They'll know what to do and when to do it."

Bays reached into a satchel that hung on one arm of his chair and pulled out a thick folder. He tossed it on the table in front of Behrens. "The families, the settlers, have all been carefully scouted and approved, and the security team handpicked by me."

Behrens quickly thumbed through the folder and closed it forcefully. "This girl is the daughter of my dearest friend. I have watched her grow up. I am the one who persuaded Breton to send her to school, expressly to get her away from the frontier. I will not toss her life aside so cavalierly."

Bays exchanged his empty glass for a full one and immediately took another hit. "The scout, the wilderness man. He will protect her. His reputation is spotless. She will be in good hands. She will never even know about our little side venture. She can lay out her town and do what her dad taught her to do. The families will be happy to settle. My men will simply break off when the time is right."

The waiter set a bowl of greens down in front of each of them without being asked. Behrens glared at the young man.

"Stop being such a priss," Bays snapped. "I ordered. Men like you," he said, pointing his fork at Behrens. "You make me sick. So full of manners. Men like you have never suffered or sacrificed for anything. You've never bled. You've never shivered through a night, lived under the stars, or taken up arms for something you believe. Yet you look down your nose at those of us who have. You don't understand an honest day's work."

"I understand fine—"

"But you've never done it. It doesn't matter. What matters is that we establish a hold on Aranwa before the Iridians do."

Behrens pushed his bowl aside. "Then why doesn't the Ministry put forth a proper expedition?"

"The Ministry," Bays said with disgust. "A collection of fools. Pointless bureaucrats."

"The president—"

"Is in a complicated position. The politicians, especially from the north, they don't understand. They won't approve a proper expedition. He understands this. He also understands the will of the people. The people want more. More land, more space, more freedom. Aranwa is the last frontier. It begs to be settled."

"Then the president should simply—"

Bays cut him off with an abrupt look. He put his powerful arms on the table and leaned toward Behrens. "Do what? Override the system? Overrule the Ministry? Would you have Cadoa turn into a damn dictatorship? Perhaps you are on the wrong side of this dispute, Mr. Behrens."

"I never insinuated—" Behrens started, backtracking. He was not a man used to being on the defensive.

"Choose carefully your words, sir. The freedom we all hold so dear is precarious. Supplanting the will of the people for the process of government is a recipe for disaster. Don't forget that, sir. This is why it is important that the entire expedition be private. There is to be no mention of government involvement in any way. The people I have chosen are…unattached. As far as anyone but a few will ever know, what happens in Aranwa will be on the shoulders and in the hearts of the individual."

Behrens, certain of the implied threat in Bays' words, softened his tone, but not his stance. "If you are so certain that the Iridians will stake their claim, aren't you leaving these poor people to die?"

Bays relaxed back into his seat and drained another glass. "A man will fight much harder for what is his than what is his government's. When the time comes to bear arms against the devils, support will come." His cold gray eyes sought out Behrens' and held them fast. "When the time is right and the stage is set. Not before. Your little girl will be on her own until then. Such is life on the frontier."

CHAPTER 7

The woman in front of him was the finest specimen he had seen in months. Border towns such as Bergstrom often offered little in the way of quality companionship when it came to women. Many of them were worn out, either from work in the fields or work of a tawdrier sort. Their manners were near non-existent and their upkeep was poor.

Though Ridge Secova wasn't above the occasional backroom tryst, a man seeking to attain status had to aim higher. The barons usually had the prettiest daughters, but they guarded their prizes fiercely, and access to a baroness was a difficult task.

Similarly, Ministry men often produced women who were nearly the equal of the baroness in terms of upbringing and manner, often without the snobbery, but their fathers were naturally suspicious, and Ridge was not a man who wanted the government looking too closely at his deeds.

So he considered himself fortunate to have stumbled across the fair beauty who was on his arm on this night. The daughter of a shopkeeper, she trailed no proper lady in beauty, with her porcelain skin, her golden hair, and her indigo eyes. A daily life of working in the shop had given her body definition that many proper ladies couldn't match. She was a startling piece of eye candy.

She was also an utter moron.

They sat across from each other in a crowded tavern frequented by farmers and shore men and hunters. The girl rambled on about her father's store and the time he took them to Norales for a holiday, or about the girls she grew up with, sneaking out into the fields at night to imbibe of stolen chibanna.

Ridge had long since stopped listening. His only hope at avoiding a total loss on the evening rested in the power of slightly more powerful drink and his own charisma. Yet even this was hard to focus on, because another of the tavern's customers had caught Ridge's attention.

This man was a beast, one of the largest Ridge had ever seen; a hulking behemoth of a man with ratty black hair and a gross beard. He was sitting at the bar, regaling all who would listen, and many who didn't want to, about the time he had taken down a full sized nita with his bare hands.

The drunkard told the story again and again, each time louder and more elaborately than the last. Ridge didn't tolerate braggarts lightly and liars even less so. As the man started telling his tale again, Ridge had heard enough. "Dear," he said to his companion, his voice smooth as glass. "I'm sure that you and your friends had a wonderful time, but I'm afraid that I just don't care. You are vapid and shallow, and even the thought of bedding you no longer appeals to me. Good night."

He pushed away from the table and strode quickly and purposely through the crowd. If he couldn't satisfy his lust for a woman, then a fight would do just as well. He pushed his way up to the bar next to the big man, who reeked of days' old drink and manure.

The brute felt the nudge beside him and turned, reflexes already dulled by a heavy night of drinking. Ridge fixed the man with a hard gaze. "I've been hearing your story all night, friend. Fascinating tale, if you don't mind my saying."

The man staggered some, but his grin showed that he was pleased to have made a fan. "Not every man could take a full-fledged nita bare handed."

"I'll say," Ridge prodded. "A nita is what, three times the size of an average man? Has four razor sharp claws and jaws like a vice? You're a worthless drunkard with almost no reflexes and average strength? No reason to doubt your story at all."

The man's mood turned quickly. "You wanna see just how strong I am? I'll break you like a twig."

Ridge smiled, and it was a smile full of menace. "Go ahead, show me how tough you are. You know what I think? I think you came across some little baby, abandoned by his mother and left to die, and you probably just smashed his head in with a boot heel, you slimy sack of pus."

With an animalistic growl the big man swung at Ridge, but he was slow and uncoordinated. Ridge easily sidestepped the wild haymaker, stepped forward, and pounded the man's face with two quick, direct shots to his nose. The nose gave way easily, spewing blood in all directions. The big man buckled and dropped off his stool, falling to a knee.

His drinking buddies then decided to enter the fray. One was too far away, and the big man's girth was between him and Ridge, but the other was coming from Ridge's backside. Most men never would have known he was there, but Ridge was far from most men.

With his right hand, Ridge reached across his chest and, under the cover of his fancy dress coat, came out with a long-bladed knife. He twirled it once in his hand, then blindly thrust behind him and felt the blade penetrate his attacker's abdomen with ease. The man screeched once before he began to gurgle and fell to the floor, clutching his midsection with both hands.

The first man was trying to climb over the prone figure of

the big man and get at Ridge. Calmly, Ridge adjusted his grip on the knife again, grasping it by the blade and flicking it at the attacking man. The knife struck home, burying itself just below his right collarbone. He fell to the floor, desperately clawing at the knife, trying to pry it out.

Ridge smirked and straightened his coat before plucking the knife out of the man. By this time, the big man had struggled to his feet. Ridge elbowed him across the nose again, then drove him backwards, bending him over the bar and quickly climbing up on the man's chest. He positioned the knife just above the man's right eye.

"I don't like you, friend. You'll never come in here again, because if I even see you walk up to the door, I'll spill your innards all over the dirt. You understand me?"

The man, blood still spilling down his face, swallowed hard and nodded his head slightly. Ridge relaxed his grip on the knife just a tad. "Your friend over there is about to bleed to death, you'd best find him a doctor."

He dismounted the large man as casually as he would unmount a steed after an evening's ride, and as the fat man struggled up to gather his companions, he whistled for the bartender to pour him another drink.

The fat man and his less seriously wounded buddy scooped up the man with the gut wound and rushed away. Ridge watched the reflection of them in the mirror behind the bar and grinned even bigger.

Ridge was, by almost any standard, a beautiful man with long auburn hair, pearly white teeth, and frost colored eyes. A killer's eyes. He enjoyed seeing his own reflection in the mirror, his fine features hiding the truth about him. Many a man more dangerous than these had mistakenly thought that Ridge's soft features were the mark of a weak man. Much blood had been spilled because of that oversight.

Bergstrom's constable, whose name was Donnelly, was not such a man. As Ridge savored his drink, he saw the constable enter the tavern, his face gray and sullen, shoulders slumped. Their eyes met in the reflection.

Donnelly approached Ridge slowly, deliberately. His eyes kept flicking to the bloodied knife on the bar next to Ridge's right hand. The crowd parted as Donnelly approached, clearly fearing more bloodshed.

Ridge waited until the constable was almost upon him. "Gord," he said politely, tipping his glass towards the mirror.

"Mr. Secova," Donnelly said, his voice shaky. Gord Donnelly had been the constable in Bergstrom for most of his adult life, and had stayed that way by knowing when to exercise his power and when to turn a blind eye. Yet the pressures of the job had taken a toll, as seen in his almost white hair and his hangdog eyes.

"Want a drink?"

"No, Mr. Secova. I...what happened here tonight...."

Ridge turned slowly, annoyed by Donnelly's presence. "You have something to say to me, Constable?"

Donnelly swallowed hard. "We can't have any more of this. Link there, he's a family man who just came down here to blow off some steam. Pence, that wound was bad. Probably fatal. Now, I don't want to have to bring you in."

Ridge laughed and smiled, a toothy smile. "Like you could bring me in."

Donnelly's hands were shaking, so he put them in his pockets and stepped back. "I know I can't. That's why I've sent word to Fort Hasten. I suspect a force will be on its way directly. I'll let them take you in. You'll face a district court, not local."

"You called the soldier boys on me?" Ridge laughed again and finished another drink. "Wonder how many they'll send?

How many do you think it would take, Constable?" He reached for the knife and held it out in front of him. "You know that they would never get here in time to save you?" Ridge let his pale eyes survey the room. "No one here would dare intercede. I could open you clear to the spine."

Donnelly swallowed again and stepped back more. "I don't want any trouble, but I can't ignore this anymore. You're a menace. I've got to do something. "So why not wait until the soldier boys come for me? Might make for a show."

"I'm giving you a chance to get out. Go south. Go to Norales. Just get out of my town." Something changed in Donnelly's face…he gained a fresh taste of confidence. "I hear the Ministry has been looking into some of your business practices. Could be looking at more than a simple assault charge."

That changed things. Ridge's smile faded as the prospect of a national prison flitted through his mind. Ridge felt he was the better of any ten men in a fight and could hold his own against slightly more, but an army was a different matter.

"Well played, Constable. It appears that I may have worn out my welcome in your fine town."

Donnelly relaxed, maybe grinned just a tad, and looked a little too cocky at someone in the crowd. Ridge moved quickly, grabbing Donnelly by the lapels, pulling him toward the bar. By reflex the constable put his hands out to brace himself, and when he did, Ridge brought the knife down in a tight, vicious arc. The shining blade caught Donnelly in the soft spot between his wrist and his foreman and cut straight through. As Donnelly screamed in pain, Ridge flicked the amputated hand away with the blade.

"Just a little something to remember me by, Constable." Ridge stowed the knife back in its place and strode quickly but confidently out of the tavern and into the night. He would have to move fast. He didn't dare return home for any of his belongings. He would have to start over.

As he mounted his steed, the thought entered his mind. *I should have killed them all, just for the fun of it.*

CHAPTER 8

Marlowe's Tavern was a low-rent dive that was populated by the harsher element of Nogales society. It was a motley collection of gamblers and thieves, prostitutes and outlaws of various types. At Marlowe's, the lights were low, the music was loud, and no one asked too many questions.

It was Bethel Hough's favorite place in the world.

Parrie Barrows stalked in the front door breathing fire. She was dressed in what was left of her uniform; iron gray pants and matching jacket with all insignias ripped off, plain white shirt, and high black boots. She was unarmed except for her fists and her rage.

Marlowe's was not the place for an attractive young woman of any age to enter, especially unarmed and unaccompanied. The door hadn't yet swung shut behind her, and already lustful eyes began sizing her up.

She stood just inside the doorway, huffing, scanning the room, certain that he would be here. She spotted him sitting at the far end of the bar, a short glass of amber liquid in front of him, laughing it up with a pair of large, hard men who looked like shoremen. He acted like he didn't have a care in the world.

Bethel Hough didn't have much reason to worry. He never had. At 6'1" and a solid two-twenty, he was a large enough man to hold his own in any brawl. His golden blond hair and piercing blue eyes allowed him to charm almost any young lady out of her most precious possession. Coming from one of Cadoa's most prominent families provided him money, influence, and the benefit of the doubt almost anywhere he went.

The problem was that Bethel knew all of that and used it to full advantage. Bethel was a rogue, a schemer and a cheat. He used his size to bully, his looks to plunder, and his name to bail himself out when all else failed. It was because of his wayward lifestyle that Bethel's father had sent him to Academy to begin with. However, his hopes that military life would straighten out his son were unfounded.

Parrie cared about none of it. All she knew was that Bethel had somehow managed to take her down with him, and now her dreams were ruined. Once she caught sight of him, nothing could have kept her from her prey.

Bethel saw her storming down the aisle towards him, drained his glass, and stood, arms outstretched and a phony smile plastered on his face. He started to greet her, but once Parrie was in reach, she reared back and punched him across the jaw with everything she had.

Parrie wasn't the biggest or strongest person, but with a head of steam and a heart of fury, she produced enough power to send Bethel stumbling backwards. She pressed her advantage, driving the palm of her left hand up under his chin and bending him back over the bar. With her right, she scooped up a glass bottle, smashed it against the bar, and drove the jagged edge into the soft, exposed tissue of his neck.

"Give me one reason not to carve you into pieces, Bethel," she snarled, her fingers turning white from the death grip she held on the bottle neck.

"Whoa, easy there, Parrie. You could hurt a guy like this," Bethel muttered as Parrie continued to push his chin back.

"That's the point, moron," she snapped again. "Why did you do it?"

Bethel tried to hide his panic with a smirk. "I don't know what you're talking about, angel. Why don't you put down that shiv and we'll talk about it?"

"Don't call me angel." Parrie pushed the bottle a little harder and a crimson tendril began running down Bethel's neck and onto his shirt and began soaking into the white fabric. "You ruined my life. You stole my dream and sullied my name. I have nothing left to lose."

"Angel...Parrie, please. I don't know what you're talking about. Just relax. Tell me what happened." Bethel began pushing back against her, forcing Parrie's death grip to relax.

"You know damn well what happened," Parrie pouted.

Parrie saw one of Bethel's drinking buddies shift out of the corner of her eye. She pressed the glass even harder against his throat. "Tell your friends to stay back or I'll bleed you like a pig."

"Everybody just needs to calm down here, okay? Parrie and I are mates, we're just having a little misunderstanding. No big thing," Bethel said defensively. To Parrie he said, "Just take the bottle down and let's go somewhere. This really isn't the place for you."

"No kidding," she spat back. "I knew my place. I was happy there and you ruined it. You slimy, rotten piece of trash." Parrie could feel herself losing control. It would be so easy to slice his throat open, to spare anyone else of the pain Bethel always left in his wake. Just one little flick of the wrist....

Then it all went crazy. Someone from behind grabbed a handful of Parrie's hair and yanked her backwards, pulling her off her feet. The broken bottle fell and shattered on the floor. Instantly there were strange hands all over her, ripping at her clothes, pulling her away.

Parrie screamed and kicked and thrashed, desperate to break free. The logical part of her brain was scolding her for losing track of her surroundings, and she resigned herself to a very short, but very brutal end. She was putting up a good fight, but half the bar must have been clamoring for a piece of her. They were spitting on her, kicking her, punching her. She felt her skin burning from a dozen different cuts. Her head was starting to swim and colored dots danced in front of her eyes. She kept kicking and struggling like a wild animal.

A large boom erupted overhead and all hands released Parrie, who landed hard on her back. She gasped for breath but immediately began scrambling, clutching what was left of her jacket and looking for some sort of shelter.

The crowd parted and there stood Bethel, pulled up to his full height, shoulders back, holding a smoking pistol held overhead. He looked like storybook hero standing there, surrounded by ruffians, a smoking pistol in his hand.

"Is that any way to treat a lady, you barbarians?" His voice boomed through the room, full of self-righteousness. He held his left hand out to Parrie and she took it, allowing Bethel to pull her up off the floor. He didn't stop his rant though.

"You see our clothes? We are your protectors! We are your officers! You treat us like some sort of rabble? You are all disgusting, pathetic vermin!"

Parrie was clutching at Bethel's arm, hiding behind him as she looked out at a room full of predators. "Bethel, let's get out of here."

He was on a roll, though. "You think I fear you? I am a soldier! I will fight you all! Do you dare stand against me?"

"Bethel, you idiot. You're going to get us killed," Parrie whispered. She was not lacking in courage, but she also understood odds, and knew that they were heavily stacked against the two of them. "Shut up and let's get out of here."

She started tugging him towards the door and he allowed himself to go. Parrie turned him, keeping his body between her and the seething mass of humanity. They reached the door without incident and Parrie was ready to run, but Bethel couldn't resist one last volley.

"Farewell, you cretins. When next I grace this establishment, I will come to you as a general and you will bow before me!" Theatrically, he held the pistol high and pulled the trigger again, only this time it clicked loudly. Bethel shrugged and tossed the pistol on the floor, then turned and bolted out the door. Parrie stumbled, taken by surprise by his sudden move, then righted herself and ran after him. They didn't dare risk a look over their shoulder, but instead ran as fast as they could until Marlowe's was far behind them.

#

Once they were clear, Bethel flagged down an elderly man in a carriage and paid him to drive the two to Bethel's hotel. They didn't speak during the bumpy ride across Nogales's pot-filled roads. The bouncing carriage finally stopped and they got out in front of Hotel Carroll, the choice resort for Cadoa's wealthiest citizens.

Parrie, who had been raised on a poorly producing farm, looked up at the towering building in wonder. "Of course you would be staying somewhere like this. I'm on the street and you are in the lap of luxury."

Bethel sloughed the comment off. "At the end of the day it's just a place to lay your head. Come on up. We'll replace those rags of yours."

Bethel led her through a lobby that was decorated in exquisite, hand-carved wordwork, with hand stitched rugs on the hardwood floors. The clientele, all dressed in the finest fashion, regarded the two of them in their torn and bloodied clothes like the lowest form of scum. An older couple clearly headed for a night on the town sneered at them, and Bethel answered with an exaggerated bow.

"Stop that," Parrie scolded, slapping him on the back. "Don't make it worse."

"To hell with these people," Bethel answered. "These are my father's people. They've lived their whole lives in priviledge. What do they know of us, or the challenges we face?"

Parrie snorted. "What challenges? *You're* born of priviledge. Look at this," she said, sweeping her hand at their surroundings. "You get kicked out of school and land here. You want to tell me about challenges?"

They began ascending the wide staircase, Parrie a step behind, thinking that Bethel was a hypocrite. He used his family's name and money to his benefit often, so how could he look down his nose at these people?

They climbed four flights of stairs before coming to Bethel's room. "You think my life is all fun and games?" Bethel said as he took his room key out of his pants pocket, opened the door, and held it open for Parrie.

"Yes, I do." Parrie stepped into the room followed by Bethel, who closed the door behind him.

"You're thinking that I trade on my family all the time and you're right, I do. But I don't do it because I think I deserve special treatment."

Parrie walked to the room's window and took a quick glance out, looking down at the people on the streets. She caught her reflection in the glass. She looked awful. Her face had been raked on both sides, leaving long fingers of dried blood on her porcelain skin. Both eyes were already turning black, and she had another, deeper cut on her scalp that was clearly visible through her shortly trimmed hair. She scowled at the image and turned sharply on her heels, the way a proper officer would. "You claim that you don't?"

"I used to, but not anymore. Academy beat that out of me," Bethel said as he took off his jacket. He tossed it on his bed and began to undo the buttons on his blood-stained shirt. There was a fine line of blood tracing down his neck and onto his sculpted chest, stopping where the shirt began to soak the blood up. "Blazes, Parrie, look at this." He felt for the puncture on his neck where she had held the jagged glass. "You could have killed me."

Parrie scoffed at him. "That was the intention. Don't think that just because you bailed me out that I have forgiven you. What you did is still inexcusable."

Bethel, who was busy scraping the dried blood off his chest with a fingernail, looked up at her with completely believable wonder. "What is it you are so convinced that I have done?"

"Like you don't know. Seriously Bethel, don't play dumb with me."

"I wish that I were playing." He threw his ruined dress shirt on the floor and put his hands on his hips. "I honestly have no idea."

"How about you accusing me of helping you cheat? How about you planting evidence in my locker? I'm not even sure how you managed to get into the barracks to do that."

Bethel began laughing, a loud, rolling belly laugh that Parrie found over-the-top, much like the man himself. "You don't think...." He pointed at himself. "Me? I didn't take you for such a fool, Parrie."

"I am not a fool," she growled between clenched teeth. "You get kicked out for cheating, and suddenly the commandant finds cheat sheets in my locker? What am I to think?"

"I didn't get kicked out for cheating, Parrie. They wouldn't kick me out for cheating. Hell, I had instructors slipping me answers and changing grades from the moment I got there. The cheating accusation is just a ruse."

"A ruse?"

Bethel strode confidently to his bed and sat on the edge. "I chose to leave," he said as he began pulling one boot off. "I had a better opportunity and I took it. The academy just needed an excuse for my absence." He let the first boot fall carelessly to the floor and stripped the second off as well.

"So how did I get involved with it?" Parrie was confused now, and she hated not knowing what was going on around her. She took a seat next to Bethel on the bed. "If you weren't kicked out for cheating, then why were those notes in my locker?"

Bethel grinned down at her like she imagined a big brother would. "You don't know? The commandant hated you. You weren't supposed to be there, and you certainly weren't supposed to last. They don't want women at the Academy, but they especially don't want women showing up the men. You were tops in your class and you were dedicated and perseverant. They knew the only way to get you out was a scandal. So they created one. I'm just the scapegoat."

It made sense. Parrie slumped, heartbroken. "I'm sorry," she muttered. "I never thought. It just seemed so—"

"Like me," he finished. "That's why it worked."

Parrie forced herself up off the bed and paced to the other side of the room. "Now I do feel like a fool." The rage was beginning to boil up again. "You know what I'm going to do?" She executed another perfect heel turn. "I'm going to go to the commandant, first thing in the morning, and I'm going to confront him. I'll call him down and leave him no choice but to take me back and issue a full apology. A public apology."

"Parrie," Bethel laughed. "You're dreaming. You'll never get in to see him. They won't let you in the gates. Let it go. Find something else to do. You're smart. You'll land on your feet."

She knew that he was right, but that knowledge didn't make it any easier to take. She stood and fumed and thought, and then an idea occurred to her. "What are you going to do? What is this new opportunity you were talking about?"

Bethel chuckled uncomfortably. "That's not really important."

"What is it, Bethel?" Parrie could tell by his reaction that he was lying. "Is it military? What is it?"

"Parrie, drop it. Really."

She stormed across the room and crouched in front of him. "You owe me. I took a fall for you."

"I didn't have anything to do with it," Bethel protested.

"Please. I don't know what else to do. My entire life has been pointed toward military service. If I can't do that...." She searched for the words. "I won't go back to the farm, Bethel. I want in on whatever it is you're up to."

"Parrie, where I'm going, it's no place for a woman."

Parrie shot up out of her crouch. "I am a soldier. You yourself said I was head of my class. Whatever you're up to and wherever you're going can't be any worse than war, can it?"

"I don't know about that," Bethel said. "It might be."

Parried sat back down beside him. "Please. I'm begging and I hate to beg. Get me in. Whatever it is. I'm no coward."

Bethel searched her eyes for a minute and saw that there was no backing down. "Fine, but if you're in, you're in all the way. You can't back out."

"I'm not the type to run from a challenge. What is it?"

This time it was Bethel who stood and paced. "I'm part of a special security detail. One of my instructors told me about it, suggested that it could be a quick way up the ladder."

"A security detail?" Parrie was excited by the prospect. "For what?"

Bethel ran a nervous hand through his hair. "For an expedition to Aranwa."

Parrie jumped off the bed in excitement. "We're going to Aranwa? Finally?" She stood excitedly and walked back to the window, looking out in the direction of Aranwa. "I have to be in on this, Bethel," she said as she turned away from the window. "You have to make this happen."

Bethel put a finger to his lips. "Quiet. I'll do what I can, but you need to understand something. We—the government, the army—we're not going to Aranwa. This is a private expedition and we will essentially be mercenaries. If anything happens to us, we get thrown in a shallow grave and forgotten about. On the other hand...." Bethel was always one to find the positives in a situation. "This new country will need an army. We'll already be there."

She saw where he was going. "A quick rise in the ranks instead of being buried at some frontier outpost babysitting farmers." Parrie's mood brightened instantly. "Well, who would have thought that being accused of cheating could work in your favor?"

Bethel smiled at her. "Welcome to my world."

CHAPTER 9

Three kilometers outside of Norales, Aribeth and Leland met Thom Behrens in a dusty field to finalize their agreement. Behrens arrived in a carriage, accompanied by two flatbed trailers loaded down with supplies.

Behrens, dressed as always for a night on the town, stepped out of his carriage, choking on the dust. He put a handkerchief to his mouth to filter out as much as possible. Aribeth and Leland exchanged an amused glance.

"Mr. Jax," he called once the coughing spell passed. "Feel free to inspect the cargo. This is, I believe, everything you asked for and more. Our backers were so pleased that you were leading this expedition that they offered to throw in some extra provisions for your family. I think that this will be more than enough to get your family through the winter."

Leland whistled at the sight of the two loaded flatbeds. "It looks that way," he said in awe as he left Aribeth's side to check out the provisions.

"What about his deed?" Aribeth asked.

Behrens nodded and reached into his shoulder bag. He produced a rolled document, sealed in wax and rolled with a ribbon bearing the official seal of Cadoa. He handed it over to Aribeth. "Would you like to review it?"

"I would," she said confidently. Father had taught Aribeth to read by giving her official documents to review. She would have no trouble reading a simple land deed. She broke the seal and read carefully over the document before looking up at Behrens. "Just a moment," she said.

Aribeth walked quickly over to Leland, who was busy checking out the cargo for the trip to the Jax family home. "These city boys," he said as he worked. "They don't know how to tie things down. Not for a load that's going out to the wilderness. This might work on regular shipping lanes, but—"

Aribeth nudged him and held the land deed out for him to review. "Everything looks good. They gave you a hundred acres, and it looks like they gave you a wide berth all the way around. Is this agreeable?"

Leland took the document from her, eyed it for a moment, then frowned and gave it back. "A hundred acres? We used to have the whole forest."

Aribeth was sensitive to Leland's dislike of encroaching settlements, but she was a realist. "It's a good deal of land that would have cost you a lot of money to purchase. This will give your family a nice area to live on. You can't stay in the wilderness forever."

Leland stopped his tying to look at her, and his gaze was enough to make her take a reflexive step back. "I might be paying for it with my life. Is that a steep enough price to pay? All of this," he said, referring to the two trailers full of supplies. "Will help my family for now. If I don't come back, what are they going to do? I'm taking a huge risk for you. Don't forget that."

Aribeth dropped her eyes to the dirt, but only for a moment. "I understand, Mr. Jax. The alternative is doing nothing and waiting for the Ministry to sell that land out from under your family. Would you prefer to take that route?"

Leland looked over at her and they locked eyes. This time,

Aribeth wouldn't flinch and Leland backed down. "No, this is fine," he sighed. "I wish I had time to deliver this to Rey myself and give him some last-minute instructions."

"Why don't we write him a letter? We can have it delivered with the cargo."

"I guess that'll have to do," Leland said with resignation in his voice.

Aribeth left him to finish his work and reported back to Behrens, who had gone back to sitting in the carriage. "He is agreeable. Thank you for making this happen. When do we set off for Aranwa?"

Behrens shifted uncomfortably in his seat. "I really do wish you would reconsider. This mission is suicide."

"A Fuller doesn't back down from a challenge. You know that."

"Yes," Behrens answered in defeat. "You will have thirty families travelling with you, plus a small security force." He leaned forward and whispered. "Understand that this is a fully private expedition. The Ministry knows nothing of it and does not condone it. Anything that happens, from the moment you leave Norales, is on your head and your head alone."

"I understand," Aribeth answered confidently. "When do I meet this security force?"

"Two more days," Behrens said. "Everything should be ready in two more days. This will be the staging area. Be here at sun up. Unless you reconsider."

"I will not," she snapped. "Thank you for your help. We will settle Aranwa; you can be assured of it. You should start recruiting the next round of settlers."

Behrens sneered at her. "You are too cocky. Let's see you get the first thirty families there safely and then we'll talk. I will strongly encourage you, one last time, take these next two days and reconsider. This is a fool's mission."

Aribeth was getting tired of the doubt and derision coming from Behrens. She opened the carriage door, squeezed in past Behrens' legs, and sat next to him. "I understand that you don't think I can do this, and that in some way you think that you're doing right in discouraging me. Please understand that I have to do this, for my father and for myself. We will settle Aranwa and we will create a new country, a place where people can live their lives without fear of the Ministry taking what they have. A land without the arbitrary laws and corruption that plague us here. I will create the truly free country my father dreamed about."

Mr. Behrens shook his head sadly. "It's a dream, Ms. Fuller. A beautiful one, to be sure, but just a dream. Even if you succeed." A look of worry crossed his face. He looked all around, checking the outside of the carriage to make sure no one was too close. He leaned in close to Aribeth. "There are things going on here, forces at play, that you don't understand. There are a lot of people, powerful people, with a vested interest in Aranwa succeeding, regardless, or maybe in spite of, who leads the expedition. If you insist on going, watch yourself and stick close to your guide out there. He may be your only true friend."

Aribeth's blood ran cold. She was suddenly filled with questions, but she knew that Behrens would have no answers for her. She looked away, hoping to hide the fear and doubt that suddenly raced through her mind.

She must have failed. Behrens reached out and patted her knee in a grandfatherly way. "No one would think less of you if you backed out. In fact, I would give you the money, out of my own pocket, if you decided that you wanted to go back to school. I fear for your future. You are a bright and beautiful young lady. You deserve a chance at a real life."

His words made sense. From the beginning Aribeth had

doubted the entire venture and her role in it. He was offering her a lifeline and she was thinking about taking it. "What about Mr. Jax? His family needs those supplies and that deed. If I back out, can you guarantee that he keeps what you've given him?"

Behrens tilted his head back and calculated. "The supplies are already loaded and ready for transport. Not much anyone could do to stop delivery now. As for the deed...." He lowered his head and looked Aribeth in the eye. "It would be voided before he made it home. Unless, of course, he agreed to guide the expedition under new leadership."

That was the answer Aribeth had expected. "I doubt it," she said. "He doesn't really want to do it at all." She thought about the night she had spent with Leland's family, how hungry they were, how undernourished, yet still full of happiness and hope. Those supplies would be a godsend, but she knew it was only a matter of time before the Ministry sold that land out from under them. What would they do then? Where would they go?

"I can't, Mr. Behrens. If it were just me, I might take you up on your offer. Mr. Jax and his family, they need this. They are why he agreed to go. I'm afraid that if I backed out, they would lose it all. I got him into this, the least I can do is go with him."

Mr. Behrens was not surprised. "Just like your father, reckless and stubborn, but also with unyielding loyalty. Please take care of yourself. Be very careful about who you place your trust in. The families I have lined up for you are solid. This security team though, I have had no hand in picking them. The investors have done that. I cannot vouch for any of them. In fact, I don't even know who they are."

"I don't suppose I could just meet the families and leave, without the security team?"

Behrens smiled sadly. "No. Besides, it would be ill advised."

"I understand," she said. Aribeth could feel the weight of

what she was about to undertake pressing down on her. "I will be careful." She shook his hand. "Thank you for all of your help, Mr. Behrens. I hope that when next we meet, it will be a more pleasant experience."

"My dear," he said quietly. "I doubt very seriously that there will be a next time."

#

Behrens took the carriage back to town while Aribeth stayed behind to help Leland finish with the supply train. They studiously checked every item on both flatbeds and secured the cargo for the rough trip to come. Then she helped Leland craft a letter of instruction to his brother.

With all of that done, they mounted their steeds and headed back into Norales. Leland had just arrived the day before and had camped in a clearing outside of town. Aribeth insisted that he return with her to the boarding house to clean up.

Leland resisted but Aribeth convinced him. They walked in together, both covered in dirt and Leland with his specially made hunting rifle at his side, to the derision of the other guests in the lobby. Aribeth was no stranger to disapproving glances, and she met them all with a cool smile. Leland looked around in wonder. As they climbed the stairs to Aribeth's second floor room, she giggled at him.

"You act like you're in the lap of luxury the way you're staring at everything."

Leland suppressed an embarrassed grin. "Never been any place like this. I go into town to trade and buy supplies, that's it."

"This is nothing. You should see some of the places down by the river. They make this place look like a hovel."

"Do you come from money, Ms. Fuller?"

"No," Aribeth said as they reached the stop of the stairs. "But my father sometimes travelled in the circles of the people who did, so it's not a foreign concept to me."

They started down the long hallway to Aribeth's room. "How did your father hang out with money if he never had any?"

"Because he had this amazing ability to make other people money. They like that. If he hadn't, neither one of us would be here right now." They reached her door and Aribeth took a moment to glance over her shoulder at Leland. "You can take that for whatever it is worth."

She opened the door and let Leland in. He was equally impressed with her relatively sparse room. He seemed particularly fascinated with her bed, and pushed down on the mattress several times.

"Ever slept on a real bed?"

"No ma'am," he said bashfully. "The floor or the ground has always been enough for me."

"Lay down on it. Take a nap if you want. Just take your clothes off first." Leland shot her a surprised look. "You're dirty. I don't want you getting dirt all over the bed."

"Couldn't do that anyway," Leland said as he stood and walked away from the bed. He went to the window and looked out. "Wouldn't be proper."

"Such manners," Aribeth answered, unintentionally sounding sarcastic. She reached into her bag and grabbed a change of clothes for herself, then started for the bathroom. "Do you have a change of clothes? We could have those washed."

"Not with me, ma'am," he answered, still staring out the window. "Got some back at the camp."

"Aren't you afraid someone will steal them?"

Leland turned around and shrugged. "If they do, they do. I can make more. Hides aren't hard to come by if you know what you're doing. Besides, I figure I'll head back now that you're safe here."

"Stay here with me. I was going to take you to dinner tonight. Have you ever eaten in a restaurant before?" Leland shook his head. "Stay. If you want, you can sleep on the floor. You can return to your camp tomorrow."

"You don't mind?"

"Not at all," Aribeth answered with a smile. "I'm going to clean up and change clothes, and then we can go eat. Make yourself at home in the meantime."

Aribeth took her time cleaning up and enjoyed a long soak. When she was done, she dressed and brushed her hair, and left it down to dry. She stepped out to find Leland still standing by the window, watching the world pass by beneath him.

"Be a good hunting spot," he said without looking away from the window. "Never thought about it before. I could pick off an issi at three hundred feet from here."

Aribeth leaned on the door jamb and watched Leland as he looked out on the world in wonder. She wondered how old he really was. She had been working on the assumption he was many years older, but she knew growing up in the wild could age you prematurely. Here, out of his element, he seemed much younger.

"I wonder if I'm going to be like that," she finally said.

Leland glanced over at her once, then did a second take. The look that crossed his face was clear enough to read, even for a girl who had never drawn a man's attention before. "What do you mean?" He looked back out the window, but kept glancing over at her.

"When we're out there in the wild. I wonder if I'll be filled with as much awe as you are. I grew up on the frontier, but not actually in the wild."

"Just listen to me and do what I say, when I say. I'll get you home alive. I got a reputation to protect."

78

She crossed the room slowly, amused as Leland tried to watch her without making it obvious. When she reached him, she took one arm in both of her hands. "Let's go eat. We're going to be spending a lot of time together, so we might as well get to know each other."

The boarding house had a tiny dining room on the ground floor in the back. Aribeth and Leland took a seat near the entrance. Leland deferred ordering to Aribeth, who ordered them both a hearty meal.

"Mr. Jax, if you don't mind my asking, how did you wind up raising a house full of children on your own?"

Leland, who was having trouble looking directly at Aribeth, shrugged. "Just happened. Daddy, he wasn't much account for anything. He died in the last war." He caught her surprise. "Not physically. But it wrecked his mind and destroyed his soul. He just drifted along, till one day he just drifted away. Haven't a clue what happened to him. Momma, she…didn't take it too well."

"How long ago did he leave? Must not have been long ago… there were some very young kids at your house."

Leland grimaced. "After Daddy left, Momma would let strangers stay the night. Sometimes they wound up in her bed." Aribeth made a face and Leland chuckled at her reaction. "I know. Used to bother me too. But it's not the kids' fault. I never looked at any of them as anything less than my brothers and sisters."

Leland's story made Aribeth appreciate her upbringing even more. "Where is your mom now?"

"Got sick and died last winter. I think she was just tired of living. She left me to raise the kids in the middle of the worst winter of my life. Wasn't easy, but we got through."

"You're a good man, taking care of them like that. A lot of men would have just left and not looked back. We used to see that a fair amount in Bretonville. Things would get tough and people would just leave."

"That's the town your father started, isn't it?"

"Yes. It started as a mining camp, but my father turned it into a proper town. That's what he did. He'd buy a mine, start a town, make some money, then pack up and start all over. We moved a lot. He was kind of like you. He didn't like being in the city so much. He liked being out on the frontier. He'd get claustrophobic once things got too big."

Their meals were delivered and Leland picked his meat up with his hands and took a large, lustful bite. "That's good," he said as he chewed. "Really good."

"Not much for utensils?"

Leland dropped the meat on his plate and looked around, embarrassed. "Sorry. I'm just not used to—"

"Don't worry about it," Aribeth said. "In fact...." She mimicked his move, feeling like a fool as the juice ran down her chin. "Saves time."

"That it does," Leland answered. He seemed pleased that she would embarrass herself on his account. They both wiped juice off their chin. "You have brothers, don't you? Why didn't your dad ask one of them to go to Aranwa?"

"Because," Aribeth said as she finished her bite. "My father didn't think they...." She paused, searching for the right words. "He didn't think that—"

"He didn't trust them?"

"It's not that. He didn't think that they were smart enough. He didn't think that they could lead people. They are big and strong men, working men, and they'll work all day for you. But ask them to do anything that doesn't involve physical labor and they're at a loss."

Leland nodded while he chewed another bite. "And maybe you were his favorite?"

Aribeth felt herself blush. "Yes. That's why he insisted on sending me off to school. He thought I needed to learn how to be a proper lady, and he wanted me to get an education. He never understood that I was a frontier kid, a prairie flower."

Leland looked at her curiously. "Prairie flower?"

"That's what the girls at school used to call me. They thought it was an insult. I took it as a badge of honor. All that ridicule, it ensured that I would never turn into them."

"So here we are," Leland said after another massive bite of meat. "Two loners about to lead a group of people into the most dangerous place on the planet."

"Lucky us," Aribeth said. She had never thought about it that way before. She was leading people, innocent people, on a trip that would almost assuredly end in death for some, if not all of them. She suddenly found that she'd lost her appetite.

"Sobering thought, isn't it," Lealand said with a macabre grin.

#

That night Aribeth lay in her bed, unable to sleep. Leland slept on the floor at the foot of her bed, still clothed except for his shoes. He was as quiet as a mouse.

Finally unable to stand it, Aribeth sat up in bed. "Mr. Jax, are you awake?"

"Yes," he said, his voice sharp and clear. "And call me Lee. Enough with this Mr. Jax stuff."

"Okay," Airbeth said. "Lee, can I trust you?

"Yes," he said, quick and sure. "Why do you ask?"

"Mr. Behrens said something earlier that's been bothering me. He said that there is more going on here than I can see. That I couldn't trust anyone."

"He's just trying to scare you off," Lee said with certainty. "He's a fancy man. He's terrified of what we're doing. And I

81

think he fancies you and doesn't want you involved. I wouldn't worry too much about it."

"But I can trust you. You're my guy, right?"

She heard him moving and then Leland's head popped up at the end of her bed. "Yes. I never did your father wrong and I won't do you wrong. If anything happens, if you don't know what to do, just stick close to me. I'll protect you. Now get some sleep."

Aribeth laid back and closed her eyes. She believed him and felt comfortable putting herself in his hands. She just couldn't shake the thought that he might not be enough.

CHAPTER 10

The sun was just starting to rise on the eastern horizon, and Echonos was still visible high overhead, his nightly watch not yet complete, when the Aranwa expedition came together in the same dusty field where Aribeth had met Behrens two days before.

Thirty families had gathered with all their worldly possessions shoehorned into homemade wagons, some almost humorously basic while others were near commercial quality. They were mostly young families with children.

Behrens met Aribeth and took her around to each family. She was inherently nervous but didn't let it show, and surprised herself in how well she handled the introductions. Aribeth engaged each family, committed names and faces to memory easily, and put them all at ease that they were in good hands.

They worked from the back of the line to the front, the introductions ending with the first wagon in line. Mr. Behrens led her to the man in the driver's seat of the wagon. He was an average looking man, rail-thin with dark brown skin, deep set eyes, and hair as black as night. The man jumped down out of his seat and shook hands eagerly with Aribeth.

"This," Mr. Behrens began, "is Jamison Gregg. He is the unofficial leader of your caravan. Mr. Gregg comes with my personal highest regards. He is a citizen of utmost standing, a brilliant man, and a fantastic engineer. I think that you will find his experience and expertise most helpful. In fact, his grandfather is one of the founders of Norales. The Gregg family has been instrumental in our town ever since."

Aribeth shook his hand. "Mr. Gregg, pleasure to meet you. If you don't mind my asking, why are you coming to Aranwa?"

Gregg's eyes slid away for a moment, then came back, full of bright-eyed optimism. "I'm just ready for a new challenge, ma'am. City life is getting a bit too…constricting. I'm ready to get back to nature. Besides, Mr. Behrens and I both figure you'll need an engineer when it comes to laying out your town. I can help with damming, irrigation, and things like that."

Aribeth had the distinct impression that there was another reason, but it didn't matter. She would need someone of his expertise, so unless the man was a vicious killer — and that seemed unlikely — she was agreeable. "Who all do you have travelling with you?"

"My wife is at the creek with our two daughters, bottling up some water for the trip."

"Well, I hope that they get back quickly, because I plan on pulling out soon. I do want to have Mr. Jax address everybody before we leave. He's the one who will be leading us."

"Sounds good," Gregg answered. "Pleased to meet you, ma'am."

Behrens gently took Aribeth's arm and led her away. "All these people are good people, good families. Lots of kids or women of childbearing age. The men are all strong and skilled in one thing or another. There's a good mixture of boys and girls among the children. They will do you proud. Please treat them well."

"I will," Aribeth said earnestly. "I like them all very much."

"Good. Now for the security team. I cannot vouch for any of these people other than to say that our investors picked them."

They walked away from the gathered caravan through a copse of trees to a small clearing on the banks of a healthy creek, where five men stood in a circle, talking jovially. They were a rough looking group of men of various age, build, and appearance. Each wore drab clothing, everything shades of gray or brown, long sleeved shirts, tight pants, and high boots. Most wore wide brimmed hats. All but one had facial hair. The other one was a young man, tall and lean, with a military style haircut and cleanly shaven. He spoke loudly and laughed heartily.

Off to one side, a single woman stood by her steed, rechecking her saddle and her bags. She was of average height for a woman, built roughly the same as Aribeth, but she moved with the silky athleticism of a predator. She wore freshly polished black boots, white pants, and a bright blue, high collared jacket over a white shirt. She had a matching blue hat perched on the horn of her saddle.

"That one's a peacock," Aribeth whispered to Behrens as they approached.

"I'm not sure who that is," he confided. "She's a late addition. Clearly she comes from Academy, as does the tall fellow over there." He then straightened up and approached the group of men, Aribeth one step behind. "Colonel Holt," he called out.

A short, older man with a brushy mustache and bowed legs stepped out of the group of men and approached. He smiled warmly as he shook hands with Behrens. "Colonel Holt, this is Aribeth Fuller. She is leading the expedition. Aribeth, Colonel Baser Holt."

"Colonel," she said politely. He took her hand in his like a true gentleman and kissed her lightly on the back of the hand.

"Madame," he said, his voice rough and deep. "A pleasure." Their eyes held each other for a moment before he turned toward the other men. "These are my command, all handpicked. I will introduce you, but first, let me tell you about myself." Holt was so smooth, so practiced, that Aribeth was sure he had done this many times before.

"I am a lifelong military man. I was a cavalry captain for many years. I led the charge at the Battle of Blackwater Draw that broke Iridian lines and drove those devils back across the river. I retired last year, but when this opportunity presented itself, I couldn't resist. I ask only that you consider me for commander when it comes time for you to appoint officers for your new city."

Aribeth was confused. "I thought you were already the commander."

"No ma'am," he answered. "I was asked to head security for the expedition. Once we pull out of here, and especially once we cross into Aranwa, you will be the leader and I want the choice to be yours. It's important that everyone in the expedition know, and respect, that you are in charge. As a military man, chain of command is very important to me. I will honor whatever you choose to do."

Aribeth was pleased. "Thank you very much, Colonel. I can assure you that you will have my full consideration, and I'm happy to have you. I will want to get to know all of the men before I make a final decision."

"Of course," he said. "Let me introduce you." Holt led her to the group of four, who were watching the proceedings warily. Aribeth looked into the eyes of each man, and she didn't like what she saw in any of them.

"First, Colonel Neal Bertrand." A plump man with thick sideburns and cigarette dangling from his mouth nodded at them. "Artillery man. Served with distinction at the Battle of Quail Creek. Lost half a foot there for his trouble." The man nodded again and held up his left leg and the half shoe he wore on that foot.

"Next," Holt said without pause. "Lieutenant Colonel Alvarez Proffitt. He's a sharpshooter who killed, what...eight Iridians at Adobe Junction?"

Proffitt, who was a tall, handsome man with deeply bronzed skin and pale green eyes, smirked at him. "Ten. Like shootin' rabbits."

"My mistake," Holt answered with a grin before turning his attention to the next man. "Lieutenant Colonel Liam Reeder. Cavalry man such as myself. He's a little too young to have seen any action, but he's chompin' at the bit."

Reeder was the shortest of the bunch but was powerfully built, slightly bowlegged, with flaming red hair and sky blue eyes. "Ma'am," he spat out, dislike oozing out of every pore.

"Finally, the young pup over there," Holt said, referring to the handsome boy she had noticed earlier. "Cadet Bethel Hough, of the Norales Houghs. He just joined in, comes to us from the Academy. He's what we old war horses call a warm body, because that's all he is at this point."

Hough smiled and bowed deeply, showing deeply ingrained manners, but Aribeth also detected a touch of the dramatic in him.

"Gentlemen," she said. Then she turned back to Holt. "What about her?" Aribeth looked over at the well-dressed woman with the white-blonde hair. They all laughed out loud at the girl. She looked over at them with a sneer and mounted her steed.

"She's with me," Hough said loudly. "Parrie Barrows. She served with me at the Academy. I fully vouch for her. She was head of her class."

"And our resident fashion model," Profitt smirked. "With her fancy clothes."

"A proper military unit should have a proper uniform," she called out. "This is based on the official uniform of a cavalry unit, is it not, Colonel?""

Holt shook his head and chuckled. "Yes, Ms. Barrows, it is." Holt turned to Aribeth. "She doesn't get that this isn't a proper military outfit. All of us are out of service, mostly due to injury. Those two young pups got kicked out of Academy. We're just a rag tag group, but we know what to do if things get hairy."

"I see," Aribeth said to Holt. To Parrie she said, "I appreciate your professionalism." Parrie tipped the bill of her cap to Aribeth in return.

Aribeth was ready to return to the families, but the sound of approaching hooves stopped her. They all turned as a magnificent painted steed edged through the trees. The rider was perhaps the most beautiful man Aribeth had ever laid eyes on. His pale blue eyes almost glowed, and his long, auburn hair flowed behind him like a mane. He was clean shaven and well dressed.

The stranger and Parrie passed by each other on their steeds, each eyeing each other cautiously. As Parrie passed, the stranger scowled, and then put his smile back on again. "I understand that the leader of this little trip is back here."

Aribeth stepped towards him. "That would be me. Aribeth Fuller."

The man grinned, dismounted in one fluid motion, and approached her. "Ridge Secova," he announced. A murmur passed through the men in the group. "I was wondering if you might have room for one more in your group. I'm no military man," he said, casting a casual glance at the men. "But I can handle a weapon as well as anyone, and I'm not lacking in courage. It would just be myself and my stud here. I wouldn't be any trouble at all."

Behrens was tugging on Aribeth's arm, but she wouldn't break the man's gaze. "Are you a criminal?"

"I have never been convicted of a crime, madame," he said

without flinching.

"You can contribute and won't be dead weight?"

Ridge looked her straight in the eye. "Whatever you ask of me."

"Then welcome aboard," she said. Ridge kissed her hand in much the same way as Holt had, but he let the kiss linger longer and she felt the heat in the touch of his lips.

"Obliged," he said, looking up at her while still holding her hand in his. "You will not be sorry that you included me."

"We need to get back to the families," Behrens said uneasily, finally managing to pull Aribeth away from the stranger. "Gentlemen, if you want to mount up and come along, I believe Mr. Jax is going to address the group before you depart."

The men in her security detail acknowledged and began checking their steeds as Behrens pulled Aribeth away. They started for his carriage. "Ms. Fuller. That man, Secova, he is not to be trusted in any way."

"Did he lie?"

"No," Behrens said. "He has never been convicted of a crime. He's never stood trial, but he is wanted in several districts. He has a reputation."

"A reputation? You want me to kick him out of the expedition because he has a reputation? My father had a reputation as well, somewhat deserved. I would need more than that to remove him, especially now."

"I tried to pull you away before you committed yourself," he scolded her. "I certainly hope that you exercise better judgment going forward. This man is a swindler, a cheat, a gambler, and, I understand, quite deadly with a blade."

Aribeth stopped and turned to Behrens. "You're afraid of this outlaw, this Talon Volpe character, right?" He nodded. "Then I would think that having a dangerous man such as Mr. Secova in tow would only help. Perhaps the best way to beat an outlaw is with an outlaw."

"It's your expedition," he said sullenly. "As of this moment, I am out of it. I will return to Norales immediately. If you secure a settlement, send word and I will assemble another group of settlers. If not...."

Behrens let the sentence dangle in the air between them, then turned and hurried off. Aribeth watched him get into his carriage and tracked it as he rode away. She rolled her eyes skyward towards Echonos, now no longer visible in the rapidly brightening azure sky, and whispered. "By your wisdom, please help me make this work and protect these people in my care."

That said, Aribeth let out a long, slow breath and turned to find Leland and begin the journey.

#

For someone unaccustomed to dealing with large groups of people, Leland handled himself surprisingly well. He had assembled the group around him. The security detail grouped together to Leland's left, the men to the center and around to his right, the women and older children standing behind. They all listened carefully as he began.

"The first part of this journey will be easy. We are a two day walk from Masterson Gulch, which will be the last settlement we see. We will resupply there. If you think that you want to turn back, this would be the time. After that, things will get difficult."

There was a ripple that ran through the families, though the security detail didn't bat an eye. It occurred to Aribeth in that moment that she had never pressed Leland for any details about the trip. She was just as in the dark as the settlers she was leading.

"Once we start down the gulch, anything can happen. The Wildorago River is the border. Crossing the river is going to be...." Leland looked slowly around the group, and then over their heads at the assembled wagons, each loaded down with provisions behind them.

"Challenging," he finally said. "The river is wide and fast, and there are razor sharp rocks just below the surface. The currents can and will sweep you away if you are not careful. Swimming across is not an option. When I crossed over the first time, we constructed a raft, started high on the bend, and let the currents push us over. We lost one of our party along the way, smashed against the rocks. "

That elicited another round of murmuring from the crowd. Aribeth slapped him hard on the arm and gave him a scolding look. Leland shrugged. "I want you to know what you're getting into. This is not going to be easy, and there is a good chance some you out there will die on this trip."

"Why cross there then?" one settler asked. "Why not find another spot?"

Leland approached the man and addressed him directly. "Because just north of there, the gulch walls shoot straight up. There's no bank, just rushing water and rocks. There's no staging ground, and you will not be able to repel down those walls. Go south, past the rapids, and you run into the pinti."

"What is that?" a woman asked as she gently bounced a newborn in her arms.

Leland walked toward her. "Fish. Vicious, flesh-eating fish. They hunt in schools. You try to cross your animals there...."

"Why not take ships and land on the coast? This approach, the way you describe it, is just stupid," said the first doubter. Leland maintained his calm and his patience throughout the questioning.

"For many of the same reasons. No big ship can get close enough, because of the jagged rocks. Little ships get swallowed up by the high tides, and there are predators along the coastline that make the pinti look tame by comparison. If the approach to Aranwa was easy, we wouldn't be making history. This is not the first attempt that has been made to colonize Aranwa. People have tried passing the mountains in the north and the sea to the south, and every attempt has failed. The only other way in is across the river. That's why we're going that way."

Mr. Gregg spoke up next. "I'd have to see it," he started. "But if we could get some guys across, we could build a bridge."

"It's too wide," Leland answered. "To support a bridge, you'd have to have posts in the water. No one's working in the water. There's no safe place to work."

Mr. Gregg considered it for a moment. "I'd have to see it. There's got to be a way. I'll think on it some. When we camp for the night, could you draw me some diagrams so I can get an idea of what I'm lookin' at?"

"I have some," Aribeth said. She pulled several worn pieces of paper out of her father's journal and carried them to Mr. Gregg. "My father made very detailed renderings. "

"We walked up and down the river on both sides," Leland continued. "The place I'm taking you to, the bend, is the best place to cross. No predators in the water at all. You just need to control your raft, keep it moving across. You slip, and the currents get you."

"What about after we get across?" another voice called out.

"Right across the river there's a forest. The trees are odd, very tall but very skinny. Not much bark, little reachable foliage, no fruit. We'll have to go around. It will take too long and it is too rugged to get the wagons through there. Then we'll pass into the wetlands. There are lots of creeks and small rivers and swampland. Not a suitable place to build, but you can graze your animals there. The water is fresh, but dirty. You'll have to watch your wagons. You get stuck in that muck and you're not getting it out."

"The area that my father wanted to build on is beyond the swamplands. There is a spring, lush vegetation, and nearby woods for lumber."

"I know the place," Leland said. "It was the most beautiful place I've seen. If we can get there, settlement should be easy. The trouble is getting there."

"All right," Aribeth said loudly, inserting as much enthusiasm in her voice as she could muster. "Let's move out." She and Leland mounted their steeds and rode over to the security team.

"Colonel," she said to Holt. "If you wouldn't mind, I'd like you to ride up front with us. After that, we've got thirty families, so each of your men can watch six families, alternating sides of the caravan. We should be able to keep a good watch on everyone."

"Agreed," he answered. Holt addressed his men. "I'll be up front. Bertrand, you take the first six families. Barrows, you get the next six, Profitt, and then Hough. Reeder take rear guard. Keep an eye on your families, and keep an eye on the two young pups too."

"I'll ride up front with you." Ridge Secova sidled his steed next to Aribeth. "I like to be kept in the loop."

Leland, surprised by Secova's appearance, rode over to Secova. "If you need to be told anything, I'll tell you. You should fall in line." Leland stared daggers at the new man.

Ridge responded with a toothy smile that was full of potential violence. "I like my current spot just fine, friend." He nudged closer to Aribeth. "I get my information first hand."

"Lee, let him ride up front. It's fine." Aribeth nudged her steed ahead and turned around to face Ridge. "You can ride next to Colonel Holt. Leland and I will take point." Aribeth called out to the crowd behind Ridge. "Mr. Gregg, if you wouldn't mind, let's move out."

CHAPTER 11

The first two days of the journey were as easy as Leland had promised. The terrain was nice and flat, the trails well-defined. Everyone was in good spirits. Aribeth routinely dropped back and rode alongside each of her thirty families, making sure that everyone was doing fine. The time and care she displayed in those first two days helped endear her to her new charges.

They reached the tiny settlement of Masterson Gulch just past noon on the second day. Some of the families wanted to push on and not waste a half day's worth of sunlight. Yet Leland insisted that the wagon train stop for the day to give the animals time to rest up. That rest would be needed in the days ahead, he assured them.

The merchants in the tiny town were happy to have the extra business, and the settlers replenished what supplies they could. A local restaurant owner cooked a special dinner for them all, and the families gorged themselves on what many of them knew would be the last prepared meal they would ever eat.

Later, as everyone bunked down for the night, Aribeth tracked down Leland, who had wandered away from the camp. She found him staring out into the darkness, apparently lost in his thoughts. So as not to scare him, she made sure to make plenty of noise as she approached.

Leland laughed. "You don't have to do that, Ms. Fuller. I

heard you coming anyway. I'm a hunter, remember? I felt you coming before I heard you."

"Right," she answered, feeling like a fool. She edged up next to him, their arms rubbing lightly against each other as she followed his gaze into the darkness. "Is there something wrong?"

"You mean, other than this whole trip? No. Everything is going fine, better than I'd hoped."

Aribeth slid her gaze from the darkness to Leland, who did a poor job of hiding his emotions. "So what are you worried about? Everyone knows what's coming. You gave everyone a chance to back out before we left. Every family back there signed up for this."

Leland looked over at her quickly and she saw anger flash in his pale eyes. "Did the kids sign up for it? I saw all those little ones back there. They were all running around the fire, playing, thinking that they're on some sort of grand adventure. They don't know what's coming. They didn't sign up for anything."

Aribeth shared his concern about the children. She'd been getting to know them along the ride. "I get that, Lee, but if we're going to start a new country, we're going to need children. You can't just bring old people. You need the next generation. Aranwa is their future."

"Not much of a future."

Leland looked away. Aribeth understood his concern; in fact, she shared it. However, this was how you settled new frontiers. She'd watched her father do it in Brentonville. Risk was part of life on the edge of civilization.

"Bentonville wasn't Aranwa," Leland said calmly without looking at her. "This is a different beast all together."

"Mind reader," Aribeth teased. She sighed and leaned her head on his shoulder. "I don't want anyone to get hurt any more than you do. I have faith that you will get us where we're going. That's what you were hired to do. The families are my responsibility."

"You're all my responsibility," he said sadly. "Every life lost on this journey, every drop of blood that gets spilled, will be on my hands."

Aribeth raised up and, taking Leland's arm in both hands, turned him to face her. She looked him square in the eyes. "Lee. No one has died yet. No one has gotten hurt. Don't beat yourself up over things that haven't even happened. And don't tell me what's going to happen. You don't know what will happen any more than I do. We will take things as they come."

"Yes ma'am," he said softly. Aribeth saw something else flash in his eyes then, like he was thinking about something else entirely. She felt it too, the crackle of attraction, pulling them together. She raised up on her toes....

"Strategy session?"

They both turned suddenly to find Ridge leaning against a tree, watching them with an amused grin on his face. "The great hunter, huh? You never heard me coming."

Aribeth felt Leland's muscles tensing under her fingers. He made a low, guttural noise, like an animal growl. She quickly let go and stepped into the space between them.

"Just getting the lay of the land, Mr. Secova. That's all. I believe Mr. Jax laid out the strategy before we left."

"Right," Ridge say coyly. "The unpassable river. Razor sharp rocks, man eating fish...just another day in the life of the pioneers. Nothing to fear there, right?"

"If you're scared, now would be the time to turn back," Leland said between clenched teeth. "No one would miss you."

Ridge laughed. He had the type of laugh and smile that could easily hold a young lady in its sway. "I don't get scared, *Leland*. I don't fear death." Ridge took his fancy, long-bladed knife out of its sheath and twirled it in his fingers. "When the reaper comes for me, I'll welcome him with open arms. Until then...." He stopped twirling the blade and held it up in front of him, the light of the moons glittering off the deadly metal blade. "I'll take my chances with anything. Or anyone."

"Good to know," Aribeth said. "Because if the stories I hear are true, we'll need someone of your skills. In the meantime, I suggest that we all get some sleep. We have a tough day ahead of us."

"Agreed," Ridge said. He twirled the knife again and slid it back into the sheath. An instant later, Aribeth felt something whiz past her ear. Ridge had just enough time to reach for the handle of his blade before Leland's own knife buried itself in the trunk of the tree Ridge had been leaning against.

"You're not the only one who can handle a knife, Secova."

Ridge relaxed and smiled before turning and investigating the knife stuck in the tree. He looked back at Leland and nodded. "Nice. Hopefully, before this is over, you and I can have a little fun." He pulled the knife out of the tree and Aribeth took a step to the side, intentionally getting in front of Leland. "I'm not going to throw it," Ridge said. Instead, he dropped it to the ground. "It's a little small for my tastes."

He turned and walked away. Aribeth let herself relax, the tension slowly seeping out of her muscles. "That man is a maniac."

"No, he's not," Leland said coldly. "And that scares me worse than anything in Aranwa."

#

Bright and early the next morning, the expedition began the treacherous descent into the gulch itself. The townspeople had cut a trail through the black rock that made up the gulch, a trail just big enough for a standard-sized cart.

Travelling down the steep ravine walls was slow going.

Everyone feared any sort of sudden movements or loud noises that would spook the steeds. If that happened, there was little to keep the attached wagon from plummeting down the cliff, taking its riders with them.

They could all hear the rushing river as they began the descent. It started as nothing more than a deep hum, but as they got lower, the sound became more intense, echoing off the canyon walls. By the time Aribeth and Leland reached the bottom, it was a roar. A fine mist hung in the air, a result of the water slamming into the rocks.

Aribeth dismounted, tied her steed to the limbs of a dead tree, and took her first good look at the river. She'd seen many rivers in her life, but never one like this. The river appeared from around a sharp bend, then immediately turned away from them. Huge, black rocks jutted out on either side of the bank both above and below them, but there were many more below. The water rushed, foaming as it passed over the stones. It was so wide that she could only barely make out the bank on the other side through the mist.

"Scared yet?" Leland was standing just behind her. "This is where it gets real. There should be enough bank for everyone to get down and rest. I hope. I'd hate to leave somebody perched on that trail. I have no idea how we're going to get all of that across though."

Aribeth forced herself to turn away from the river. "That's what Mr. Gregg is for."

She stepped past Leland, desperately hoping that he couldn't see the terror she was feeling. Jamison Gregg had just eased his wagon down onto the bank and was pointing it south, trying to get out of the way of the others. At his side, Gregg's wife, a portly, gray-haired woman, clutched his arm, her face as white as a ghost. Behind them, their two teenage children, one boy and one girl, looked in wide-eyed wonder at the rapids.

Aribeth walked along the wagon and tried the best she could to transmit confidence. "I think right about now is the time to start coming up with some ideas."

Gregg looked past his terrified wife and across the river. "I want to walk the bank a bit," he said calmly. "See what we're working with."

"Good idea," Aribeth agreed. "I'll be right back." As she turned to head back, she caught Gregg's children, who were only a couple of years younger than she was, staring at her. She gave them a wink as she walked away, and heard them muttering between themselves as she went.

Leland was still standing where she had left him, watching as Ridge eased his steed up to the water. "Mr. Jax," she called out, trying to sound professional. "Mr. Gregg wants to walk down the bank to get the lay of the land. Would you please join us?" Leland nodded and started walking. Behind him, she saw Ridge turn his steed. "Mr. Secova. If you could please oversee the rest of the wagons coming down the trail?"

Ridge was tracking Leland with his eyes. "I'd rather go with you."

"You said anything I ask. Remember?" She waited for Ridge to acknowledge. "Good. I'm asking you to supervise the rest of the wagons coming down the trail. I don't want to leave them unsupervised." Colonel Holt was easing his own steed out of the way. "Colonel, would you please assist Mr. Secova in watching the wagons?"

"Certainly ma'am," Holt said with a tip of his hat.

"Very good," she said, her eyes going back to Ridge. "Thank you."

Aribeth hurried back down the bank and found Leland assisting Mrs. Gregg out of the wagon. Mr. Gregg was already standing on the bank, watching the river flow. He whistled as she approached. "Sure does look nasty," he said.

"There's a corridor," Leland said from behind them. He pointed up river, to the start of the bend. "You see the big rock there? If you look, you can see the space before the water really starts rolling there. That's your corridor. If you launch right by that rock, you can use a pole to force yourself across but you have to keep your raft moving. If you lose control and the currents grab it, you're done."

"You get spattered on the rocks," Gregg agreed.

"Or you get swept down river and into the feeding zone. Either way, the rest of your life is very short and unpleasant."

Gregg watched the water run for another moment, then started further down the river, with Aribeth and Leland falling in stride.

"So, ideas on how we get the wagons and the animals across?" Aribeth asked.

Gregg kept his eyes on the water as they walked. "I could construct a simple pulley system, set one end on this side and have someone take the other half over on a raft. We could use that to transfer the supplies. Maybe even some of the young ones. But the heavy stuff, that's another matter. Have you tried walking a steed across your corridor?" he asked Leland.

"No. We left our steeds on this side and we walked from here."

Gregg stopped walking and looked back at Leland quizzically. "You walked all over Aranwa?"

"Not all over," he responded flatly. "There's too much ground to cover. We walked a large area. When Mr. Fuller found the area he liked, we explored that area very well. Then we turned back. We only saw a small portion of Aranwa."

"What do you think?" Aribeth asked. "Do you think you

could walk a wagon across?"

Gregg rubbed his chin in thought. "I'd be willing to try it, if I had a cart to spare. The question is, who is going to risk losing their cart to try? I wouldn't risk mine."

"What if we attached some ropes and pulled it across? We could raft a couple of the stronger men over." Aribeth was brainstorming.

"That's not a bad idea, but who is going to risk their wagon?"

"If you can't get a wagon across, doesn't matter one way or another," Leland finally spoke up. "You either leave it on the bank or you risk losing it in the water. At least if you try to cross it, you have a chance. That walk, it's a rough one, and you'd be carrying a ton more supplies than we were."

"Yep," Gregg agreed, then he started walking again. "I still want to see the area where the river slows down."

They walked further down the river, to the area where the rapids stopped and the water calmed down. Aribeth picked a handful of grass from the bank and tossed it into the water and watched the currents rush it away. "Still moving pretty fast."

"It moves fast all the way to the sea," Leland said. "I don't know how far down the fish go, but I'm assuming all the way down. It would take a week, maybe more, to reach the sea. We don't have the time to waste."

"Why not send a couple of those security guys down there? They could make better time with no wagon to pull."

"That's not a bad idea," Aribeth agreed. "It might only take three hard days' ride to make it to the end."

"And another three days back," Leland countered. "We could have everybody across by then, if we can find a way. And besides, with so few men I don't know that we want to send half of them on what might be a pointless trip."

"I don't even see why we need a security team," Gregg

said in a huff. "Every man in this caravan, and a good chunk of the women, can handle a gun. What do we need soldiers for? Certainly the animals aren't that dangerous."

Aribeth and Leland exchanged glances. She debated whether she should broach the subject of the purported outlaw. She wasn't even sure she believed he existed herself.

"Extra eyes and hands," Leland finally said. "You all need to be focused on guiding your wagons and watching your kids and your animals. If something came charging out, you wouldn't have time to reach for your gun. The security team, they're trained to react on a moment's notice. That's why they're here."

"Makes sense," Gregg finally said. Then he turned back to the river. "You get away from the rocks a little and it's as smooth as glass. You sure about those fish?"

Leland walked over to a young tree, just beginning to bloom with purple and yellow flowers. He broke off a good sized branch, carried it to the water's edge, and with a flick of the wrist, tossed it out into the middle of the river. Almost instantly, several fish began to attack the branch, their needle-like teeth flashing in the light reflecting off the water. After a moment, they disappeared back under the water.

"You can bet that there were a good dozen more. When something falls in, the first three or four hit it to check it out. Once blood hits the water, the others start attacking."

"Well that sounds nice," Gregg said. He fixed his gaze on the far bank. "Be a great place for a bridge, but without being able to get in the water, it'd be a heck of a challenge." Gregg stared across the widening expanse of the river for a while longer, then turned to the others. "What do you say that we try and edge one of those wagons across upstream first, see if that will work?"

"If someone will volunteer," Leland said. They both looked down at Aribeth.

"I guess I'll try to convince someone."

They took a slow walk back up the river and were pleased to see that most of the wagons had made it down by the time they got back, though the area was getting crowded. As they approached, all three kept a sharp eye out.

"There," Gregg said, pointing ahead.

"Dr. Grant?" Aribeth looked where the doctor had stopped his wagon and she saw it. He was piloting a wagon with his wife and their belongings, while his grown son piloted a second one that was weighted down with his medical gear. "Two wagons. It's worth a try."

They approached the doctor, a black skinned man with shortly cropped white hair, and his wife, lighter skinned and with dark, almond-shaped eyes. "Dr. Grant? Might we have a word?"

"Sure," he answered uncertainly. He slowly climbed down off the wagon, giving his wife a tender pat on the leg as he went. They waited for him to make it to the ground and gather himself. "What can I do for you?"

Aribeth stepped forward, reminding herself to sound confident. "Our engineer, Mr. Gregg," she said, pointing the man on her left. "He believes that we can walk a wagon across the river up there, by the bend. We need someone to volunteer their wagon so we can try it. You appear to be the only person with two wagons."

His son, a frail-looking man with his mother's features and his father's white hair, stared down at them in shock. "You want me to drive this across that river?"

Dr. Grant shook his head. "I have all of my medical supplies in that wagon. If something were to happen to them...."

"We would unload the wagon first," Gregg said. "And if something happened to it, I would personally pack your equipment in my wagon."

"I still hate to risk it. And my son—"

"A man would have to be crazy to try to ford that river," the younger Grant said.

"Not necessarily," said Aribeth. "Would you be willing to let us try if I find someone else to drive it?"

The two Grants looked at each other and the younger one climbed out of the driver's seat. "Have at it, I guess," the younger Grant said. "If you can find someone crazy enough to do it."

"I already know someone." Aribeth turned to Dr. Grant's son. "Why don't you unload the supplies and I'll be right back with our lucky volunteer." As the younger Grant started to unload the wagon, Aribeth stepped away from the crowd and spotted Ridge sitting atop his steed, pretending to watch out for the last few stragglers to make it down the trail. Aribeth called out to Ridge and he promptly turned his head her way. "Come here, please."

He grinned when he heard Aribeth yell and started toward her. Aribeth walked back to the group, trying to suppress her own grin. When she heard the hooves of his steed right behind her, she turned around.

"You needed me?"

"Yes, we do," Aribeth started. "You're the man without fear, right?"

Ridge grinned wider. "I sure am. You have something dangerous in mind for me?"

"I sure do," Aribeth answered. She walked over to the smaller wagon and patted the front wheel. "I need you to drive this across the river. Right over there by the big rock."

Ridge followed her gaze. "You want me to drive this across? What about the jagged rocks and the rapids and all of that?"

"We're not sure it will work," Leland said with a smirk. "Mr. Gregg thinks that it might. You've got this little gap before the water hits the rocks. We think that you ease a wagon on through there." Aribeth got the impression that Leland was enjoying this.

Ridge again turned around and pointed to the area in question. "Right over there? Just, ride it across?"

"Right," Leland said coyly. "Just be easy, we don't know what kind of footing there is. You wouldn't want to break the steed's leg."

Ridge looked back, then sized up the status of the steed that was hitched to the wagon in question. "I'll do it." He dismounted and handed Aribeth the reins to his own ride before climbing up in the wagon. "Watch this."

He started the wagon moving and Aribeth, Leland, Gregg, and the Grants all moved to watch his effort. Aribeth heard hooves behind her and found the two cadets, Hough and Barrows, watching intently as well.

Ridge led the steed and wagon to the water's edge, then Leland called out. "Go up river a little more. I mean, right behind that big rock there." Ridge did as he was told. Leland then walked up next to the wagon. "What you want to do is to angle across, but not too sharp. You'll want to stay north of that area there," he said, indicating the area where the rapids began. "Go easy at first until you have an idea about how deep it is or what the footing is like. Once you get out there, if you feel comfortable, you can make a run for it." Leland pointed to a spot on the other bank. "You're aiming for a spot right along there."

Aribeth watched them collaborating from a distance. She was amazed at how, for the moment, all pretense of rivalry had been abandoned. They had been presented with a challenge and were now completely focused on meeting that challenge.

"You think he'll make it?" Parrie Barrows asked from up on her steed.

"No, I don't," Aribeth said coldly. "I'm surprised he's even trying."

"He'll make it," Bethel Hough said. "Watch. That man is a legend. He's got this."

Leland stepped away from the wagon, Ridge gave the steed a little start, and forward they went. The steed easily stepped down into the water, wobbled just a little, then stabilized. Up in the wagon, Ridge was a tightly-coiled ball of nerves. The steed pulled forward slowly and the front wheels of the wagon dropped down into the water. It was a hard landing that jostled Ridge, but he held on.

"So far, so good," Gregg said beside Aribeth.

Ridge nudged the steed forward still. It continued to wobble but stayed upright, and finally, the back wheels dropped off the high bank and into the water.

"Nothing broke," Gregg said. "Nice start."

"I don't like the way the steed keeps wobbling," Aribeth said. She was chewing her thumbnail as they watched. "The footing looks treacherous."

Gregg shrugged. "Yeah, well, what do you do?"

As they watched, Ridge continued to edge his way across the water. Everything looked good at first, but then the rushing water began to push the little wagon downstream. Ridge nudged the steed a little harder, hoping to pick up some speed. Then the wagon shifted suddenly and all progress stopped. Ridge looked back over his shoulder. "Wheel's stuck," he yelled back at them. "Let me see if I can get it out."

He snapped the reins and the steed started forward, then stopped. He snapped them harder, but the steed resisted. He tried several times to get the steed to move and it refused. Meanwhile, the wagon was rocking in the rapid water. Finally, he lost his patience, pulled his pistol, and fired a shot right over the head of the stubborn animal.

Aribeth was astonished. "What the hell is that fool doing?"

The steed bucked and pulled away, and the wagon came free. For a brief instant, it looked like Ridge's plan had worked. Then everything went wrong.

The steed wobbled again, losing forward momentum. This time, the water grabbed ahold of the little wagon and wouldn't let go. As it started moving downstream, the steed, with no footing, was powerless to stop it. Ridge was desperately maneuvering the reins, but had lost control of the situation. The wagon took off down the river, pulling the steed off its feet. Ridge came up off his seat, struggled to hold on, and then the wagon went over on its side and he went into the river.

Moments later, the wagon slammed into the rocks and shattered on impact. The poor steed was whipped up onto a large rock jutting out of the surface, and everyone turned away from the animal's gruesome end. The water briefly ran red from the steed's blood, but soon even that was washed further down the river.

"Well," Parrie said, sounding somewhat pleased. "So much for your hero," she said to Bethel. "Damn fool." She spurred her steed away as Bethel looked out over the scene in shock.

Aribeth stared at the water where Ridge had been just moments before. She felt sick. Less than three full days out and she had already lost a man, and had no idea how she was going to get the rest across. She had failed before she'd ever really started.

"Ah, ah," Bethel started saying, his voice rising with excitement. He pointed at the far bank of the river. "Look. Look."

All heads turned as Ridge crawled his way up the far bank. He was soaked to the bone and cut to shreds. Blood ran down his face and arms and legs, but he emerged on the other side, pulled himself up and looked over, and then bent his head back and screamed up into the air.

"How's that? Challenge accepted!" A hearty cheer went up from the crowd.

"How in the hell?" Leland asked, stunned. "I thought that he was a goner for sure. I don't believe it."

"The man is a hero," Bethel said admiringly.

Parrie wheeled her steed back around and watched as Ridge let out his primal scream. "He's a lunatic," she replied.

"One thing is for certain," Mr. Gregg said. His eyes were focused on the red foam that was washing up on the bank. "We're going to have to find a different way across."

CHAPTER 12

Mr. Gregg went back to brainstorming as the rest of the caravan began to camp for the day. Leland took two men and they started back up the river. Leland had stashed the raft he and Breton Fuller had built in a cave up above the bend. He didn't expect to return before nightfall.

On the other side of the river, Ridge's celebration was short-lived. He was freezing cold and bleeding from a dozen cuts. No one dared attempt to cross the river to give him aid, and he wouldn't try to cross back. Finally, he stripped his clothes off completely and climbed up on a rock to soak up what little sunlight was left, while mothers and fathers did their best to keep their teen daughters from looking.

As the sun began to descend and Echonos began his nightly watch from straight above, Mr. Gregg called Aribeth to his tent. He had been scribbling fiercely in a notebook. "A pulley system will work," he said excitedly. "I can make it strong enough to carry the equipment and most of the people. If Mr. Jax's raft has held up and if he can replicate his landing, then we can have some of the men raft over and construct their side. I'll supervise over here. It will take time, but it will work."

"How much time?"

Gregg looked up at the top of the tent while calculating. "Working hard, a week at the least. First thing is we're going to have to walk further down river to find the timber we need. You gotta cut the timber, haul it back here, then construct the end over here. You have to put at least three men on the other bank, and you have to either raft the wood over, or they have to do their own cuts over there. Then someone will have to run the line, hook it up over there, and raft back over here. Not an easy job, but it is doable."

"Supplies will start running low. I don't know that we can take that long," she said. "And we'd have to leave the steeds and wagons here."

"We've got no choice. I can't build a pulley strong enough to carry something that heavy."

Aribeth thought about it for a moment, and then she had an idea of her own. "What if you didn't have to lift it over the water?"

"What do you mean?"

Aribeth took his pen and began to sketch on a blank sheet of paper. "Attach the pulley to the raft. If you built a big enough raft, you could just ferry everything across. You could build a harness up here, and attach it to the raft like this."

Gregg studied her drawing, then took the pen back and made some minor adjustments. "Could work. Hell, it will work. But again, you're looking at a week to build it. Maybe more. Like you said, supplies will start running low."

"If anyone has any money, they can run back to town. Otherwise, the only option I see is to send a scouting party over and out ahead of the rest of the caravan."

"That might be smart. Give you a chance to do some advance scouting. I hate the idea of us all riding blind into God knows what."

A commotion started outside. Moments later, one of the many teen girls on the trip poked her head in the tent. "Ms. Fuller, come quick. It's Mr. Secova."

Aribeth scrambled up and out of the tent. A crowd of people were pointing across the river. Ridge had fallen off the rock he had been laying on and was writhing on the ground in the water's edge, shivering uncontrollably.

"He must be freezing to death. We've got to get over there. Where's Leland with the raft?"

Dr. Grant, who was standing on the bank, shook his head. "They're not back yet, and judging from what I'm seeing, I doubt that Secova has much time left."

Aribeth started to panic, but she forced herself to be calm. She assessed the situation and made a quick decision. She scanned the campground and saw Parrie Barrows reclining on a blanket by the feet of her steed. "Barrows," she screamed. "Go find Mr. Jax. Now. Tell him we need that raft immediately."

Parrie shot up off the ground, threw her coat and hat on, mounted up, and was gone in an impressive amount of time. Aribeth didn't have time to admire it. "Dr. Grant, get me anything I need to attend to his wounds." She ran to her own steed and yanked a pack off the saddle. "I need blankets."

Two women came running with blankets. She took them and shoved them into her pack, took off her jacket, and shoved it into the pack as well. Dr. Grant returned with bandages and medicine and a bottle of liquor. She threw them in the pack and cinched it up tight. Then she slipped her arms through the straps.

"What are you doing?" Colonel Holt asked, concerned.

"I'm swimming over."

"You can't," Gregg said. "Especially with that strapped to your back. You'll drown."

"If you don't freeze to death first," Holt continued.

Aribeth stepped past them both. She knew in her heart that they were right and that she probably wouldn't survive the trip.

111

"I can't sit here and let him die. I'm a strong swimmer. I can make it."

"A strong swimmer in a pool may be one thing," Holt continued. "That's no pool, or even a creek. You must wait for the raft."

"There's no time," she said, determined. She stared across the water at Ridge's shivering form, thrashing around on the opposite bank. "Colonel Holt. If I don't make it, you and Leland are in charge. Decide what's best."

He started to protest, but Aribeth was already running for the bank, and when she got there she dove in headfirst. The cold hit her like a rock. It stole her breath and threatened to short circuit her mind. She felt the rocks underneath. This part of the river wasn't deep enough for the dive and she felt them slicing her before her buoyance pulled her up off the bottom. Strictly working on instinct, she began to paddle. The rushing water tried to push her off course and she couldn't see from the splash in her eyes. Aribeth said a silent prayer and kept paddling, hoping that she had enough strength to make it.

#

Leland and two of the younger men from camp had started up river looking for his homemade raft immediately after Ridge's attempted crossing had failed. The walk along the bank was more difficult the further north they got. As the walls to the gulch began to get steeper, the bank got narrower. When they finally found the cave, he had stashed the raft in, the group was walking in shallow, icy water.

The cave was more of a hole really, not very deep into the bank and barely bigger than the raft itself. Leland had jammed the craft in, so extricating it without damage was time consuming. In the depths of the gulch they lost sunlight quickly and, after the three of them carried the raft far enough back down river to get back to the bank, they decided to rest for the night.

They scavenged some wood and had just gotten a decent fire going and stripped off their boots and wet socks when they heard the rapid approach of a steed's hooves. Each man had their guns pulled and ready to fire when Parrie came galloping into the camp.

"Mr. Jax, Ms. Fuller needs you to hurry up with that raft. Secova is dying on the other side of the river. We need to get clothes and medicine to him."

Leland put his gun aside. "Well, that's not going to happen. We're tired and we're camped for the night. He's just going to have to tough it out." The other two men agreed. None of them wanted to lug the heavy raft through the rocks and the darkness.

That answer didn't satisfy the young cadet. "You're just going to sit there and let a man die? A man who is only in this situation because he did what you asked him to do?"

"I didn't ask him," Leland shot back. "Aribeth did. It's not my fault that he was fool enough to try it. He knew the risks."

"And you wouldn't be so cavalier because you're afraid that Ms. Fuller has feelings for him, would you?"

"Why should I?" Leland paused, looked away, then looked back. "You think Aribeth has a thing for him?"

"Every girl in camp does," Parrie said with disgust. "And yes, I see the way she looks at him. There's definitely something there, but clearly that doesn't concern you."

Leland continued to resist. "Nope. Like I said, we're tired. Our feet are sore and wet, our clothes are wet, and we can't drag that thing in the dark."

"Fine," Parrie answered. She hopped down off the steed, took a rope off the saddle, and began tying one end to the saddle horn.

"What are you doing?"

Parrie ignored him and continued. With a mighty effort, she dragged the raft to the water's edge and tied the other end of the rope around it. "I'm gonna take it back for you." She shoved the raft into the water and then quickly mounted her steed.

"You damn idiot," Leland shouted, standing up quickly. "You're gonna get yourself killed."

"At least I'll die trying. Unlike you." Parrie rode her steed over into the shallow water. The strong currents were pulling the raft along, and Parrie's steed struggled to hold on with the weight of the raft tugging her down the river. Parrie kept her weight back on the saddle, then out of the saddle completely, riding on the steed's rear end to keep the rushing currents from yanking them in.

"Moron," Leland called out, but it was too late, she was gone. Leland looked at his partners and grimaced. "Better get your stuff. Let's go follow her before she gets killed." The others groaned and forced themselves up, everyone putting on their soaked socks and boots and trudging after the headstrong cadet.

"If she lives through this," Leland moaned. "I think I'll kill her.

\#

At a certain point, the animal side of Aribeth's brain took over. At first, she consoled herself with thoughts of all the laps she had swum at school. She thought about the summers as a kid, swimming in creeks and lakes or whatever body of water happened to be nearby. She tried to remember those days, the sun warm on her skin, cutting through the water like a shark without a care in the world.

The freezing temperature and the pounding currents destroyed those thoughts. She couldn't pretend that this was some pleasant afternoon getaway. A man was dying on the other side of the bank, she was his only chance.

Yet with every stroke, her arms burned. She gasped for air, but the cold kept her from getting the deep breaths that she desperately needed. Her legs and arms tired and the bank never seemed to get any closer.

Then the tiny voice in the back of her mind began telling her to let go. Just let the water take her away. She would be done with all of this, done with Aranwa. She could see Father again, and they would lay in the cool grass on endless warm summer days, watching the puffy purple clouds pass by overhead.

For a fleeting second, Aribeth almost did just that. It would be so easy to give her aching arms a rest; to quit kicking. The rocks would make a short end for her....

That was when the animal took over. She screamed out and pushed harder. Aribeth would not fail. She found a second wind she didn't know she had and began kicking harder, swimming faster, beating the rushing water at its own game. As the bank finally came close, she began to curse Aranwa in her mind. It would not beat her.

With one last push, she thrust herself out of the water and up onto the bank. Her lungs burned as she gasped for air, but Aribeth only had a moment to rest. Ridge was still dying. She could hear his shivering and his teeth chattering. She scampered up and crawled on all fours over to Ridge, who was laying in the water in a fetal position. "Hang in there," she said as she hooked her hands under his arms and began pulling him up, away from the rocks and the water.

Once she had pulled Ridge clear, she tore open the pack. Luckily, she had managed to keep the pack out of the water, so all the things inside had stayed dry. She wrapped the blankets around Ridge, covering him from head to toe. Only then did she stop to consider herself.

Aribeth dug out a fresh pair of clothes and her jacket and

changed quickly. She was too exhausted to care about the fact that she was giving a show to those on the other side of the bank. Darkness was falling quickly anyway, and between that and the mist in the air she doubted anyone saw much.

With that done, Aribeth crawled up beside Ridge and wrapped her arms and legs around him. "You'll be fine," she whispered in his ear. "You'll be fine. Just hang on."

\#

They never give me credit.

Parrie was angry. Leland and his crew were walking behind her, urging her to stop, to pull the raft out of the water. They didn't think she could hold on.

She ignored them. Parrie pushed her steed as hard as she could. The frigid water splashed up, soaking her clothes, but she didn't stop. With every step, the raft threatened to break away or to pull them in after it.

Parrie refused to budge. She wouldn't even allow herself to consider the possibility that she would fail. The rope would not break. Her steed would not stumble. She would not fall.

As they drew closer to camp, they could all smell the burning campfires and hear raised voices. No time to quit now. Parrie pushed harder and her steed responded. The river widened and the raft drifted further out into the middle. Parrie held fast.

Leland and the others went ahead, only now when they yelled, they yelled in support. "Almost there," one called out. "Just keeping going! You're doing it," yelled another. Then Leland was there beside her, hauling in some of the slack, easing the burden. He groaned and strained with the effort, but it helped and together, they made sight of the camp, then pulled the raft up onto the shore.

Parrie slid off the steed and onto the ground, exhausted. Leland looked down at her slumped figure with approval. "Good job, kid. That took some guts." Then he and the other two men heaved the raft up and carried it the rest of the way.

In that moment, Parrie let herself smile. *Let them tell me I'm no good. I'll prove them wrong.*

#

Grant, Holt, and Gregg all rushed up to Leland as he and the boys finished hauling the raft in. "Where's Aribeth?" he asked, scanning all over for her.

"Over there," Holt said. "Crazy woman swam across."

Leland let go of the raft and the other two almost dropped it, just managing to regain control before it hit the ground. "What?" He pushed through the crowd and looked across. All he could see through the mist was a huddled mass of humanity. "She made it?"

Holt eased up alongside him. "Yes, she made it. Never seen anything quite like it. Like running headfirst into a bayonet charge and living to tell the tale. Tell you what though." He turned to look back toward camp and Leland did the same. "I'd say that she won this group over today. No doubt who the leader is anymore."

"Was there ever a doubt?"

"More than you think," Holt said cryptically. "More than you think."

#

High above the settlers at the top of the gulch, Lon Kinson kept a careful watch on the settlers. He was sprawled out on his stomach, pointing a looking glass down through the leaves of a large bush. Between the light from the campfires and Echonos shining brightly overheard, he was able to get a good idea of the size and condition of the wagon train.

Lon took detailed notes. He would not leave until he could account for every person, every animal, every piece of equipment, even every weapon down there. He'd been on them since they left Masterson Gulch. A townsperson eager to keep his family safe from predations had sold them out for a pair of gold coins and a handshake promise. When you terrorized people, they didn't ask for much more than that.

This was not the first group of travelers to attempt this crossing. The others had learned the hard way what happened when they trespassed, as would these.

This group was more impressive than the others. They had professional soldiers watching their flanks, and courage appeared to be in plentiful supply. Lon was also pleased by the outstanding number of women in the group. The men had been short on entertainment for a while now; some fresh meat would be welcome.

He could go ahead and report and they could sweep down upon the settlers by morning, but they would be outnumbered and there was no need in rushing. The travelers were trapped in the gulch. A crossing would take days. A retreat would be equally time consuming. Best to wait and watch and see what they decided to do before reporting back to Talon. Lon didn't believe in taking unnecessary risks.

Especially when the prey was oh so easy.

CHAPTER 13

Leland ferried Dr. Grant over to tend to Ridge and Aribeth while he scouted for wood to build a fire. Ridge was coming around, his color returning, though he was still shivering badly. He did take ample advantage of the bottle of liquor to warm his insides.

Aribeth insisted that Grant focus on Ridge first, doing her best to ignore her own cuts. Feeling was just starting to creep back into her extremities, and the tingling was the most painful thing she'd ever experienced.

Though she knew she couldn't help, Aribeth insisted on tagging along with Leland as he hunted for firewood. He wouldn't look at her or acknowledge her in any way.

"Are you mad at me?" she finally managed to ask, trying hard to keep her teeth from chattering. She kept her hands in her pockets and her arms drawn in tight against her body. Her wet hair still hung in front of her face.

"No," Leland answered. He was still looking every which way but at her.

"Liar. You are mad at me. What for?"

Leland wheeled around quick as a lion, and it startled her. "Because you took a stupid chance." Then Leland regained control, the quick flash of anger subsiding. "That wasn't a smart move. You could have died. You're the leader here."

119

He turned away again, but Aribeth maneuvered to try and stay in front of him. "Should I have let the man die? He's only here because I told him he could come. I told him to try to cross the river. Everyone on this expedition are my responsibility, but you and Ridge are the only two who I'm directly responsible for. I take that seriously."

Leland stood and sighed. He had a nice collection of small branches cradled in his arms. "I know." He looked skyward before looking back at her. "What you did was very brave."

"So why are you so mad? Should I have sent someone else? What if they had drowned? Then I'd have two lives on my hands."

"No, you shouldn't. You should have waited for us. You just...you shouldn't be so careless."

Aribeth stepped closer and forced him to look her in the eye. "We're okay then? You forgive me?"

"Yes," Leland said with a shake of his hand. "By the moons, you are so...hardheaded." As he said the last word, his voice trailed away and he focused on something up above. Aribeth turned and followed his gaze.

"What?"

Leland kept staring, then stepped forward. "Take these," he said absently, shoving the firewood into her arms. He quickly stepped past Aribeth, his eyes scanning the top of the gulch far overhead.

Aribeth was trying to secure her grip on the wood and see what he was seeing at the same time. "What? What do you see?"

Leland continued looking. "Nothing I guess. Just thought that I saw something up there."

"Like an animal?"

"No. Something shiny. Like metal." His eyes kept scanning. "I could be going crazy, but I doubt it."

"Mr. Gregg thinks we should send a scouting party ahead

while he works on getting the pulley system built," Aribeth said over his shoulder. "Do you think that would be a good idea?"

Leland finally dropped his gaze and looked back at Aribeth. "That would be a very good idea. I'll put together a group in the morning."

Aribeth shoved the wood back into Leland's arms. "I'm going. And I want to take Parrie too. I like her, she's eager to please."

"I don't know," Leland said. "Parrie's got guts. I like her too. But you should stay here and supervise."

"I'm no engineer," she protested. "I'd just be in the way. Besides, I'm the one with the journal that includes all the maps. You, me, Parrie, Ridge, and the sharpshooter, Proffitt. That should be good. Parrie, she rides a steed like she was born on one. You and Proffitt are the ace shots, and Ridge is fearless. Come on, we should do it."

Leland kept glancing up the canyon walls but finally relented. "Fine. I don't know about taking your boyfriend over there, though. He's not in too good a shape."

Aribeth glanced back over her shoulder at Ridge, who was getting his wounds attended to by Dr. Grant. "We'll see how he's doing in the morning," she said. Then she turned back to him, a curious look on her face. "Why would you say that he's my boyfriend?"

Leland shrugged and went back to picking up sticks. "Just a hunch, I guess."

Aribeth watched him again going out of his way not to look at her, and she suppressed a smile. "Well, he is very good looking. Very rugged, and with an air of mystery. What girl could resist?" Leland kept walking and picking up wood, trying very hard to ignore her. She finally couldn't resist and broke into a huge smile. "Lee?"

He finally forced himself to look up at her.

"There's nothing between me and Ridge. He's just a guy along for the ride, okay? I would have done what I did for anybody in the camp."

"Okay," Leland answered, trying to be casual about it. Still, Aribeth thought she caught the edge of a smile from him before he went back to picking up wood.

#

Morning broke in shades of purple and orange and high blue, a perfect day ahead. Leland and Aribeth rafted back across the river, each using long guide poles to push the craft along and to hold the raft against the currents. As they reached the other side and pulled the makeshift boat out of the water, Leland shook his head.

"Every time we cross, we run the risk of losing it. It's only a matter of time before it gets away from someone."

"It's a risk we have to take," Aribeth said. "Beats trying to swim across. Hopefully Mr. Gregg's pulley system will work and crossing will get much easier."

Leland stared out at the rushing river. "I hope so. This river, it's bloodthirsty. I'm amazed that we didn't lose anybody yesterday." Then he forced himself to look away.

Aribeth gathered everyone around and explained the plan. It was decided that the two strong young men who had helped Leland with the raft, Bryson Lane and Dak Allenbaugh, would raft back across along with Liam Reeder from the security team. They would begin building their end of the pulley system while Gregg supervised the construction on the other side. Parrie Barrows and Alvarez Proffitt would also cross, and would accompany Leland and Aribeth on climbing out of the gulch and scouting the area. They would have to go on foot as no one wanted to risk riding their steeds crossing the river given the precarious footing.

122

As preparations were being made to cross, Leland took Colonel Holt and the rest of the security team aside and warned them to stay vigilant and keep an eye on the top of the gulch. They all understood just how vulnerable the caravan was down in the hole.

Crossing took longer than expected. The raft would only hold two at a time, and the added weight of equipment made the raft sit lower in the water. While that helped stem the effects of the current, it made pushing the boat across that much harder. By the time Leland came back for Aribeth, he was drenched in sweat, despite the cool temperatures. It had taken them almost all morning to execute the crossing, and they still had to find a way up out of the gulch on the other side.

Aribeth ordered Leland to sit and rest. He took a seat next to Ridge by the still smoldering fire. Ridge was rebounding well, and had managed to force down a little bit of food and get himself dressed, though he was still pale and weak. They did not talk to each other, or even acknowledge each other's presence.

Aribeth, Proffitt, and Parrie examined the gulch walls, hoping to find a trail, or at least something that they could turn into a trail. They did not, and it made them appreciate how much work it must have been for the townspeople to cut the trail on the other side.

Leland rested for an hour before joining the hunt. The group kept working their way south, still unable to find a suitable path for them to pull up out of the gulch. "How did you get out the first time?" Proffitt asked.

"We climbed the walls. It was just three of us and it was very hard. Took all day. I don't want to do that again if I don't have to. Besides, even if we climb out, what about everybody else? We've got to find a passage.

"The land has to flatten out eventually," Aribeth said. "The bank is fairly passable. We just ride the bank until we pull up out of the gulch."

"Yes, but how far do we have to go? How many days' ride is that going to take? We need to know."

The group wandered south, far past where Lane and Allenbaugh had stopped to start cutting trees along the bank, when Leland called for a rest. They all stopped, snacking on food they had in their packs. "All right," Leland finally said. "This is what I want to do. Girls, you walk back to camp and keep an eye on things there. Alvarez and I will keep going south and find a way to get out of this canyon. We might have to camp overnight; we're going to run out of sunlight soon."

"Why do we have to go back to camp?" Parrie said, challenging Leland. "I am perfectly capable of —"

"You're a junior officer," Alvarez said. "Hell, not even an officer really. At best, you're a private. So as the senior officer here, I am ordering you back. You have no experience at all, and neither does she. If we run into trouble, you will both be liabilities. Back at camp, you have help and you have numbers, so do as you're told."

Parrie looked to Aribeth for support, but Aribeth saw the logic in the move and simply shrugged. "It makes sense, Parrie. Besides, with Reeder watching over the cutters and everyone else on the other side of the river, there's no one to watch Ridge and Dr. Grant."

Parrie, her eyes almost spitting blue fire, wanted to argue, but she didn't. "Fine," she finally spat out as she stood and gathered her pack. "I'll head back, Lieutenant." She started stomping back up the way.

Aribeth stood and gathered her pack as well. "She'll be fine. Just hurry, and please be careful. We'll wait for word." Aribeth and Leland exchanged quick, worried looks, and then she started back up the path after the still steaming Parrie.

They arrived back at camp to find Ridge in good spirits, sharing a drink and a tall tale with Dr. Grant, who appeared to be enjoying himself as well. Allenbaugh and Lane had started an impressive stack of logs and had gone back to make more cuts. Reeder, they were assured, was around, keeping a steady watch.

As Parrie stalked off by herself and sat down to pout, Aribeth climbed on top of the rock where Ridge had been drying on the previous day and peered back across the river. Through the misty air, she could see progress being made on their end of the pulley system as well. Maybe, she thought, it wouldn't take a week after all.

"They sent the girls to watch over us," Ridge smirked as Aribeth climbed down off the rock. "I feel so much safer now."

Aribeth saw Parrie, who was sitting behind Ridge, turn to glare at the man. Aribeth blew it off. "A girl saved your life last night," she said. "You might want to consider some gratitude." Ridge and Grant looked sideways at each other and laughed. "Something funny about that?"

"I was never in any danger," Ridge said. "I've been in worse spots than that. I did appreciate the cuddling though. That was a nice touch."

Parrie growled behind him but Aribeth laughed. "Whatever you want to believe," she answered. "When you were laying in the water writhing around, shivering and unconscious, you weren't so flippant." She walked past the men and took a seat next to Parrie.

"Pigs," Parrie said.

"Don't take it so personally," Aribeth said. "The best way to shut people like that up is to prove them wrong. Let your actions do the talking, and eventually they will learn."

Parrie rolled her eyes and looked away. They sat silently

for several minutes, and Aribeth was about to join the men with Parrie finally spoke again.

"How much daylight do you think we have left?'

Aribeth looked to the sky. The sun had just passed high point and was starting its descent. "Down here? Two hours, give or take a few minutes. Why?"

Parrie stood up, dusted her pants off, and started digging through her pack. "I'm going up."

"What?"

Parrie nodded. "I see a way up and I'm going to take it."

"Don't be foolish," Aribeth started. "You heard Leland. It took them all day to scale that cliff. You've got two hours. And what if you fall? I can't afford to lose anybody."

"I won't fall," Parrie answered, still focused on the cliff in front of her. "I can make better time. I'm lighter and I won't be carrying a pack. We had to do rock climbing exercises at the Academy. I can do this."

"You're going to go up there without a pack? I really don't think this is a good idea."

Parrie checked the pistol in a holster on her right hip and then threw her rifle across her back. "This is all I need."

She walked to the face of the cliff wall, took a moment to get her bearings, and then started up. Aribeth followed her to the cliff and watched her start up, fearing the worst. She was afraid that Parrie was simply doing this to prove to the men that she could, and that was a foolish chance to take just to make a point.

"What is that moron doing?" Ridge had come up behind Aribeth and she hadn't heard. She recovered quickly from the surprise.

"She's climbing to the top."

Ridge stood, watching her go as well. "Gonna make a hell of a mess when she hits the ground. I'm not even that stupid."

Aribeth turned to argue with him, saw the bottle of liquor he held loosely in his hands, and took it instead, taking a long drink and handing it back.

"No coughing or gagging? I'm impressed."

She gave him a coy smile. "I was the bad girl in school. You grow up on the frontier, you experience things."

"Really? I'm intrigued."

"Keep dreaming, Secova," Aribeth said, but she said it with a wink. Then they both turned to check on Parrie, who was making good time. "I sure hope she makes it."

#

The doubt began to creep in about halfway up the wall. Until then, the climb had been as easy as Parrie thought it would be. But the further up she went, the harder it became to find handholds. Her footing became more treacherous. She realized that she was wearing dress boots, not climbing boots, and that any slip, even a minor one, would likely send her plummeting to the ground.

Just past halfway, she got stuck. She was standing on a toe-wide ledge, plastered against a flat area on the cliff face. Parrie blindly felt along with both hands, but could find no crack or crevice she could slip her fingers into or an outcropping to grab.

Panic tried to seize her, but Parrie held tight. She had plotted the course in her mind…she had to be missing something. She risked a look up and tilted her head back. The movement was too sudden and she started to lose her balance.

Quickly, Parrie tightened the muscles in her back and willed herself to hold the position for one heartbeat, then two, and finally, she bent back and reestablished her footing. Regrouping, Parrie looked again, moving much more slowly this time.

She spied a handhold above her and to the right, higher than she'd thought. Parrie reached out, stretching as much as she dared, but it was just out of reach. She looked some more, but found no other suitable option.

If she could just reach it, Parrie could pull herself along to the right and there was a short ledge she could stand on. She kept looking, and felt that there was a way up from there. She just had to reach that small outcropping.

The sun was dipping rapidly and Parrie knew that she had to make it up soon. She did not want to be stuck on the rock face in the dark. She ached all over, her calves threatened to cramp if she didn't relax her legs soon, and her fingers and hands were sore.

Parrie thought about easing back down and admitting defeat, but one glance beneath her killed that thought. There was no way. She'd certainly fall if she tried it. She had to go up.

Resigned to the fact that she either reached that handhold or she died, Parrie decided that she would have to jump. She didn't need much lift, maybe two inches. If she missed or if she couldn't grab hold, she would fall and that would be it. If she stayed, eventually she would give out and fall. Best to die trying, she reasoned.

Taking a deep breath and stretching her arms out as far as she could, Parrie readied herself. It seemed so close, so easy. With a solid launch it would be easy, but she had almost no room, no surface to push off from. If the rock she was standing on broke....

Parrie cleared her head of such thoughts. In a few moments, none of it would matter. She would either be dead or on her way up. She counted to three in her head, then pushed up with all the force she could generate out of her legs. Parrie's fingers found the shelf, hit loose dirt, and slipped. She clawed desperately at the rock, digging with her fingernails for a grip, and found it. She was dangling, twenty feet in the air over jagged rocks, holding on with her fingernails.

Parrie took a second to catch her breath, then pulled herself up, got one arm up on the shelf, then the other, and relaxed again, letting the tension go out of her leg muscles. Now she just had to edge her way over. There was a nice ledge that she could pull up on and stand just a few feet to the right. She got a grip with her right hand and slowly lowered herself back down, then grabbed on with her left. Parrie's hands were on fire, but she maintained her grip.

Slowly and painfully she edged to her right. Small gains felt massive now. The opportunity to stand, to rest, drew closer by centimeters at a time. The ledge was just a short reach away.

Parrie reached out for the ledge, confident the worst was about to be over, but her finger slid off the edge. Again, she had to scramble to hold her position. Parrie's heart felt like it was about to beat out of her chest. She had to calm herself down. She took several deep breaths and let herself dangle for a minute before reaching up again. This time she found her grip, and moments later pulled herself over and sat, back to the cliff wall, and gave thanks that she had made it.

She might have stayed there, but the shadows that were rapidly climbing the cliff walls forced her to move. She had to get up out of the canyon. Parrie took her time getting back up and in position, planned the rest of her moves, and started up one more time.

#

Lon Kinson had been faced with a choice that morning. He could either stay and continue watching the camp, or follow the small group that broke off to the south. He took his time, then decided that there was likely nothing to watch at the camp, so he decided to follow south.

He had to crawl on his belly back away from the lip of the crevice far enough that no one could see him from below. Somehow, the night before, he had almost been spotted by the scout. Lon attributed it to moonlight glinting off the looking glass. Damn Akil and her nightly jaunt across the sky. In the light of both moons, he would have been easy to see had he not camouflaged himself so well.

Another near miss. In ducking, the looking glass had started to roll away toward the cliff's edge. He barely managed to corral it in time and tuck it back underneath his body before the scout started looking too closely.

Lon wondered all night if he had been given away. He hadn't, but the scout was suspicious. He had warned the other soldiers, and throughout the day they had kept a careful watch in his general area.

When the scout led the small group to the south, Lon had to wonder if they were going to try and find a way up and flank him. He couldn't allow that. Lon waited until they had been gone awhile, then slowly backed out of his hiding spot in the bushes and followed along behind.

Then the group had broken up, with the two women returning to camp and the men continuing south. Lon wrote off the women at first, sticking with the men as they continued south. As they approached the end of the gulch, Lon lost his nerve. The last thing he needed was to be face-to-face with two experienced guns and having nowhere to run.

Lon started back the way he had come, calculating as he walked. The men would find the way up out of the gulch, but crossing the entire party was going to take time. He doubted that the men would travel far. Should he alert Talon now, or continue watching? Was there a second wave waiting in the wings?

Lon had almost decided to hold tight and keep watching as he approached his lookout. That was when he saw the woman with the white-blonde hair suddenly emerge out of the mouth of the canyon. She was dirty and sweaty and bleeding, but there she was, rising out of the crevice and falling flat on her back in exhaustion.

Lon hit the deck, for the moment getting lost in the waist high yellow grass. He pulled his pistol and held it ready. Once she started looking, she would see his tracks in the grass. Should he attack now, while she was prone? He could be seen from the other side of the river and he was certain that the men on the other bank could hit him with the long rifles. Plus discovery would erode the element of surprise.

He began to crawl away from the cliff. The woods were a short distance away; he could easily lose himself in there. He risked a quick glimpse and saw the woman was getting to her feet, recovering quickly. She wore a uniform and had brought nothing but weapons with her.

They knew, and had snuck her up the cavern walls to surprise him. She moved like a panther and had the cold blue eyes of a killer. He had no choice now. Lon dropped back to the ground and waited for darkness to come. Then he would make his move for the woods.

Talon had to know. They had to act quickly.

CHAPTER 14

"What do you make of this?" Alvarez Proffitt stood in the early morning sun, the smell of their still smoldering campfire fresh in the air. He was studying a large bush on the edge of the gulch. More specifically, he was studying some broken branches on the bush. He held his rifle in both hands, barrel down but ready to swing and fire at a moment's notice if need be.

Leland hunched down in front of the bush and rubbed his face while he studied the scene. "Somebody has been watching us."

"Animal of some kind?" Parrie was standing behind them both, her pistol in her hand and her eyes scanning the terrain for any signs of danger.

"No. I'd say human." Leland stood and pointed to an area of tall grass. "See how the grass is down through there? These are human tracks, not animal. At least, no animal that I've ever seen." He then circled around the bush. "And back here, you can see where he would get down and crawl into the bush."

"Trying to stay out of sight," Alvarez said coldly.

Leland, who had hunched back behind the bush, nodded. "Yep."

"Who would be watching us? Aranwa is supposed to be deserted," Parrie responded.

"Could be the Lost Tribe," Alvarez said, trying to keep his

voice flat. His eyes gave him away. Parrie glared at him.

"I'm too old for ghost stories, Lieutenant."

"A scout maybe?" Leland said. "For the Talon Volpe gang?"

Alvarez grunted and took a cautious look around. "Most likely." He then turned to Parrie. "The Lost Tribe may be a ghost tale, but Volpe and his gang are very real. They've been terrorizing settlements along the border for years now. Ministry's never been able to catch them."

"If they're living in Aranwa and crossing over, that could explain why," Leland opined as he came around to join the others. "They might have a secret crossing somewhere."

"Or this could be their crossing," Parrie interrupted. "Scout was on his way to make sure the coast was clear and stumbled upon us."

"I don't think so," Leland said. Like the other two, he was suspiciously eyeing the immediate landscape. "This is a hard cross, and it would take a while to cross a large group of people."

"How many?" asked Parrie.

"Nobody knows," Alvarez answered. "No one has ever gotten a solid number. Could be a dozen or more. I've heard as many as twenty men."

"Or could be five or six," Leland continued. "You come sweeping out of nowhere in the dark, or ambush some poor travelers out on the road, a handful could seem like a lot more."

"Either way," Alvarez continued. "It's bad news. We're sitting ducks down there in that canyon. We've got to get those people across. And fast." He turned his attention back to Parrie. "Burrows. Climb back down and warn the settlers."

"Forget it. Commanding officer or not, I'm not climbing back down that rock face. You're crazy if you think I am."

"I could toss you off," Alvarz responded, but there was no humor in his voice. "That would save you some time."

133

Leland stepped between them. "Nobody's going back down that cliff. We know how to get up here now. I say we go back down, get some supplies and a few more men, and then we come back up here and sweep the area. I want to get back into those woods a bit, see if I can find a trail."

"Are you suggesting that we track down Talon's men?" Alvarez seemed excited by the prospect.

Leland surveyed the surroundings a bit more, then nodded. "I'd rather find them and know where we stand than go on our way and just wait for them to swoop down on us."

"I'd love to track down that monster, but we don't have the manpower for that. Our men, there's only six of us, and three of them have never seen any action. I don't want to go up against twenty hardened bandits with three experienced soldiers and three newbies crapping their pants at the first sign of trouble."

"I'm not afraid to fight," Parrie said. "I've been preparing my whole life to fight,"

Alvarez grinned at her smugly. "You think so now. We'll see what happens when the shooting starts."

"It wouldn't be just you six either. I can handle myself," Leland said. "I've fought some. And Secova is a dangerous man."

"Secova's a duelist," Alvarez said. "He gets by on a sprinkling of guts and a handful of cockiness against men who have neither. He's really nothing more than a swindler. And you're a hunter. I doubt the animals you track shoot back."

Leland took one step forward, his cold eyes locking in on Alvarez's. "I've seen my share of fighting. I've been shot at. It's not something I liked, but if I had to, I would."

Parrie had seen enough of the men's posturing. "Well, while you boys work it out, I'll head back on down the track. Somebody's got to start putting this thing together." She holstered her pistol, straightened her hat, and started walking away."

Leland and Alvarez sized each other up for another few heartbeats before Leland smiled brightly. "She's right. Let's get going. For all we know, could just be some cannibal tribesman lining up his next meal."

Alvarez reluctantly holstered his own weapon. "Sure, Jax. You keep thinking that."

#

Ridge Secova woke that morning to find Aribeth asleep facing him, shivering in the cold. She'd used her jacket as a pillow, and had nothing but her shirtsleeves and pants to protect herself from the cold night.

He threw the blankets off him, feeling like himself for the first time since he had made the foolhardy attempt to cross the river. That wasn't the first time his arrogance had gotten the better of him, and probably wouldn't be the last.

Ridge laid beside Aribeth and studied her in the early morning light. Here was this woman, just a girl really, who'd risked her life to swim across that raging river with a heavy pack on her back, just to save him. Ridge sat up and peered across the water, trying to make out the camp on the other side through the morning mist. How many others would have tried that? How many had hoped that he'd die that night?

Ridge smiled at the thought. People had been wishing him dead forever, but the Reaper hadn't caught up to him yet. People would just have to get used to disappointment.

Ridge glanced down at Aribeth. She wasn't pretty, he thought, but cute. She hadn't really blossomed yet. Her face still held a little adolescent chubbiness in the cheeks, and she lacked the feminine wiles that true ladies knew how to wield. She was very much a tomboy. He'd seen her kind many times. The daughters of farmers or miners, pressed into service before they were ready. It suppressed the soul.

Yet he admired her in a way he admired few people, regardless of sex. She had a steely resolve to her that was rare. He could see it in the flash of her violet eyes and in her stance when she was challenged. She had a presence.

"Don't think too hard about it," Dr. Grant called from behind. He had been off somewhere a little further up the river, and Ridge didn't realize that he'd come back. "That's a nice girl there. Doesn't deserve the likes of you."

Ridge looked up at the old man and sneered. "You don't know what I was thinking. Don't try to read my mind, geezer."

Grant found a seat on a large boulder and rubbed his hands together. "Don't have to read minds to know what you're thinking. I've seen that look before. You got dark intent written all over you."

Ridge looked away. "Why don't you butt out?"

"Why don't you act like a man and throw one of those blankets on her? You ain't sick no more."

Ridge glared back up at the man, picked up the blankets he had been sleeping under, and threw them over Aribeth. "I was getting to it." With that done, he stood and stretched. His body felt like it had been wadded up, and it took several minutes to get the muscles to unwind.

He walked down to the river's edge and splashed cold water on his face. The cold bit hard and woke him up. He rubbed his face and felt the stubble of several days without a shave. That wouldn't do. Ridge trudged back to their makeshift camp and found his knife in its sheath on top of his old clothes. As he plucked up the knife he grinned menacingly at Grant, then returned to the water. It took only a couple of minutes and several careful strokes with the knife to clear away the unwanted facial hair.

On the ground, Aribeth stirred, mewing softly as she did. Ridge smiled down at her. "She doesn't seem so tough, just to look at her," Ridge said, an edge of appreciation in his voice. Grant, still watching him warily, nodded in agreement.

Aribeth groaned and stretched, eyes still shut tight. As she released the tension, she half-groaned, "Are you talking about me?"

"What gives you that idea?" Ridge asked. He stowed his knife and picked up his clothes, which had been laid out on the ground to dry. They were still a tad damp.

Aribeth sat up and began rubbing the back of her neck. "I don't see anybody else over here." She stretched again and then began looking around. "Any word from Lee or Parrie?"

"Lee?" Ridge stopped in the middle of buckling his pants. "Are we on a casual first name basis with our guide?"

Aribeth's dark eyes slid over to him. "Yes, we are," she answered. "Are we jealous?"

Ridge scoffed and resumed dressing. "Why would I be jealous of that...hillbilly?"

A slight smile touched her lips. "Mmm. Don't know. I don't suppose there is much of a reason for a man of your...stature... to be jealous of a man like Lee. No immediate reason anyway."

Ridge glanced back over at her, and he knew that Aribeth knew what he had been thinking. Somehow this frontier girl, this prairie flower, had seen right through him. The thought made his blood run cold. He looked away from her, unwilling to allow her another look behind the curtain, and slipped into his shirt. "I'm glad we got that settled."

"Me too," she said. "Now, what about the others? Any word?"

Grant answered from behind her. "No. I heard them up there, rustling around, earlier this morning. "

Aribeth struggled to her feet, groaning as she did, and turned. "So the others made it up as well?"

"I'm sure," Grant said. "I couldn't see them up there, but unless that crazy girl was talking to herself, there's more than one person up there."

Aribeth put both hands against the small of her back and bent over as far as she could, still trying to work out the kinks. "Good. We needed some good news. How about the boys, have they said anything about how things are going?"

"No. They just get up and they get to work." He nudged his head in the direction of the other side of the river. "On occasion, I can hear them working over there. We might be able to see for ourselves once this mist clears." They both craned their heads skyward. "Still a couple of hours before the sun gets high enough to burn it off."

"Okay then," she said as she continued to massage out the muscles in her neck. "I'm going to go check on the boys, see how they're coming along. I'll be right back."

"I'll come with you," Ridge said eagerly, falling in step with her as Aribeth started down the bank.

"I think I can handle it on my own."

"I don't mind," he answered. "You're far better company than that crusty old man any way. He doesn't like me very much."

Aribeth's eyes again slid over to him. "From what I hear, you're not a very likeable guy. Almost no one wants you here. The security team, Mr. Behrens, Lee, they all say I shouldn't trust you. I figure that there must be a reason for that."

Ridge kept his eyes focused straight ahead. "Life on the frontier is hard. Sometimes a man has to be hard to make his way." He looked down at her and forced a smile. "I have no problem being hard. That sometimes rubs people the wrong way."

"Oh," she said, but Ridge didn't think that she believed him.

"So, if I may ask, why did you allow me to come?"

Aribeth shrugged. "Just a feeling. My father taught me to

listen to my instincts. My instincts told me that I should let you come." She reached out and gently took his arm and stopped walking. Ridge stopped as well. "Please, Mr. Secova, don't make me regret that decision. I'm responsible for those people back there, for all of those children. If something happened to them...."

"You have nothing to fear from me, dear. I am a man who does not shy away from confrontation, but I am also a man of honor and loyalty. I owe you that loyalty, and you shall have it. You will reach your destination. I promise you."

Aribeth exhaled slowly. "I hope that you're right." They studied each other for a moment in the morning light. Contrasted against the dark rocks behind her, Aribeth's pale skin almost seemed to shine. How was this plain and simple girl vexing him so?

"I'm always right," Ridge said arrogantly. They started walking again. "I've never run into an opponent I couldn't beat, and Aranwa won't beat me."

#

Leland, Proffitt, and Parrie made it back to the camp by early afternoon. They were all dusty, sore, and exhausted from the walk. Aribeth saw them coming and rushed to the river's edge to gather water for them to drink. They each took a canteen eagerly and gulped it down, while Dr. Grant prepared them plates of berries and fresh fish.

"So you found a way up? How far is it, and can we get the wagons up?" Aribeth grilled them as they drank.

Leland held up a hand to slow her down as he greedily chugged more water. After he finished his gulp, he gasped for breath and wiped his mouth with the back of his hand. "The cliffs gradually lower, and there are areas along the way that you can make it up. The best place is several kilometers down river, but we'll be able to get everyone up. The terrain is rocky but not impassible. Individuals can get up sooner, but I wouldn't risk a wagon up any of those passes."

"Great. That's great." Aribeth took a seat between Leland and Alvarez, squeezing into the space.

"Not so great," Proffitt snarled. "Is the fact that someone has been watching us."

Aribeth's eyes widened and she snapped her head around to him. "Someone's watching us? There's not supposed to be anyone here."

"They think it's the outlaw," said Parrie, who was sitting to Leland's left.

"Talon Volpe?"

"It's possible," Leland said, trying to diffuse any unnecessary worry. "All we know for sure is that someone has been up there," he said, his eyes tracking to the edge of the cliff and the approximate location of the large bush. "And fairly recently. It could be anyone. We can't rule out the possibility that someone has already gone across. We don't know that there aren't settlements over there. It could also be savages."

"The dreaded lost tribe," Proffitt said in mock fear. "If you believe in ghost stories."

Aribeth switched her attention back to Proffitt. "You think it's the outlaw?"

He nodded solemnly. "If it were settlers, there's no need for them to watch us. If it were savages, they would either see us and run or gather forces and attack. The fact that someone sat up there and watched, and we both believe he was up there for a while, indicates something else. There have long been rumors that Volpe was based out of Aranwa, but no one would follow up on it."

Aribeth had a sinking feeling in the pit of her stomach. "What does that mean for us?"

Leland choked down a bite of fish. "I want to sweep out ahead of us a little bit. Once you get up on the cliff, you've got a narrow stretch of prairie grass and then some woods about a kilometer back. I want to get some men and walk through those woods. I also think that we need to get a couple of people up on that ridge to keep watch. Right now, everyone down here is an easy target."

"And we need to get word across the river," Parrie said, picking up the thread. "If they are crossing at some unknown place upriver, they could sweep in behind us."

"Trap us down here," Ridge said. "How many men are we talking about?"

Proffitt shrugged. "We were talking about that. Could be twenty or more, could just be a handful. No one has an exact idea."

"If you're right," Ridge said as he stabbed his own piece of fish with the point of his blade. "Then their next move will tell us about their strength. If they've got twenty or thirty men, there's no reason to wait. They'll have us outgunned and boxed in. If they wait, then that tells us that the numbers are close enough that they don't want to risk a direct run at us. They'd be better off letting us get everybody up, and waiting for opportunities to present themselves."

"If it's even them at all," Parrie said, her voice showing the depth of her doubt. "All we have to go on is some trampled grass and drag marks on the ground. For all we know, there could be some sort of predator up there dragging victims away."

"No blood, no bones, no carcass. There's no reason to believe an animal made those marks," Leland countered. He looked sternly at Aribeth. "You're the leader. What's your call?"

Aribeth took her time thinking it over. She looked around their little camp, checking the eyes of each person. "First, we send someone back across to warn the others. Then I agree with you, Lee. We should scout out ahead." She stared across the circle at Dr. Grant. "I want you to stay here, in case one of the boys gets hurt, you can tend to them."

"I wouldn't be much help up there anyway," he said.

Leland laid his hand on Aribeth's leg. "I think you should stay here with Dr. Grant. It could get dangerous up there."

She pushed his hand away with disgust. "I'm the leader, I need to be there. I don't want to sit down here in this hole and just wait for some bandit to swoop down on me."

"What about Grant?" Ridge asked, picking up Leland's thread. "He'll need some protection."

"We'll leave a man here," she said coldly. She fixed Ridge with a cold stare. "Are you going to tell me that Dr. Grant and I would be a match for this Volpe character and his gang? I'd be better off up there with you."

"She's right," Grant croaked. "No offense to our fearless leader here, but I'd feel much safer with one of you military boys watching this side of things. I'm no fighter, wouldn't know what to do with a gun if you gave me one."

Aribeth was pleased. "There you have it." She turned back to Proffitt. "Lieutenant Proffitt, if you would ferry across and report to Commander Holt. The rest of us will start back up."

"Can we get some steeds over here?" Parrie asked. "That's a brutal walk."

"Not a chance," Leland answered quickly. "That little raft of mine wouldn't stand a chance with that much weight on it. We'll have to walk. We do need more provisions though." He leaned forward and looked past Aribeth to Proffitt. "You and I should go over and stock up. Fresh packs, food, ammo, medicine—"

"I've got all of the medicine," Grant interrupted. "I'll put together a kit for you of the most common needs."

"Good," Leland said. "Get warm clothes. I know its spring, but the weather can be unpredictable over here."

"Excuse me," Aribeth interrupted. Leland ignored her.

"Who is our fisherman here?"

Ridge poked his knife at Aribeth. "She's the one who caught this scrumptious little meal." Leland glanced over at her with a new appreciation.

Aribeth was fuming. "Listen, I'm still in charge here…."

"And now you're in charge of catching us some food. As much as you can pull out. Go past the rapids here. You can get some big ones."

"Hey, wait a minute—"

Leland kept talking. "The rest of you, rest up and make any preparations you need to make. Let me or Lieutenant Proffitt know what you need from the other side."

"Hey!" Aribeth grabbed Leland's arm and forcefully turned him. "Where do you get off…?"

"Ms. Fuller," he said, and he put some emphasis on it. "You may be the leader, but I'm the one that has been here before. I've travelled those woods and I know what we're looking for. You made the decision on what to do…now let me take point on how to do it. Okay?"

Aribeth, still fuming, relented. "Fine."

Leland returned her angry stare for just a moment, then smiled and pointed downstream. "Go catch our dinner. Please."

#

The girl was sobbing quietly in the corner.

Talon Volpe, drenched in sweat from head to toe, lay back and listened to her cries, drank them in and savored them the way the fancy men up north savored their fine wines. Her terror was intoxicating, but like all highs, the buzz was quickly wearing off. He could tell that he had already broken her. She was nothing but a naked shell now, bruised and bloodied and worthless.

He exhaled slowly and stroked his long black beard. She was the last of his stash. Business had been too good for too long. The settlers were either preparing better or leaving for the safety of the cities. The money, and the girls, were drying up. He had already lowered his normally impeccable standards once.

"Talon, get up," he heard a voice call from outside his fur-lined tent. It was his second in command, an olive-skinned man who went only by the name Drak. Only Drak dared call him by his first name.

Talon looked lazily at the whimpering girl in the corner. "I'm all done with you now, sweetie." The girl, slightly overweight, looked through her stringy, blood-soaked hair at him, eyes flashing with the faintest glimmer of hope. "Time to pass you on to the boys. It has been a pleasure though."

As he pushed himself off the ground, his words penetrated and the girl began to screaming out. Volpe stood over her and smiled. "Oh, how nice of you to save a little fight for them. I'm sure that they'll appreciate it."

The girl was restrained with binders fastened to a metal stake by a short chain, just long enough for him to maneuver her. Now he picked the key up off a chest that contained his most prized possessions, his guns, and released her. She tried to bolt but he snatched the chain quickly and yanked it hard, pulling the girls arms up over her head. Any more force and he might have dislocated her shoulders.

"Now, now. I can't be selfish. I'm sure you'd rather stay here with me, but my men will lose respect for me if I don't share." He dragged her out of the tent. She tried to dig in her heels but had no strength left to put up much resistance.

He emerged into the brilliant sunshine of another fine day to find Drak standing there, arms crossed and clearly annoyed.

Talon held up the end of the chain like a trophy. "Play time."

Drak took the chain, yanked the girl ahead, and passed her off to another man standing to Drak's right. He never partook of the trophies like the rest. "Here," he snarled.

The second man took the chain with delight and hurried off to the rest of camp, calling out to the men. "Hey fellas, play time! Play time," while the girl bucked and screamed in terror.

Talon watched her being led away morosely. "The pickings are getting slim, my friend."

Drak was all business. Drak was *always* all business. "Lon just came back. You need to hear this."

"Well, bring him to the tent," Talon answered. "No need in standin' around out here with our peckers in the wind."

Drak scowled at him. "Yours is the only one in the wind."

Talon looked down and admired himself. "Indeed." He looked up and grinned bigger. "If ya got it…." Drak didn't smile. Talon had been trying for years to get Drak to loosen up and have some fun, but he never did. "I'll get dressed. Bring him," he said with a sigh.

Talon dropped inside the tent and picked out the day's clothes; tight black pants and matching boots with silver pointed toes, and a dark red shirt with frills at the end of the sleeves and a high collar. He dressed and stood in front of a full-length mirror. He checked carefully to make sure that he looked proper, then brushed through his flowing black hair.

Talon Volpe could have passed for a man of money in the cities with his impeccable manners and style. Volpe's mere presence could stop all talk when he entered a room. Talon Volpe was an unusually tall and rangy, with hair and eyes dark as coal and skin permanently bronzed by spending his life outside. Still a relatively young man, his face was only beginning to show some lines. Talon liked the lines. He felt that they made him look distinguished.

That was his public face. The one he put on when he took leave of his gang and headed into Norales for a few days, his pockets lined with coin and with a thirst for civilization eager to be satisfied. He allowed himself these creature comforts only on rare occasions.

Those fools strode with him, shoulder to shoulder through the streets, never thinking that they were in the presence of the most wanted, and most deadly, outlaw Cadoa had ever known.

Only his men, his beloved Gang of Eight, knew the real Talon Volpe. They knew him as a reckless, fearless, and completely depraved leader that they would follow into the very depths of hell if needed.

Though he liked to play with his toys, what he had told the girl was, in part, correct. He maintained his men's loyalty through one part generosity — keeping coin in their pockets and girls for their carnal welfare — and through one part brutality. He had often found it necessary to make an example of someone, and when he did, Talon made sure that it was public and extremely bloody. Even Drak, who Talon secretly believed was of Iridian ancestry, would never go so far so to openly challenge Talon's authority.

As Talon finished primping in the mirror, Drak ducked inside with Lon Dickson in tow. Lon was Talon's best scout, with hair just a shade lighter than his sandy skin, and almost white eyes. Lon could blend in and disappear in almost any situation. He was also the coward of the group, which was why Talon sent him away from camp often. Lon never actively participated in raids, instead acting as an advance man and lookout.

So far, no settlement had figured that when the yellowed man on the pale steed came riding into town, death and destruction were soon to follow.

"What is it, Lon?" Talon asked as he smoothed out a wrinkle on his shirt.

"They've finally done it," Lon said, panic rising in his voice.

"Done what?" Talon often had to pry information from the soft-spoken man, a particularly annoying habit.

"Launched an expedition," Lon said nervously. "They're camped down in Masterson Gulch right now. I counted 127 people, mainly families."

Talon smiled into the mirror and studied the shine on his perfect teeth. He paid great money to a dentist in Norales to keep them that way. "Girls? Did you see girls?"

"Yes," Lon stammered. "But that's not all. They've sent soldiers with them. Heavily armed. Some in uniform, some are not. I counted eight, possibly nine."

Talon turned away from the mirror. The terror in Lon's face was evident. Lon always dreaded the raids. He didn't have the stomach for the bloodshed, though he didn't seem to mind the booty too much. Beside him, Drak was stone faced.

"Were these wealthy travelers or were they hovel?"

Lon swallowed hard. "I saw a few who might have some money. Most appeared to be farmers and laborers. I couldn't say how much they have in valuables."

"But there are girls?" Talon turned away from the mirror and gave Lon his full attention. "You know, our supply is gone."

"Yes, but the soldiers—"

Talon didn't want to hear any of Lon's worrying. That always brought him down. This was good news and not to be rained on. "That will be all, Lon, thank you. If you hurry back to camp, you might still get in on some play time before Sidor bleeds the poor girl out." Talon paused and studied the yellow man, then shrugged. "Then again, maybe it doesn't matter so much to you."

Lon tried to hide his disgust, but bowed quickly and ducked

out. Talon watched him go, then stepped closer to Drak. "Eight soldiers protecting 130 people, down in the gulch? Easy pickings."

"Eight on eight, against professional soldiers," Drak said. "Those aren't great odds. They know we're out here."

Talon laughed heartily. "They're not professional soldiers, and that is not a sanctioned expedition," he said as he slapped his second on the shoulder.

"How do you know that?"

"Because, my friend, a sanctioned expedition would be more heavily guarded. Besides, they wouldn't send families into an area like Aranwa without sending in a proper military sweep force first. What you have is a private expedition with some hired guns riding along for protection. If I had to guess, I'd bet that they are military washouts or just mercenaries. They're probably not even getting paid enough to risk their lives for a bunch of farmers."

Drak was clearly not convinced. "Before you do anything impulsive, let me send Lon back out to take another look."

"Are you still afraid that the Ministry is baiting us? You've been jumping at that shadow for years now."

Drak looked at Talon through cold, flat eyes, his face expressionless. "Have you ever spent time in a prison? A real prison with hardened criminals? I have. It's not something I care to do again."

Talon huffed in defiance and turned back to the mirror. "No. And I never will. If they get the drop on me, I'll go out blasting." He took another few moments to primp himself. "Send Lon out. And send Sherald out too. Have him cross the river and sweep around behind. Tell him to go all the way to town and make sure that there's no one following. I want him to come right up on them, as close as he dares, and get us a better idea of what we're looking at."

Drak, who was a stickler for having solid intelligence, was satisfied with the answer. "Right away." He turned sharply, like an officer receiving orders from a superior.

"Wait," Talon called out. Drak slumped his shoulders, stopped, and turned slowly.

Talon took a black, wide brimmed hat with silver accents and placed it on his head, then straightened it up. "You get Sherald. I'll get Lon. I want to take a look myself."

"Are you sure that's a good idea?"

"Of course it is," he said jovially.

CHAPTER 15

It took the rest of the day just to hike back up to the bluff overlooking camp. In the advancing twilight, the group moved quickly to collect wood to build a fire, which fell to Aribeth and Parrie, while the men made a tentative sweep of the immediate area, but no one was willing to go too deep into the woods in the dark.

The group now included Bethel Hough, who took the place of Alvarez Proffitt. Proffitt elected to stay behind to guard Dr. Grant and the boys as they worked on the far side of the river, and to watch the opposite cliff side. They all agreed to keep the news from the families for the time being, as no one felt it necessary to spread panic if there was no good reason for it.

As darkness fell, they ate some of the fish that Aribeth had taken from the river before they left. Aribeth, though somewhat insulted that she was reduced to "fetching dinner," was excellent at fishing, thanks again to the tutelage of her father. After dinner, Lee prepped and dried the remaining catch so that they would have enough food to last them on their exploration, while the rest sat around the fire and made idle small talk. The entire time, everyone kept a careful watch on their surroundings, each fearful of what secrets the dark woods might hold.

Eventually most of them slept, while Ridge took first watch over the camp. Armed with his knife and pistol, Ridge walked a wide circle around the camp, stopping periodically to listen for any sounds that didn't fit. Once he was sure that nothing was out there, Ridge gingerly slid deep into the same bush their mystery guest had used and positioned himself so that he could keep an eye on the woods.

After two hours, Parrie stirred. She had, during her time at Academy, trained herself to wake up at set intervals. She sat, stretched, yawned, and picked up her rifle before looking around for Ridge. When she didn't see him, she jumped up and began a frantic visual scan of the area.

"Calm down, kid," Ridge said quietly from the bush. "I'm right here."

Parrie, who was looking around wildly, spun on her heels. "What...?"

"Don't look over here," he said quietly but with a tone. "If somebody's watching I'd rather them not know that I'm in here."

Parrie processed that for a minute, then nodded and strolled casually to the edge to look down over the camp. She saw numerous campfires on the east side of the river, and one on the west side. With her back still turned to the camp, she whispered, "See anything?"

"No. I think we're jumping at shadows."

"Maybe you're right," Parrie answered. "But I'd rather be prepared for nothing than be caught completely off guard." Satisfied that all was right down below, Parrie began making her own sweep of the area, walking far outside the light cast by the fire and right up to the edge of the woods.

At one point, for no reason other than instinct, she stopped and stared intently into the woods. There was no sound, no smell, no reason to believe that anything was amiss. Yet she was certain that there was something out there, watching. She peered intently into the darkness, trying to force her eyes to penetrate the thick black curtain, yet she could make out nothing. As Parrie stood, rifle at the ready, she debated going in, but already the light of the fire was small, and if she got turned around, lost out there, there was no telling what she would run into.

Finally, with a heavy sense of unease, she headed back to camp and sat with her back to the woods, and as close to Ridge's post as she could.

"Something you don't like out there?" Ridge asked as she sat down.

Parrie propped her rifle up next to her and held her hands out to the fire. "Just a feeling." Ridge didn't immediately answer, which made Parrie feel foolish. She was being paranoid.

"I got that same feeling," he finally responded. "At that same spot."

#

Lon and Talon, both now wearing thick coats to guard against the chill of night, sat silently, hunched behind a fallen log in the woods just outside of camp. They took turns peering through the looking glass, assessing their targets.

"Look at this one," Talon whispered excitedly. "She's a dandy. Check out that uniform. She thinks she's something," he said as he watched Parrie make her rounds.

Lon took the glass and got a long look. "She looks like a boy."

"That's because all you see is the haircut," Talon criticized. "She doesn't have a boy's body. Nice and hard, that one. I'll enjoy my time with her. I bet she puts up a fight. But the one I really like is the other one, the young one. She's a beauty."

Lon grunted and shifted his weight carefully so as not to make too much noise. "The men, they look tough."

"The other cadet is big, but he's just a cadet. The guide, I bet he can shoot. He's got that stance, that attitude. He'd be tough in a fight. You say that there are more down below?"

"Several," Lon whispered.

"We'll have to wait and find out what Sherald says. It's too bad," Talon said. "We could walk up there right now. You suppress the girl, I knife the men, and we drag the two girls back into the woods. The people below wouldn't know."

"We could," Lon agreed. He was a coward, but the thought of first turn on one of the girls overrode that trait.

"We would, if it weren't for the guy in the bush." Volpe swung the looking glass to look at Ridge's hiding spot. "I don't like the look of him. He looks like a killer."

"We could fire a shot in the bush and then charge the camp. Still have surprise on our side."

"No. If he's laying down in there, the shot goes over his head and he's firing back at us. Too many unknowns there." Talon took the glass away from his eye. "Best to wait. I'll make my way back to camp and wait for Sherald. I want you to stay on them. Stay back, especially in the day."

Lon grunted an acknowledgement, which was not enough. Talon plucked Lon's arm in a vise grip and pulled him close. "Listen to me," he snarled into Lon's ear. "Don't let them catch you. If you give this away, if you warn them, I'll personally cut your intestines out and feed them to you. Clear?"

"Y-y-yes," he stuttered.

"You'd better be." He started to stand but then the female cadet, mere feet from them, stopped and began staring intensely in their direction. Talon froze instantly, his eyes locked on the figure silhouetted by the campfire and the light of the twin moons.

"Do you think she sees us?" Lon whispered, barely audible.

Talon shushed him. She kept staring. Talon, ready for trouble, slowly moved his hand to the pistol at his side. If she moved wrong, if she knew, he'd kill her in a heartbeat, even if it meant losing a toy.

153

Finally, she moved away warily. They both released long, slow breaths. "I'm serious," Talon warned again, his voice full of unspoken menace. "Don't get caught."

#

Aribeth woke to the now familiar sound of birds chirping in the trees. When they'd first arrived, she'd never heard a call anything like what these strange, and still unseen, birds made. By now it had become normal.

She sat up slowly, feeling stiff and unrested. She had been haunted all night by strange dreams and the feeling that someone was watching her. Now, in the first rays of light, she scolded herself for being paranoid.

The others were all waking up as well, except for Ridge, who came scuffling out of the bush with exhaustion written all over his face.

"Were you up all night?" Aribeth asked him as he took a long drink of water from his canteen.

"Couldn't sleep," he grunted between chugs.

"There's something out there," Parrie said cryptically. She took a cautious glance over her shoulder. "I swear that there is. I felt it."

Bethel yawned on the ground beside her and chuckled. "What are there, ghosts out there? Ooooohhhh. Look out. Parrie feels something."

She glowered down at him. "You're going to feel my boot up your butt."

"Promises, promises," Bethel grinned back at her.

"Shut up," Parrie snapped.

"Both of you shut up," Leland finally said. He already seemed fully awake and alert. "These woods do that to you, Cadet," he said tensely. "If you haven't felt it yet, you will. Now everybody needs to grab a bite to eat and do it quick. We've got a lot of ground to cover today."

They did that and were soon ready to move out. Leland gathered the group around. "Okay, listen. Those woods get dense in a hurry. The coverage is thick up high, so the light is going to be poor. Try to keep your bearings. Look for anything that looks out of the ordinary."

"Not all of us are trackers like you," Bethel snorted. "How do we know what we're looking for?"

Leland patiently answered. "If you see something that you think looks unusual, call out for me and I'll come look. If you pay attention, you'll notice things. Watch the ground for tracks or footprints. Watch the grasses and short vegetation for evidence someone, or something, walked through. Watch the branches on the trees for breakage." Then he shifted his attention to the whole group. "We're not just watching for humans. I saw signs last time of very large predators. I'd like to know if there is something out there. Look for feces, especially big clumps of it, or carcasses, bones, that sort of thing. Any more questions?"

No one had anything. "All right. Everybody check your supplies and your weapons and we'll get started." He went to each member of the group, assigning them each a section to explore, making a half circle outward from the camp. He came to Aribeth last. "Are you ready to go?"

"Which section is mine?" Aribeth said eagerly as she fiddled with the strap on her father's bag, which she had slung across her chest.

"You and I are going straight ahead," Leland answered.

"Why am I going with you? Why can't I have my own section?"

"Because, Ms. Fuller, you're not experienced—"

"Hell. I've been wondering around forests all my life. You don't think I can walk around a bunch of trees?" She pointed at Parrie and Bethel, who were standing side by side a few feet away. "I've got more experience than those two."

Leland maintained his cool. "I'm sure you can find your way in the woods, but can you handle it if you stumble across some beast out there? What if there are bandits in the woods? What are you going to do? Have you ever even fired a gun?"

"No," she said softly, eyes dropping to the ground.

"That's why I want you with me. I don't want you to get hurt."

That got Aribeth's blood boiling again. "I don't need you to be my protector, Lee." She reached out and plucked Leland's knife out of its sheath on his left thigh. "I'll take this. If anybody tries to grab me, I slice. If I find an animal, I run. I can take care of myself."

She started to storm past him but Leland hooked her arm and turned her around. "This isn't like Bretonville," he snapped at her. "This is an untamed land. There's a difference between exploring a tame forest and an unexplored wilderness."

Aribeth leaned up on her toes and got right in Leland's face. "You don't know that there's anything out there, and I think that's what really scares you. You keep talking about how dangerous it is here. How foolish this whole thing is. You don't know anything. I have yet to see one thing to make me think that this land is any different, any more dangerous, than when Father first packed us up and took us to Bretonville."

"And you've seen how much?" Leland shot back. "Your father and I walked hundreds of kilometers, saw animals unlike anything anyone else has seen. Who are you to judge Aranwa over me?"

Aribeth settled back on her heels but wasn't about to give in. "I'm not. But I'm also not afraid. I can take care of myself. I need you to quit treating me like a tagalong. I'm the leader. I have my father's journal, his maps, his notes. I've studied them and committed them to memory. I can do this."

"It's different when you're really out there."

"No, it's not." She tucked Leland's hunting knife inside of her belt. "Trust me. We'll divide that section in half. I'll take the left side. You'll be on my right, and Bethel is on my left. If anything happens, I'll scream. Okay?"

Leland was reluctant, but Aribeth wouldn't back down, wouldn't break his gaze. Finally, he relented. "Any trouble, any at all, you scream. Got it?'

"Sure," she said flippantly before she turned and strutted off into her section, proud of herself for winning the battle of wills.

#

Lon, exhausted both emotionally and physically from the long night of watching, almost made a crucial mistake. He had fallen asleep hunched over the fallen log and in plain view. He might have slept right up until the search team swept over him.

Until the girl started yelling.

Lon awoke with a start. Disoriented, he stumbled backward and fell. Quickly he scurried back behind the cover of the log, and after a few tense heartbeats, worked up the courage to look out.

The group was spread out, each about to enter the woods. The tough looking man was nearest to Lon, almost on a straight path to him. Yet, the girl and the scout began to argue and everyone had stopped to watch the show.

He had to move, quickly. He had no desire to tangle with the man who even Talon had seemed wary of. Lon started working his way deeper into the woods and to his right, hoping to take himself away from the tough man's path.

The argument lasted only a minute, but it was enough to give Lon the chance to lose himself deeper in the forest. With only five people, there would be plenty of gaps in their search. He just had to stay sharp and keep his distance.

Soon, the search spread out into the woods, but by that time, Lon had already lost himself deeper in the forest, far out in front of their search.

#

Bethel was bored, and when he got bored, his mind wandered. As he absentmindedly tromped through the forest, his thoughts were back home. How had he wound up here?

Of course, his father would find this all so…typical. While Bethel's brothers were busy making money and courting women, Bethel the Baby was walking through a forest, stepping in God knows what, insects constantly flying in his face and feeding on his exposed skin.

He could see them all now, sitting around the dinner table, eating the finest food, swilling drinks afterwards, and trading laughs on what a failure Bethel was. They'd all have a great time making sport of him, just as they always had.

He should have been there. His brothers didn't have anything that he didn't have, other than pure, blind, stupid luck. They weren't any smarter, didn't work any harder. But somehow, where they had always managed to scrape by and avoid trouble, Bethel always found a way to fall face first into it.

Hell, it was his brothers who had told him how to cheat his way through Academy. He'd done everything they'd said. Yet, he was found out. He wondered now if his brothers had turned him in out of pure spite.

Bethel knew that he could never tell Parrie about that. He had made up the story of being recruited for this trip off the top of his head. In truth, he had been approached with the opportunity just a few hours earlier, *after* he had been dismissed. The only reason Bethel had taken the offer was because he knew that there was nowhere else to go.

Bethel had no doubt that Parrie would kill him if she found out the truth.

So far, Aranwa was proving to be far from the land of riches he'd been promised. The professional soldiers treated him like an errand boy. Parrie viewed him as an incompetent fool, and the others largely ignored him.

The deeper he got into the woods, the more Bethel convinced himself that this was all a gag. They had set him up to be the stooge. They had probably all doubled back to camp and were sitting around laughing as he got himself lost in these damn trees. Bethel the Baby, lost forever in the stupid trees with the stupid bugs biting him.

I should turn around, Bethel thought. Screw all of this tromping through forest garbage.

He should turn around, go back, and not stop until he reached civilization again. He wasn't a bad looking guy. He could find a rich girl, maybe one with limited prospects, and still have a life of relative leisure. He could handle marrying an ugly girl if she were rich enough.

That was when he heard the whuff.

Bethel felt it as much as heard it, a sudden, strong outflow of air. Bethel immediately stopped and turned to the right.

The lumbering giant rose off the forest floor. Even on all fours, the creature was a head and a half taller than Bethel. It had a short snout, floppy ears, and thick, brown and green mottled fur that had allowed the creature to disappear into the environment. Now it locked on to Bethel and let out a nasty, snarling howl that revealed two rows of pointed, glistening white teeth.

"Whoa, whoa," Bethel muttered as he began backing away from the creature. He fumbled for the pistol at his side, but his hands were shaking and he was stumbling along the uneven ground.

The creature lumbered forward with its nose low to the ground, a deep rumble coming from its throat, slowly stalking its prey.

Bethel finally managed to free the pistol and took a quick, panicked shot that sailed high. He dodged right, putting the trunk of a large tree temporarily between them. With another roar, the creature rose partway on its hind legs and swatted a huge paw through the air. The animal shattered the tree trunk to splinters. As the top of the tree crashed to the ground, Bethel turned and broke into a dead run, finally finding the voice to begin screaming for help.

He could hear the pounding footfalls as the creature began to give chase. Without slowing to look, he fired another blind shot over his shoulder, but was immediately certain that he missed. The creature's breath reached out ahead of the beast. Bethel could feel it on the back of his neck.

Bethel was certain that he had no hope of outrunning the beast. He risked a look over his shoulder and found, to his relief, that the monster wasn't as close as he'd imagined. However, it was closing fast. Bethel turned, took his time, aimed, and fired a perfect shot that hit the creature between the eyes.

It stopped, reared back, and roared again. This was a roar of anger, not pain. Bethel ran again, winding his way, looking to put any sort of obstacle between them. Almost immediately the creature resumed the chase, his heavy footfalls shaking the ground and rattling the branches on the trees.

With nowhere to go and no cover to speak of, Bethel knew he was a dead man. He wasn't even sure where he was in relation to camp anymore. The forest seemed to stretch on forever in front of him, while the pounding strides of the beast drew closer and closer.

He kept running, all the while preparing for the end. Bethel expected to feel the crushing weight of the animal's paw slam into him, or its teeth slicing into his flesh. He was going to die in these horrible woods and be eaten by a creature that didn't even have a name

Two shots rang out from Bethel's right and the creature roared again. Bethel skidded to a stop as Parrie, running at full speed, emerged from the trees suddenly. "Run, idjit," she screamed before bringing up his rifle, sighting, and firing two more shots.

Instead, Bethel turned and watched. It had been hit in the side and now blood dripped out of the wound, yet the beast only seemed more enraged as it changed course and charged Parrie. She glanced quickly over to Bethel and again yelled "run" before firing another shot and taking off herself.

Bethel swerved in her direction, trying to catch up to her. Parrie caught sight of him heading her way. "What are you doing? Get away."

Bethel took another shot with his pistol and smiled as it found its way home, hitting the creature in the hindquarters and temporarily slowing it. "I'm coming with you."

"Dummy," Parrie yelled back. "He'll get us both." She stopped, turned, and fired again. Bethel, even in the midst of running for his life, admired the speed of the move. She was a dead shot, but the creature just kept coming, though it had been slowed. Parrie shook her head and took off running, crossing Bethel's path. "Keep zigging. It doesn't change direction very quickly."

He fell in step behind her, the two crashing through the forest, periodically changing course, hoping now that they could simply outlast the enraged monster.

It kept coming and kept gaining, in spite of everything Parrie and Bethel tried. Parrie readied her gun on the run, turned, and prepared to fire again, but Bethel was too close and running too fast. He crashed into her and they both fell. She dropped her rifle, instinctively reaching out to brace herself for the fall. As she landed with Bethel crashing on top of her, Parrie screamed, her wrist caught underneath her.

Obviously sensing victory, the animal let out a scream. Parrie ignored the pain in her wrist and began desperately feeling for her dropped weapon, while Bethel hit the ground and rolled, too afraid to stop moving to do anything else.

A loud crack split the air, and this time the animal stopped dead in its tracks. Bethel stopped rolling and Parrie sat up. Leland was there with his long rifle, smoke pouring out of the barrel, and he let loose and there was another loud crack, and the creature bucked and whined and stumbled.

Leland took one deep breath and fired again. Another crack and the beast went down as blood began spurting out of a gaping hole in its neck. Leland lowered his gun and studied the creature from a distance before approaching it slowly, still ready to fire if needed.

The beast was whimpering now, twitching spasmodically as it lay on the bloody ground. Leland quickly hung his rifle on his shoulder and reached for his knife, found it missing, and shook his head sadly.

He was soon standing beside the beast, showing not an ounce of fear. As Bethel and Parrie watched in stunned silence, Leland laid a hand on the creature's side and began to pet it gently. He did that for a minute, which seemed to soothe the beast. He stepped up to the still bleeding wound and reached inside, forcing both hands into the creature's neck. They could see him feeling around inside the beast before finally finding what he was looking for. With a powerful yank, Leland pulled and blood quickly poured out of the wound and onto the ground. Leland, looking greatly disturbed, removed his hands and stroked the animal again until it finally, mercifully, died.

162

CHAPTER 16

Ridge was no frontiersman by any stretch of the imagination. He was a man who was fond of society and the trappings that came along with it. He had been born and raised in the country, but never far from town and in areas that were largely settled, so the experience of searching unexplored wilderness was new to him.

Hunting men was not.

Ridge walked carefully, slowly into the forest, his eyes constantly on the move, his senses all sharply attuned, waiting for any sign of a presence. He kept his knife in his left hand and his right hand close to his pistol. He was a coiled spring, ready to strike.

During the night, Ridge had fixed on a location, roughly the same area that Parrie had also fixed on. Despite his assurances to her that they were jumping at shadows, Ridge had a keen sense for when the hunt was on. He could sense it in the air…the slight traces, the vibrations that let him know that someone was near. That someone was watching.

His walk steadily took him to the log where Talon Volpe and Lon Kinson had watched them from the night before. Ridge instantly noticed the spot because, if he were spying, he would have used the same spot.

He circled the spot and began to pick out the tiny telltale

signs. Strange impressions on the moss that covered the top of the log, shuffle marks along the ground, and a near perfect half circle impression in the soft dirt that was the perfect shape for a man's knee.

Ridge tightened up even more now. His suspicions had been confirmed. He unholstered his gun and began tracking further back, still deliberate in his movements.

He stalked the woods throughout the day, always feeling as if someone were right there, just beyond the reach of his senses. This person, whoever it was, was taunting him, teasing his presence. Ridge took it personally. This was his type of hunt and he did not accept defeat, especially to cowards who hid in the shadows.

He was aware, from somewhere off to his left, of a disturbance. He heard what might have been screaming and possibly some gunshots, but Ridge did not let it distract him from his purpose. He kept going, pushing further and deeper, and eventually, the woods began to thin out and he could hear water running nearby...not rushing like the river, but gentle, like a small creek.

Ridge wanted to push on, but darkness was quickly approaching and Echonos was already beginning to appear in his perch high atop the world. If he were to have any chance at making it back to camp by nightfall, he had to go now and move fast. Even then, it was unlikely he would make it back.

Instead, Ridge decided to keep going.

#

"What happened out there?"

Aribeth had just emerged from the woods, having rushed back after hearing the shots and screams emanating from the forest. She found Parrie and Bethel sitting at the campsite looking haggard and beaten. They were both dirty and bleeding from tiny cuts across all exposed areas. Parrie had stripped off her jacket and rolled up her sleeves, and was busy placing a wrap on one wrist. Bethel had taken off his boots and opened his shirt, and was reclined against a rock, head tilted back and eyes shut when she called out to them.

Parrie looked up. "Animal attack. Almost killed us."

"Oh no." Aribeth jogged the rest of the way into camp. "What kind of animal? Are you okay?'

Bethel chuckled. "A demon animal. Biggest thing I've ever seen. Kinda of like a nita, but bigger and meaner. I almost walked right over him."

Parrie picked up the story. "I heard him yelling and ran over. Shot it…I don't know, three, maybe four times or more. Direct hits and it barely slowed down. Then the genius over here ran into me and nearly got us both eaten." She glared at Bethel and then returned to the task of wrapping up her arm. "I think I sprained my wrist, and we're both pretty bruised and cut up, but other than that we're fine."

Aribeth took the wrap from Parrie's hands and began to do it herself. "You're not getting it tight enough," she said. "You need pressure." She finished the job and asked Parrie how it felt.

"Better," she answered.

Aribeth stood and dusted herself off, then began looking around the camp. "Where's Lee?"

"He's back there with the beast," Bethel scoffed. "He saved our hide. I'm not sure what kind of gun that is he's shooting, but it took that thing down."

"Then he reached inside of the thing and killed it with his hands. I guess he opened a vein or something," Parrie said in awe. "He seemed really upset by it though."

"Where is he? I'll go in after him."

Parrie pointed the way. "We came out right over there. Keep walking straight and you're bound to find him. I'm staying here."

"Me too," Bethel called. "To hell with this place."

"Have it your way," Aribeth said. "Has Ridge come back yet?"

They both shook their heads. "Haven't seen him," Parrie answered. "It's like he just disappeared."

"I hope he's okay." She stood and debated if she should go find Leland or Ridge. Leland apparently was fine but distraught, while Ridge was just gone. She checked the sun in the sky and determined that it was too early to worry about Ridge, so she decided to go find Leland instead.

Aribeth hadn't gotten too deep into the woods when she heard him. He was grunting loudly, and she could hear tree branches breaking underfoot. Adjusting her trajectory slightly, Aribeth soon found Leland huffing and puffing as he struggled to drag the animal back to camp. Her eyes widened in shock as she took in the sheer size of the animal.

Leland was dripping sweat as he looked up at her. "A little help?"

Aribeth rushed to his side, picked up one massive paw, and began pulling as well. "What is this thing?"

"Good question," he said between grunts. "Mean sucker. Real tough hide, thick bones." He stopped pulling and dropped the paw he was holding. "Look at this fur. Perfect camouflage. He's really something. Shame I had to kill it."

"From what I hear, it was going to eat Parrie and Bethel."

"Yep." He picked up the leg he had been dragging and resumed the labor. "I could feed the family for a month, maybe more, with a beast this size. When I get it back to camp I'll carve him up, and then we should send someone back down to camp with a bunch of this meat. We won't need near this much."

"I'll send Bethel. He doesn't seem too thrilled to be here anyway."

"Good call."

"Parrie said that you seemed upset about killing this."

"I am," Leland said. "He was just doing what he's born to do. He needs to eat and Bethel just happened to stumble across him. He didn't deserve to die for that, but I couldn't let him kill somebody. I did what I had to do."

"For someone who survives by hunting I find that surprising."

"I hunt for survival and I'm good at it, but that doesn't mean that I don't respect the animals I hunt. I don't take pleasure in killing. It's just a part of my life. "

When they were in sight of the camp, Aribeth called out to the others and together the four of them finished bringing the animal in. An exhausted Leland collapsed in a heap and lay motionless for several minutes. Aribeth tore a swatch of fabric off the tail of her shirt and soaked it in water from her canteen, then laid it on his head to cool him.

"He's not as scary up close," Parrie said as she surveyed the carcass.

"He's not chasing you," Bethel responded. He was still angry at the beast and kicked it in the stomach. The beast released a belch of gas when he did.

Leland sat up suddenly. "Don't do that again. Leave it alone."

"Why shouldn't I? Damn thing tried to eat me."

Leland pushed himself up off the ground and stormed toward Bethel. "Because I'll kill you if you do. You're the trespasser. *You're* the one who walked into *his* hunting ground."

"I can't believe that you feel sorry for this...thing. What should I have done, huh? Should I have just stood there and let him eat me?"

Leland shoved a finger in Bethel's face. "I saved you because it was the right thing to do and because your life is my responsibility. But there's no need for you to be cruel about it. I won't abide it. Show some respect."

Aribeth forced her way between them. "Stop it. It's over now." She pointed at Bethel. "You leave the animal alone. And rest up. I'm going to send you back to camp soon."

"Oh, come on," Bethel cried out as he threw his hands in the air. "You're sending me back because I kicked a dead animal?"

"I'm sending you back," Aribeth snapped, "Because Lee is going to carve this up, and I'm going to have you run a bunch of the meat back to the others. Is that a problem, Private?"

Bethel stood and huffed, and sneered before finally relenting. "Fine."

Aribeth turned to Leland. Without a word, Leland plucked his knife from Aribeth's belt and started toward the animal. Aribeth knew that Leland needed time to cool off and let him go.

"I suggest that we let Lee do his work in peace. Have either one of you seen or heard any sign of Ridge yet?" They both shook their heads. Aribeth looked out in the direction Ridge had been travelling. "He might have gotten lost. We should go looking for him."

"It's getting late," Leland said without looking up from his grim task. "I wouldn't advise going too deep, if you go at all. Personally, I think he'll be all right. He's seems to be able to take care of himself."

"But what if he's hurt? What if one of those things got ahold of him?"

Leland finally quit cutting. "I doubt that. I don't think you'd find two of these that close together. Not as big as he is. If so, that'd be one hell of a turf fight."

"I'll go look," Parrie volunteered. She slipped her jacket back on and slung her rifle over her shoulder. To Aribeth she said, "We can split the distance between us. Shout out every so often so we can keep tabs on each other."

"What about you?" Aribeth asked Bethel. "Are you going?"

"No," he said as he plopped down on the ground. "I'll stay and guard the butcher." Leland glared at Bethel from over the top of the bloody animal body, but didn't respond.

"Fine," Aribeth answered. "We'll be back."

#

The search went nowhere, and with darkness closing in, Aribeth called it off. By the time they made it back to camp, Leland had fully skinned the animal and made a sizeable dent on carving up the meat. Bethel was sound asleep on the ground.

"No luck?" Leland asked, still focused on slicing up the remains.

"No luck," Aribeth answered. "I'm afraid that he got lost back there. I called out, but I never heard an answer."

"He'll be fine. Why don't you start a fire and we'll roast up some of this meat? I could go for some dinner right about now."

"Sounds good to me," Parrie called out from behind them. "I'm famished."

"Okay, fine," Aribeth reluctantly agreed. She toed Bethel's prone body in the ribs and he woke with a start. "Get up and help us gather some more wood."

Bethel rubbed the sleep out of his eyes and grunted. "How about mixing in a please?"

Aribeth was in no mood to play games with him. "How about if you don't help, you don't eat? How does that work for you?"

Bethel rolled his eyes but got up, and together they all set out to gather wood. They got the fired started and Leland cooked a steak for each of them. The animal turned out to be tasty, and a welcome relief from the fish and dried foods they had been eating. Bethel finished his and licked his fingers. "I bet that would be a delicacy back home. How much do you think some of those bankers and lawyers would pay for a dinner like that?"

"No clue," Aribeth answered. She was still working her way through her piece. "Maybe you just found your calling. Good luck with that."

"What do you think about Secova?" Parrie asked. "You think he found something out there?"

"If he's got any sense, he doubled back and took off," Bethel said. "We should all have our heads examined for being here. There are reasons nobody has settled Aranwa."

Aribeth rested her piece of meat on her lap. "I know that it's been tough so far, but the land my father described in his journal is like a paradise. Just stay the course and you'll have a plot of your own to do with as you please."

"If we even make it there," Bethel started. "If something doesn't eat us or—"

Leland suddenly shushed him and held up a finger to indicate that everyone should be quiet.

"What?" Aribeth whispered.

"Someone's coming," he whispered back. "I hear the footsteps." He slowly reached for his rifle and readied himself to shoot.

"Maybe it's Ridge," Aribeth answered. Leland glared at her out of the corner of his eye, and Aribeth realized that she had sounded a little too eager.

"Wrong direction," Leland said, turning his attention back to the approaching stranger. "Ridge would be coming from the woods. What I hear is coming from there." He nudged his head to indicate the area just south of camp.

"I hear it," Parrie said, quickly picking up her rifle. Bethel grabbed his as well and they all pointed their weapons into the dark.

"Don't shoot," a familiar voice cried out. "It's me. Alvarez." Parrie and Leland dropped their weapons with a sigh. "I brought news," Proffitt called out. "What are you eating up here anyway? It smells delicious."

"Come get some," Aribeth called out, and held up her meat for him to see. Soon enough he emerged from the shadows and went straight to Aribeth. As they watched, Proffitt devoured the other half of Aribeth's steak.

"That was great," he said as he finished up. "I gotta get some more of that."

"Well, the next time we come across one of these, you're more than welcome to hunt it," Bethel said. "Be our guest."

"I may take you up on that," Proffitt said with a snap of his fingers.

"What is your big news?" Aribeth asked.

"Mr. Gregg says the pulley system is almost done. They got the anchors up on both sides and a heavy-duty raft built. Tomorrow they're going to run the rope across the river and string it all up, and then we're going to test it. If all goes well, he thinks we can cross the whole lot by tomorrow night."

"That's wonderful," Aribeth said. She desperately needed some good news. "I'm so glad to hear that. How is everyone doing down there?"

"Everybody is holding up well. Got a few people who are sick, but Dr. Grant says that it's nothing important. People are getting restless."

"I imagine," Leland said. "Any sign of intruders hanging around?"

"Not that I've seen," Alvarez answered. "I did spend a good chunk of the day helping the boys build the anchor, though. I felt bad, watching them working so hard and me just sitting there, looking around. You find anything up here?"

Leland poked his knife in the direction of his makeshift spit. "Just dinner," he said. "No sign of any people."

"We lost Secova though," Bethel pointed out. "He walked into the woods this morning and vanished. I figure he took advantage and is probably on his way home by now."

"Maybe," Proffitt said doubtfully. He considered the possibility for a moment.

Aribeth read Proffitt's expression. "What are you thinking?

"Have we considered the possibility that he might be part of Volpe's gang?" He anticipated Aribeth's argument and moved to cut her off. "Think about it. He just shows up, unannounced, the morning we're about to leave. He's got a bad reputation for being a swindler, and he's bragging about how tough and dangerous he is. This trip wasn't exactly a secret. What if he's been waiting for a chance to slip off and go report to Volpe?"

"What if he is Volpe?" Parrie interrupted, only half kidding. "Nobody knows what he looks like. Volpe, that is."

"Don't be ridiculous," Aribeth chided her.

"You don't know the man," Leland said. "You should at least consider the possibility. He did just wander away. It makes sense."

"I don't believe it," Aribeth said, outwardly confident. In the back of her mind, she was seeing the logic behind the argument, but she wouldn't believe. She had made the call on Ridge. If he did turn out to be an outlaw, it would be her fault. Aribeth couldn't stomach the possibility that she had welcomed a killer into their midst. "You'll see," she said. "When we find him. You'll see."

"Anyway," Proffitt chimed in, changing the subject. "Mr. Gregg and Colonel Holt both believe that you should be there tomorrow to oversee the crossing, since you're the leader and all. That's why they sent me up here. If we leave at dawn, we should make it back just in time."

"But I'm needed here," Aribeth protested.

"Go on," Leland said. "I think we made a pretty good sweep

today. I'm confident that there's no immediate danger." He nodded at Parrie. "The two of us will stay up here and keep our eyes open. You and Alvarez and Bethel head back down and help with the crossing. We need to get those people across, and the sooner the better."

Aribeth felt better with Leland's approval of the plan. "Okay then," she said with a smile. "Let's go bring civilization to Aranwa."

CHAPTER 17

Aribeth, Bethel, and Proffitt set out just before daybreak, each carrying as much meat as they could in their packs. Leland and Parrie stayed on the ridge. Parrie was assigned to watch over the camp and keep an eye on the opposite side of the gulch, while Leland watched the woods.

Walking hard and talking very little, the group did make it back down and into camp by late morning. As they came into sight, Aribeth was relieved to see a pair of steeds milling around on the west side of the river, contentedly munching on the available grass.

"They did it," she exclaimed.

"Looks like it," Proffitt said, trying to sound casual, but he couldn't hide the smile on his face as well.

Dr. Grant saw them coming and hobbled out to meet them. "I'm glad to see you made it back in one piece, dear," he called out.

"There was never a doubt," Aribeth said, beaming as she hugged the old man. "So it works, I see."

"It does," he said proudly. "They moved it further down the river to the deeper water. They crossed those two steeds with no problem. Raft's back on the other bank now."

Aribeth put an arm around Dr. Grant and the four made their way to the landing spot. The boys were standing by the anchor point, ready to receive the next boatload. They both held up a hand in recognition. Across the way, Aribeth could make out Jamison Gregg coordinating the next pass. They were pushing a wagon, without steeds, up on the elongated raft.

"I assume the steeds over here belong to that?" Aribeth asked.

"Yes. He wanted to test it a couple of times before we put anybody on it." Another hulking young man stepped on after the wagon was loaded, carrying a long, thick pole with him. "One person poles, another pulls the rope, and the boys here pull as well. Four people pulling and pushing across. It takes a while and it's tiring, but it works. If they can get this wagon across then we should be fine."

"How do you know all of this?"

"Mr. Gregg came across yesterday to examine the anchor point on this side and make sure it was up to his standards. He was explaining it to me. If this works, we'll start moving families across. We're just not sure how it's going to handle the weight of the wagons."

"Wouldn't it make more sense to cross the people and worry about the wagons later?" Aribeth asked.

"If you cross all the people and then can't get the wagons over, then you've got a bunch of people over here and no supplies. Besides, it's too late now. Here they come."

They all looked across the river as the boys began pulling the rope and the pole man starting pushing. The raft sank low in the water and the displacement put some strain on the rope, but it held and they slowly worked the raft from one bank to the other. Everyone on both sides of the river cheered as the raft reached the other side and they pushed the wagon up onto the bank.

"Excellent," Aribeth called out. "Let's start moving some people." She turned to Proffitt and Bethel. "Jump on. Let's ride over and help. The more hands we've got, the faster this goes."

175

#

Ridge reached the forest edge by the time Akil joined Echonos high overhead. He had found no other evidence of the watcher, but was more convinced than ever that he was out there. Ridge took one furtive glance at the gently running brook that cut across the land running from northwest to southeast. He didn't dare camp for the evening in the clearing, and didn't risk even a small campfire. Instead he huddled up with his jacket in a thick copse of trees and managed to grab a few hours of intermittent sleep.

This land reminded him of home. He had started his journey as a teenager, helping his father sell forged land deeds to Ministry controlled lands similar to these. When his father had wound up on the wrong side of a pistol, Ridge was left to his own devices.

Yet his father had instilled in him a keen ability to read people, pick up their weaknesses, and play them to his advantage. Those skills had enabled Ridge to make a nice life for himself. He still sold forged land deeds, only he did it better than his father had. In the meantime, he gambled, courted wealthy women and, when the opportunity presented itself, engaged in the odd act of burglary.

The advance of civilization was making it harder and harder for a man of questionable means to make his living. The frontier kept pushing, and Ridge kept finding himself squeezed into tighter and tighter quarters.

Then a drunkard had spilled word of the impending expedition to Aranwa during a low stakes game of poker in the backroom of a notorious brothel. In Aranwa, Ridge saw a chance to wipe his slate clean and start over. Ridge was not opposed to an honest life, as long as he was still free to make a little dishonest money on the side. In this new land, he figured that he could do both.

Which meant that these bandits, the Talon Volpe gang, were

his competition. Ridge only tolerated competition so long as the odds were tilted in his favor. If he tracked them down, helped take them out, he would be a hero in the eyes of the settlers, especially in the eyes of young Aribeth. A man could do worse in marriage than Aribeth, who was strong willed and had a good head on her shoulders. They would make a lovely pair.

If not her, Ridge had noticed several young ladies in camp who would be coming of age soon enough. There were definite possibilities. So long as Volpe and his crew didn't ruin them.

As morning broke Ridge edged out of the forest and into the clearing. He saw no evidence of people and took the time to drink from the brook. The water was cold and crisp, a welcome relief, and he quickly refilled his canteen.

This would be a good spot to lay out a town, he thought. The vegetation was lush on the other side of the creek, with good sightlines. To the west, the grasslands stretched out forever, an endless sea of green, occasionally dotted with patches of red, blue, or yellow wildflowers, the land gently rolling along the way. To the east the land was slightly more flat, and he could see that further along the way the woods flanked the clearing, though from a distance they didn't appear to be as dense.

That, he thought, was the perfect place for an outlaw to make his camp.

#

Two nights without sex and Talon Volpe was cranky. He had been too quick to discard his latest plaything, and now the pressure was building in his brain. The only releases were sex or violence, though the combination of the two was always the best remedy. It was too late. The poor girl was carrion by now.

Talon sat in the dewy grass outside his tent, drinking hot bala and thinking about the expedition Lon had discovered. They were down there now, camped by that raging river; fat, easy targets just waiting to be hit. He wished that he'd had a chance to look down there himself, but he hadn't dared.

He was still waiting for Sherald and Lon to get back and report. Two other members of his gang had been gone for days, scouting for other possible targets, while three others had gotten bored and left to round up wild sobas, which ran plentiful on Aranwa's sprawling prairies. The wild steeds brought a pretty penny at the markets.

Drak was pacing nervously. The gang had been idle too long and everyone was itching for a new score. Security was getting tougher and the targets harder to hit. This caravan coming right at them was a blessing.

"Talon! Talon!" Talon snapped out of his daydreams at the calling of his name. He looked to find a disheveled Lon half running and half stumbling into camp. "Talon, we got trouble," he said breathlessly.

Drak, always the good lieutenant, was right there to hand Lon a cup of water, which he drank eagerly.

"What is the problem?" Talon asked coldly.

"The tough guy, the one in the bush. He's here. He's at the creek. He followed me the whole way."

"He followed you here?" Talon's anger immediately began to boil over and he reached for his weapon.

"Not directly," Lon said, desperate to cover his tracks. "He never saw me, but he just kept coming. I had to keep moving to stay in front of him. This morning, I saw him on the far bank of the creek. "

"He can't find us here, Lon. You know that," Talon warned.

"I know," he stammered.

"Is it just the one man?" Drak asked. "Or are there more?"

"Never saw anybody else," Lon reported. "I never felt that anyone else was close. This guy though, he wouldn't stop. I figured he'd give up at nightfall, but he kept coming."

Drak nodded solemnly. "I'll take care of him." He dutifully ducked into his own tent and emerged moments later with a pistol, a knife, and an axe he had made himself. "He won't get to us."

"Take Lon," Talon said. "This guy looks like he's fought a little bit. You might need the help."

Drak scoffed. "How is he going to help me, except to run for help if I'm wrong? And I'm never wrong."

"You can't afford to be wrong this time," Talon responded calmly. "Take him. Bring me back his head."

Drak nodded in acknowledgement, grabbed Lon by the arm, and they started out of camp, intent of taking out the meddlesome stranger.

#

The crossings were going well, but taking time. The physical toll of moving the large, heavy raft across the river was draining the men, and the process continued to slow as the day moved on. Any hopes of completing the move by the end of the day were abandoned. Aribeth and Mr. Gregg agreed that they should focus on moving the people across and leaving the wagons for the morning.

As the sun began to drop and long shadows began to creep over the gulch, Bethel and Aribeth loaded the raft for one last run across the river. They were joined by the two largest families in the group; the Maywoods, who had seven people, including five children, and the Nueva family, which was six people, three of them children, and one dog.

As they prepared to push off from the bank, Bethel sidled up next to Aribeth. The children on the raft gathered around the edge to look down into the water. The dog, a small brown, black, and white pup, yipped excitedly at their heels.

"Going pretty smooth," Bethel said confidently. "I think your boyfriend was just trying to scare us with all the big talk."

Aribeth rolled her eyes at him. "You weren't saying that yesterday when you were running for your life. Aranwa was a pretty scary place then."

"Well, that was scary, but we've got scary animals back home too, you know. But this, I mean, look at this." Bethel bent down and dipped his hands in the water. "This water is as smooth as glass. This is easy."

In the distance, there was a splash as a single fish jumped up out of the water and splashed back down. Then another, and another, each one closer than the last. "See? Even the fish are giving us a sendoff."

With a grunt, two large men pushed the raft away from the bank, hopped on, and began pulling on the overhead rope, working the boat slowly across the water. The children squealed with delight.

"I've got to admit," Aribeth said with a sigh. "I'll feel a lot better when we've got this river behind us. We've lost so much time here already."

"It's all downhill from here," Bethel said. "Hey, look." Bethel pointed in the water, where a school of the leaping fish had gathered just under the boat. "Hey kids, look. You can see them swimming alongside." He knelt next to a towheaded little boy and pointed again, his finger just above the water. "See the fish? They're seeing us across."

The boy leaned over just as one of the fish leapt out of the water. Bethel saw the flash of teeth an instant before it clamped down on his index finger. Bethel screamed and fell backwards, trying to flick it off his finger. When he did, he kicked the boy, who started to fall forward. Aribeth acted quickly, grabbing the boy by the collar of his shirt, and pulled him back. The other children panicked and ran for the other side of the boat. The sudden movement caused the boat to rock violently and sent everyone tumbling down. The oarsman dropped his pole into the water and, in trying to brace himself for the fall, knocked the puppy into the water.

Moments later the fish converged on it, tearing the tiny creature to shreds and turning the water red. The children cried out, and one, a ten-year-old girl with her dark hair pulled back in braids, lunged over the side, trying to grab at the dog.

Bethel managed to shake the fish off his finger, though it was dripping blood. Seeing the girl headed over the side, he lunged after her. He hooked his right arm around the railing of the boat and with his left hand, he caught her by a braid, held her above the water line, and then spun her back onto the boat just as another fish jumped up out of the water after her.

The railing wasn't designed to hold such weight, and it cracked under Bethel's weight. Aribeth and the oarsman both grabbed for him; Aribeth caught his arm and the oarsman grabbed him by the waist, and together they stopped him from falling completely into the water. His right arm did go in and was immediately attacked by the swarming creatures. As Bethel howled in pain, they pulled him back onto the boat and began tearing the vicious creatures from Bethel's arm.

The oarsman pulled one fish off and tossed it aside, where it skidded along the boat and then latched onto the arm of a little boy who had fallen and was still laying on the deck. His parents raced to help him. Aribeth pulled off another fish, only to have it chomp down on her left hand. She screamed in pain and began punching and slapping at the bloodthirsty animal. Bethel and the oarsman got the third and final fish off Bethel's arm and tossed it overboard, while the other father finally killed the one attached to Aribeth's arm with his knife.

"Everybody get in the middle of the boat," Aribeth called out. "Get away from the edge." All around, children cried while parents tried to shield the young ones from the sight of the poor dog being torn apart. Bethel, Aribeth, the oarsman, and the little boy were all bleeding from deep cuts caused by the razor teeth of the fish.

Aribeth reached out for Bethel's arm and turned him around. "When we get to shore, do me a favor. Stay away from me. You're a magnet for trouble."

Bethel shrugged his shoulders, trying to hide the pain he was feeling. "Story of my life."

#

On the ridge overlooking the river, Parrie had kept a keen eye on things. So far there had been nothing to see, so she occasionally took time out to look down and check on the progress of the river crossing.

Leland paced, more out of boredom than nervousness. He kept his rifle in his hands and his eyes on the woods. They did not talk except when he asked Parrie to report. Her response was always, "Nothing to report, sir."

They heard the commotion rising out of the gulch. Parrie took a quick look down at the camp. "We've got trouble," she called. Leland hurried to her side and they both peered down on the scene, completely helpless. Parrie held up her rifle and glanced through the scope. When she saw the blood in the water she turned her face away. "My god, people are falling into the water. There's blood everywhere."

Leland made angry fists at his sides. "I told them. I warned them. This place…." He started pacing again, now out of anger. "This place doesn't want us here."

"I'm beginning to agree with you," Parrie said with a heavy sigh. She forced herself to look anywhere but down. Her eyes soon focused on a figure on the lip of the other side of the gulch. "What is that?" Again, she brought her rifle's scope to her eye. "Mr. Jax, we've got a watcher." Leland spun around and peered across the way as Parrie continued to report what she was seeing. "Single man, with a mount. You think he's one of ours? Maybe Ms. Fuller sent him up to keep watch."

"He's not one of ours. I'd recognize him."

Parrie lowered the scope and looked over at Leland, incredulous. "You can see him from all the way over here?"

"Sure," Leland answered. He squinted and leaned forward slightly. "He's armed."

"You can't possibly tell that from here." Parrie peered through the scope again and saw the holstered pistol on his hip. "Well I'll be...." She let her words drift away as she took aim at figure across the way. "I don't think I could hit him from here, but I could scare him."

"Don't. We don't know who he is. It could be someone from town checking on us, or someone sent by Mr. Behrens. I don't want to fire on an innocent man."

Parrie agreed with the logic, though she secretly wanted to take the shot, just to know if she could hit him across the expanse. She let the gun drop. "Can't be the guy that we're looking for. How would he have crossed?"

Leland was still glaring across the way. "If it's bandits he might have. There could be a secret crossing. This is a big river. I doubt that it's been fully explored."

As they watched, the figure, who had been crouching by the cliff's edge, stood, quickly mounted his steed, and rode away, hard and fast.

"Wherever he's going, he's in a hurry," Parrie said.

"We need to let the others know. Will you go down? I'll keep watch up here."

"I'm on my way," Parrie answered sharply. It appeared trouble was on the way, and the very thought excited her.

#

Ridge had almost reached the eastern edge of the grasslands and the woods again rose in front of him. He'd followed along the south bank of the creek, not wanting to track through the water. Now as he approached the woods there was no longer any doubt that someone was out there.

The man was heading right towards him, and making plenty of noise.

Ridge had been hearing him tromping along for a bit, but now the man emerged from the tree line, caught sight of Ridge, and began to wave. "Hey there! Hello!"

Ridge was instantly wary. He held up his right hand in greeting while resting his left on the hilt of his knife. Ridge was not one for taking chances with strangers in the best of settings, and these were far from the best of settings.

As the man shuffled closer, Ridge saw that he was a largely unremarkable man with a leathery face and stooped shoulders. His eyes kept sliding away to the tree line on Ridge's right.

"Hi there, stranger," he called out when they got closer. "Ain't used to seeing people in these woods. You get lost?"

"You might say that," Ridge answered. Again, he watched the other man's eyes glance away. "Are you lost as well?"

"No sir," the other man chuckled uneasily. "I live here, back in the woods a way." The man turned and pointed back the way he'd come.

"I didn't think anybody lived over here," Ridge said, trying to sound friendly. He was slowly easing his knife free.

"There aren't many of us. We came over here to get away from the Ministry. You know how those devils are. Over here a man can live in peace." They were close enough now that the stranger held out his hand for a shake. "Name's Lon, what's yours?" Again, the eyes slid away, only this time, not all the way to the trees but just a tick to Ridge's right.

Ridge held out his right hand and tightened his left fingers on the knife. When they shook, Ridge gripped tightly and locked down on Lon's hand.

Lon began frantically trying to pull it away. "Let go," he called out, trying to yank his hand free but lacking the strength. "Let go." Then the man's eyes got wide. Ridge darted to his left and pulled Lon forward. Lon stumbled, pulled almost completely off his feet, and then an axe blade sliced through the air and imbedded itself in Lon's neck. Lon gurgled and fell to the ground, dead.

Ridge moved quickly, stepping over Lon, his own knife in his hand. "Some welcoming committee you've got here," he said with a smile that was all teeth and promised violence.

"We don't like strangers around here," the second man answered. He slid forward quickly, jabbing with the knife, but Ridge danced away.

"You're gonna have to be faster than that, friend," Ridge taunted.

"The name's Drak," the man answered. "And I'm not your friend."

Drak lashed out once, twice, but still couldn't get close to Ridge. Ridge began to toss his knife from one hand to other. He was having fun and it was clearly making his attacker angry. Once more the man lashed out and this time Ridge circled away, reached out, and punched the man in the side of the head.

It was a glancing blow, but it had put Drak off balance and he scrambled to get back in position. Ridge thrust and caught Drak in the left bicep, his blade easily slicing through the muscle. The man dropped the arm to his side and cried out with the pain.

"You're going to pay for that."

"I doubt it," Ridge said coldly.

Drak jabbed again and Ridge sliced across Drak's forearm. The man was now growling, which made Ridge enjoy himself that much more. "Why don't you try the gun?" Ridge asked. "You can't beat me with a knife. No one can."

Drak scowled and started to jab again, then stopped. He tossed the knife aside and went for the gun on his hip. Ridge flipped his knife, caught it by the backside of the blade, and tossed it all in one smooth motion. The knife entered Drak's shoulder just as he was clearing the gun, and Drak shot into the ground as he screamed.

Ridge launched himself at Drak, hitting him with a flying tackle in the midsection that sent Drak slamming into the ground, his head rocking back and cracking against the ground. Before he could recover his wits, Ridge had reclaimed his knife and was holding it to Drak's throat.

"How many more of you are out there?"

Drak smiled up at him through bloody teeth. "Enough to kill you. You don't know who you're messing with."

"Neither do you," Ridge snarled, and he started to draw the knife across Drak's throat, a sliver of blood oozing out of the cut. "Tell me. How many? Where's your camp?"

"I'll rot in hell before I tell you anything," Drak growled. If the man felt an ounce of fear he wasn't showing it.

Ridge laughed. "We'll see about that, friend."

CHAPTER 18

As twilight approached Talon was getting anxious. Sherald had not returned with his scouting report, and Lon and Drak had not returned from confronting the stranger. He was alone in the camp, surrounded by the woods and the strange noises that arose every night. Even Talon, for all of his bravado, disliked being alone in the woods of Aranwa at night.

Talon had been aware for some time that his window was closing. He wasn't fool enough to believe that he could elude the Ministry forever. His band was slowly shrinking and the settlers were getting braver and better prepared. In these moments, his mind began to flood with images of himself wasting away in a Ministry prison somewhere, or reduced to nothing more than a crazed mountain man, living off whatever he could scavenge.

If it came to that, he'd eat a bullet first.

The familiar sounds of hooves approaching snapped him out of his darkness. Sherald came into camp riding hard and fast. Instead of bringing his steed to a stop, he slid off while moving and let the creature stop itself further down the way.

"Lon was right," he said breathlessly the second his feet hit the ground. "Big caravan, lots of targets, and just a few guys for security. But we gotta move fast. They're already crossing the river. They built some sort of...contraption to get across."

"A contraption?"

"Yeah. It's this thing with a rope on top, and it's attached to a raft and—"

Talon put up his hand. "I get it. Drak thinks it might be too big for us to hit. He's afraid that we'll be outgunned. What do you think?"

Sherald grimaced. "Drak always thinks we'll be outgunned."

Talon smiled. Sherald was the youngest, and most enthusiastic, member of the gang. He said exactly what Talon wanted to hear, which was that there was no target they couldn't hit.

"I already sent word up the line to Cord and Gibbons to get back here."

"Good. The others are on round up. Take my steed, track 'em down, and get 'em back here. Tell 'em to leave the damn sobas and move fast. I don't want to lose them."

Sherald nodded and took off at a full run for Talon's steed. As he started to ride out of camp, Talon called out to him. "And if you see Lon and Drak, tell them to get back here too." A look of confusion crossed Sherald's face, but he tipped his cap and took off at a full gallop.

#

An equally breathless Parrie entered the riverside camp shortly thereafter. She had run almost the entire way, and was never more thankful for the endurance training she'd received at Academy. At the time, she'd thought she'd never need it. Maybe, she thought, there were reasons for some of the things they'd been forced to endure.

A lookout saw her coming and called out. She identified herself with what little breath she had left. A call resounded through the camp, which was now extremely crowded after the crossing. More than a dozen small campfires had been lit, each surrounded by settlers as the children ran around and explored the area.

She was escorted into the middle of camp, where Aribeth, Jamison Gregg, and Baser Holt stood to meet her. Aribeth handed her a canteen, which she took gratefully.

Aribeth patiently waited for her to finish before speaking. "What is it, Parrie?"

"We saw him, the watcher. Up on the other bluff. He rode out of here fast. Mr. Jax thinks it could be trouble."

"And we're down here in this damn valley, sitting ducks," Holt spat out. "Just a big, juicy target to the likes of Talon Volpe. They could be on their way here now."

Aribeth looked from Parrie to Gregg and Holt, who each met her stare with one of their own. She took just a moment to debate it internally before making her decision. She turned to address Holt and Gregg. "We need to cross those wagons now. Get every able-bodied person and let's start working."

"We can't do that," Gregg protested. "Not at night. Not after everybody worked so hard all day. People are exhausted. They need to rest."

"Colonel Holt is right," she said calmly. "If that was a member of the Talon Volpe gang they could be on their way here right now. We need to get up out of this ravine as soon as possible. We need to get up there."

Holt backed her up. "We get up on the ridge, we can circle up and put the cliff behind us. Look around you." Holt pointed up and down the bank. "Look how scattered we all are. Up there we'll be in a much more defensible position."

Gregg was still unconvinced. "I just don't think the men have it in them. It was such a tough day."

"By the light of the moons, we can do it," Holt answered with enthusiasm. "We're Cadoans, there's nothing we can't do. Come on, man. Last thing we want is a band of outlaws catching us down here. We have to move."

"I know it's not perfect and everyone is tired, but we don't have a choice," Aribeth continued. To Holt she said, "We need to tell the families, at least the adults. I think that if they knew, they would agree."

"Could start a panic," Gregg protested.

"I think they have a right to know," Aribeth answered.

"This isn't a surprise. Everyone knew when they signed up that we'd be travelling through Volpe's territory," Holt jumped in. "At least this way everyone knows what's in front of them. They deserve to know."

"Parrie," Aribeth said. "Get your steed and Mr. Jax's steed and head back up to the top. Let him know what we're doing. If you see anything, fire a shot. We're not keeping this a secret any longer."

"Yes, ma'am," Parrie answered and she started off.

Aribeth looked at the two men. "Let's get to work, gentlemen."

The three of them made their way quickly through camp, taking aside the heads of families and explaining the situation. There was some worry, but as Holt had predicted, many families had come prepared for the possibility of running into Volpe's gang.

Soon, a large group of people, largely men but also some of the women, gathered on the bank to begin the night time crossing. Half the group went on over and began to organize the wagons on the east side. Once everything was ready they sprang into action, working hard to push each wagon onto the raft and work it across the river. There another group would pull it off and send the raft back, along with a fresh set of people to help.

The shuffle continued through the night. Aribeth kept a cautious watch on Akil as she wandered across the night sky. They needed to get all wagons across before they lost her light.

Beside her, Gregg was keeping a careful watch as well, afraid that the work was putting too great a strain on his pulley system.

As Akil began to slip away, there was just one wagon left to cross. There was never any hesitation on the part of the last group of men on the eastern bank; they would cross, light or no light.

By this point, almost everyone on the west bank had gathered at the river's edge, anxiously watching the proceedings. The other wagons were hitched to their steeds and ready to roll out. The entire process was surprisingly easy given the circumstances.

Six men rolled the last wagon onto the raft and pushed off the bank. On the other side, a group of men, including Bethel Hough, began pulling on the rope, dragging the heavy wagon across the river. The rope had been fraying for some time, but without the time to replace it, the only chance was to pray that it would hold out. Now, with Akil's light gone, no one could gage the status of the rope.

Until it snapped.

Immediately, the raft nosedived into the water. The men scrambled, jumping off the side as the wagon rolled into the water. Cries began rising from the bank, and the family whose wagon it was collapsed in tears as their life's possessions disappeared in the dark water.

Almost instantly the fish began jumping, making a beeline for the helpless men in the river.

Bethel didn't hesitate for a moment. He ran to the river's edge, pulling his knife as he ran and slicing into his forearm. He ran into the water, thrusting his arms in the water, and waving it vigorously for three seconds. He then stepped back and ran further down the way and repeated the process, hoping that the smell of blood would draw the fish away from the other men.

Several others rushed into the water, swimming hard to get to their friends and bring them across. The men in the water who

191

could swim began pedaling hard against the tide. Others grabbed on to the pieces of debris that floated to the surface. Another man grabbed the broken end of the rope and was quickly pulled ashore.

Eventually they all made it to shore, not a single man bitten in the ordeal. A sigh of relief rose through the crowd as an exhausted Bethel left the water and collapsed on a heap on the bank. Aribeth moved quickly to comfort the family whose wagon had been lost, while Holt sought out Bethel.

The crusty veteran plopped down on the ground next to Bethel and gave him a solid pat on the back. "Damn good thinking, boy. You saved those men's lives tonight. I'm proud of you."

Bethel looked over his shoulder at the man, who so far had barely spoken two words to him. "Thank you, sir." He couldn't remember a time anyone had ever said such a thing to him. "Just doing my duty, sir."

"Well, that didn't come from no Academy training. A man takes action like that, it comes from inside," Holt said as he tapped Bethel on the chest. "That's the mark of a man with heart, son, and you can't teach that. You're gonna be all right."

Bethel was too exhausted and too proud to outwardly show just how much those words meant to him, but as he peered up at his commander he knew that, if need be, he'd follow Baser Holt into hell.

There was no time to rest. The group was still vulnerable and fearful that an attack could be sprung at any moment. At Aribeth's urging, the families jumped on their wagons, while those who had lost theirs found rides with friends. Holt and Aribeth took the lead, lighting their way with torches as the caravan began the long, hard ride that would finally take them up out of the canyon and away from the raging river they'd all come to hate.

As they rode, Holt called out to Aribeth. "I sure hope that you were right about this. Hate to go to all this trouble for nothing."

"About Volpe? That's funny," Aribeth smirked. She waited for Holt to look at her before finishing. "I'm hoping that this *is* about nothing."

#

Cord and Gibbons, two of Volpe's oldest gang members, arrived from their scouting trip around midnight, their steeds exhausted after a long ride. Volpe met them with a huge smile on his face and gave each a manly hug as they dismounted.

"Good to see you boys. Glad you made it back. Are we ready for some fun?"

Cord, a graying, dark skinned man with a weathered face, showed a smile full of yellowed teeth. "Always ready for some fun, Talon. What's the score?"

Gibbons, who despite his age was the only one of the group who could challenge Talon when it came to attractiveness, dusted himself off. "Sherald said something about a wagon train into Aranwa?"

"Sure enough, boys," Talon said. He felt immensely better now that he had two of his best soldiers at his side. "Seen it myself. A group of citizens apparently got tired of the Ministry dragging their feet and took settling Aranwa into their own hands. I believe its past time to roll out the welcome wagon."

Cord, the elder of the group, was no dummy. "People come settlin', we're gonna get squeezed, sooner or later. Can't fight progress."

"Which is why we need to disavow those poor people of their colonial spirit. We need to hit them hard and send a message. A very plain, very brutal message. We need to hit them so hard it will be decades before anyone tries to invade Aranwa again."

"We're not just talking about a smash and grab then," Gibbons said.

"No," Talon said, slowly breaking out into a menacing smile. "I'm talking about destroying them. Utterly and completely."

"With eight guys?" Cord asked.

"We'll catch them at night, when they are sleeping. We'll take out their lookouts, then sweep down on them and take them. Kill the men first. Once all the men are dead, they won't put up much fight."

"Sounds good to me," Gibbons said. "Been a while since we had some fresh meat around here."

Cord was less agreeable. "Pretty ambitious. How many people are we talking about here?'

"Thirty families, give or take. But once we take out the armed guards, the rest will fold up. Most of these people will be thinking that if they just give us what we want, we'll leave them alone. We are the Talon Volpe Gang. No one stands up to us."

"If you think so, boss," Cord said, though he still seemed doubtful. "If you say we go, we go. You know I'll follow you."

"I know," Talon said, pleased. "I'm just waiting on Sherald to get Roeth, Betsch, and Sidor down here." Then, almost as an afterthought, he asked. "Have any of you seen Drak and Lon?"

#

By mid-morning, the head of the caravan appeared. Leland and Parrie were both exhausted from a long night of watch, and the sight of Holt and Aribeth with wagons in tow was a welcome relief.

"Well at least we're out of that ravine," Leland said. "Crossing that river was always going to be a huge challenge. I'm sure glad we made it."

"Not out of the woods yet, are we?" Parrie asked.

"Not by a longshot," Leland admitted. "Aranwa still has plenty of surprises up her sleeve without Talon Volpe adding to the mix." He paused, taking a long, slow look around at the surroundings. "I'll feel much better once we get moving and get away from here."

Parrie studied him as he kept up his vigil. "You're scared of him, aren't you?"

"Not exactly scared," he said without looking at her. "If it came down to me versus him and I had to kill him, I would. If I died, I died. But it's not just him and me. I'm scared for the families. I can't stomach the thought of them getting ahold of any of these girls, or you. Or Aribeth."

Parrie shrugged. "I'm not. I figure that most of what you hear is just legend. People exaggerate, blow things out of proportion. He's just a man and he can die like a man."

"I admire your bravery," Leland said. "I think you might underestimate him. A lot of what you hear is true. His band, they are vicious. They kill readily and they take women as prizes. Some of what you hear may be exaggeration, but not all of it. If he were that easy to kill, someone would have done it by now."

"I'll do it," she said without hesitation. "You worry about keeping the people safe. But I'm a soldier, and taking out people like Volpe is what I became a soldier for. We'll get him if he shows his face around here."

Leland didn't respond to that boast and they sat in silence until Aribeth and Holt drew closer. Parrie noticed Leland watching them approach. "That Aribeth, she's something," Parrie said. "She called for that nighttime crossing just like that. No hesitation at all."

Leland made a grunting noise, but said nothing. He was watching Aribeth intensely.

"A woman like that would be some sort of a prize for some lucky guy," Parrie continued to prod.

"Would she? I never considered another person a trophy." Leland turned away from her. Parrie thought that she had seen him blush.

"You know what I mean," she said.

"Drop it, Burrows," Leland snapped at her. "Keep your eyes open for any strangers. I'll worry about Aribeth...I mean, Ms. Fuller."

"Whatever you say."

#

The last three members of Volpe's gang rode in with Sherald just before morning. Talon took a few minutes to explain the situation. He was concerned that no one had heard from Drak and Lon, but he believed that they would catch up. Despite his worries, Talon felt that there was no time to waste and the band rode out. The plan was to fix the expedition's location, then wait for nightfall to launch a surprise attack against the convoy.

They used a well-worn path that would bring them to the cliff's edge north of the encampment. Once they reached the edge of the woods, the group left their steeds in the woods and crept through the high grass to the edge of the cliff. A gentle rise in the terrain helped shield them from the position the lookouts had taken up.

Talon came to the edge and peered over eagerly, expecting to see their target waiting for them down below. Instead, they saw nothing but the remains of a dozen campfires and some rutted tracks. The expedition was gone.

"Can't be," Sherald said. "They were there yesterday. When I left, they were still crossing people. They had wagons left to go. They couldn't have moved all of that this quickly."

Talon was embarrassed. His men had ridden hard to get to him and now their booty was gone. He sneered at Sherald. "Do you see them down there? I don't see them. I don't see anyone."

"They were there."

Talon, no longer concerned with concealment, stood and

started towards Sherald. "Maybe you should go down and take a closer look. Let me help you down."

The others stood quickly and got between them. Cord gently pushed Talon away. "They gotta be somewhere nearby. We'll find 'em. Where's their lookouts?"

Talon jerked his head to the south. "Just over the rise." He was still glowering at Sherald, who was doing all he could to disappear.

"Let's go look then, Talon," Cord said. "Just you and me. The rest of you go tend the steeds." He didn't think twice about giving orders, even with Talon right there. The others did as they were told as Talon and Cord walked south.

"You gotta keep your composure, Talon," Cord said. "We don't have the men we used to. Can't be tossin' perfectly good men off cliffs anymore. Stay calm."

Talon was still pouting even though he knew that Cord was right. "I'd feel better if Drak was here," Volpe said. "Don't know where those two ran off to."

"Let's see what we've got here and then we'll go look for them. Not gonna hit 'em middle of the day like this anyway. Let's just look."

As they approached the rise, the two got down and crawled the rest of the way. The tall yellow grass hid them from view, but they had to be careful to move slowly or the waving blades could give them away.

"There they are," Cord said as they finally peeked over and found the entire group camped on the bluff. They had arranged the wagons in a half circle out from the cliff's edge, with the settlers barricaded behind them. Mounted gunmen kept watch just outside the makeshift fort. "Man, that sure is a lot of booty."

"It's beautiful," Talon said, his anger fading. "But we'll have to rethink the approach. Hitting them like this would be suicide."

"They musta worked all night to get up here. It's quiet. Must all be sleepin'. We could hit em' now."

Talon thought it over for a moment, carefully watching the guards on steedback, looking for signs of fatigue. "Not worth it. We don't know how many people are inside there or what kind of guns they've got. By the time we got past the guards, we'd be riding into a shooting gallery. We'll have to catch them on the road."

"Right," Cord agreed. "Let's go tell the others. Then we'll see if we can find Drak."

They slipped away from the rise and rejoined with the rest. "We found them," Talon said, much more calm now than he had been. "We'll have to hit them when they're moving. Sherald, you keep an eye on them. If they start moving, I want to know which way they're headed. The rest of us are going to split up and go find Lon and Drak. We meet back here at twilight. Questions?"

There were none and the group broke up. Talon waited until they were gone. "Sherald, you lose them again and I will throw you off that cliff."

#

Ridge took his time with Drak, but the man was strong and never gave up his secrets. He finally tired of the game and took the man's life. After that, he rested. He thought only occasionally about the rest of the expedition. This was no longer about them. Volpe had sent men to attack him…that meant he was getting close.

In the morning, Ridge moved out. He had taken the time to relieve his victims of any articles of importance: two guns, ammo, two knives, and a couple of handfuls of Cadoan credits, plus two coats that helped fight off the cold of night, and some dried meat and water.

He started into the woods, moving deliberately. It would be

198

easy to take a wrong vector and miss the camp entirely. In the early afternoon, he caught the faint hint of smoke and followed it. Walking into the wind, he traced the sent as it got stronger.

The camp came into sight gradually, first as flashes of color that didn't quite fit in the forest and the sound of fabric moving gently in the breeze. The smoke smell was much stronger now, and was accompanied by the smell of food.

The camp was built in a natural depression that was deep enough that only the tops of men's tents were visible from a distance. There were eight tents in a circle, around a fire pit that was still smoldering. Off to the side, a much larger tent stood alone in front of its own fire pit.

That had to be Volpe's quarters, Ridge reasoned. He crept silently up on the camp and took his time inspecting each tent. The camp was empty now, but it had been occupied recently.

He checked Volpe's tent last. While the other men led a meager existence, Talon lived large. He had furniture: a proper bed, a small wardrobe, a dresser, a full-size mirror, and a chair covered in tanned hide. Ridge rifled through his belongings. He was a fancy man, a man of taste. An outlaw, trying to pass himself off as a man of status. Ridge took a moment to admire his clothes. They had a similar sense of fashion.

He was almost done with his sweep when something else caught Ridge's eye. In one corner of the tent, not far from Volpe's bed, a tree stump squatted with a metal ring firmly attached to it and a chain running through the ring with shackles on each end. The entire corner — the tent, the chain, the stump — was stained red with splatters of blood. There were pieces of fabric laying around and other, smaller white particles that did not appear to be cloth. He bent down close and picked one up. The particles were fragments of teeth and bone, and they littered the ground in a wide circle out from the stump.

Ridge sat back on his haunches and rubbed his chin. This was a torture pit, and Talon Volpe was much more than an outlaw. He was a monster.

CHAPTER 19

That night Aribeth took Leland, Jamison Gregg, and Colonel Holt aside to discuss their next move. After the hard crossing the night before, everyone was given the day to rest. With the exception of designated lookouts, everyone slept most of the day away.

By the light of the campfire, Aribeth laid out her father's journal and opened it to a hand-drawn map that spread across to pages. She located their position and began to trace a path with her finger.

"This is where my father wanted to settle. In the morning I want to start moving out as soon as possible. We might want to warn the families about those…whatever it was we ran into out there," she said to Leland.

"What?" Holt asked. "What did you run into?"

"Large predator," Leland said matter-of-factly. "Hard to kill. Gotta shoot it in the neck, right where it meets the skull. It nearly killed Parrie and Bethel. They're camouflaged well, so you might not see one until you're right up on it. There is one good thing though."

"What's that?" Gregg asked nervously.

Leland smiled at him. "They're damn good eating." Gregg turned away, disgusted. To Aribeth, Leland said, "We'll have to swing around further to the west. Here. We're not getting wagons through those woods. Probably take most of a day just to get around. From there, we're good to here," he said, pointing at another area of the map. "This is where it gets tricky. The wetlands. We'll have to advance scout that whole area and carefully plot our path through to here." He pointed at another area of the map. "After that, it's smooth sailing."

"Anything else we need to know about out there?" Holt asked. "Any other man eating animals or the like?"

"Not that I know of," Leland said. "Then again, I didn't know about the last one until we stumbled upon it. Just stay alert."

"What about this Volpe character?" Gregg asked, looking more and more nervous by the minute. "What are we going to do about him?"

"Stay alert," Aribeth said calmly. "That's why I want to get going as soon as possible. The sooner we get away from here, the harder it will be for him to track us down."

"I hope so," he said.

Holt was less concerned. "Let him come. My men will shoot him right out of the saddle if he comes at us now. When we were down there…," he said, eyes sliding over the cliff's edge, "he had the advantage on us. Not anymore."

"But at what price?" Gregg asked. "How many would die before you took him out?"

Holt slapped Gregg hard on the back and laughed. "Mr. Gregg, I have fought against the elite Iridian Guard. It's going to take more than a handful of thugs with guns to get to me and my men."

"I wish I had your faith," Gregg answered.

"Let's not worry about the Volpe gang," Leland intervened. "Let Colonel Holt worry about them. That's why he's here. We need to worry about getting these people to their destination."

Aribeth shut the journal, tied it up, and slid it back into her bag. "Okay then, if nobody else has anything, let's get some rest. Tomorrow we head out for paradise."

#

Talon and his gang spread out through the woods, looking for any sign of their lost comrades. The search was slow and tedious. As night fell, there was still no sign of Lon or Drak.

Sherald was still smarting from Talon's rebuke earlier in the day. Talon was losing it. When Sherald had first signed on as a wayward teen, Talon had been something of a father figure and a hero. Sherald had been proud to ride with him and learn from him. Over the years, he'd been watching the man slowly descend to a level of depravity that he could scarcely imagine.

Sometimes at night, he would be tormented by the piercing screams of the young women Talon took into his tent. The punishment he inflicted was grotesque. It hadn't taken long for Sherald to start making himself scarce when Talon got through with one of his playthings. The other men lived for the calls of Playtime, but for Sherald it was a call to vanish.

As he searched through the woods, Sherald tried not to think about the convoy they had found. He tried not to focus on the bloodshed that would surely follow or the countless prisoners Talon would take. He tried, without success, not to dwell on Talon's rebuke of him, but he failed.

Maybe Lon and Drak had seen the same things and decided to make a break for it. They all had enough money. Sherald himself had been thinking for some time of making a break. Only the fear that Talon would track him down kept him in line. However, if others were breaking free, then maybe it was time for him to do the same.

Sherald knew that wouldn't be the case. Drak was as loyal as they came. He would never betray Talon, and Lon was just as depraved. If they were missing, then something had happened to them.

Sherald broke into the clearing and rode to the creek, where he and his steed both stopped for a drink. It was a nice night, still a bit chilly. The wind was gentle, carrying with it all the scents of the wildflowers. He liked it here, could see himself making a life here, but not with Talon around. No one would ever be safe with him around.

He wondered if, by some happenstance, Talon should happen to be killed in the coming raid, would anyone think too hard about who fired the fatal shot? It was something to think about.

He knew that they were supposed to meet back by the bluff, but Sherald decided to make a quick stop by camp first. He wanted to change clothes and check his stash. If he were going to make a play, or a break, he needed to know exactly what kind of funds he had.

Mounting back up, Sherald splashed through the creek to the other side and started back toward camp. The entire ride he debated, run or kill. He had just about made up his mind to run when the smell hit him.

It was intense and coppery, a smell of blood and feces and rotted meat. Sherald pulled his shirt up over his nose and mouth to block the smell and dismounted. Leading his steed by the reins, he approached camp slowly. He could hear the tents flapping gently in the breeze when dark figures scurried on either side of him.

Two large trees marked the entrance to camp, and on each, a figure slumped. He knew before he looked, but Sherald approached each figure, getting as close as he dared. The heavy canopy of trees blocked much of the moonlight, but enough seeped through that he made out what was left of Lon, his head nearly cut completely off. The scavengers of the forest had been working on him for a while, and most of the tastiest parts were long gone.

Sherald forced himself not to throw up as he walked to the other figure. Drak looked much worse. There was a similar level of animal damage, but his face, or what was left of it, was contorted in a grimace. He had been in terrible pain when he died, and there was much more blood around him. Had he still been alive when he was left here?

In that moment, Sherald knew that the mystery man they had been sent to track was truly a dangerous one. Lon was a fool, but Drak was an accomplished warrior, a former soldier, and a tough man. He would not have died easily. This man had taken them both.

The urge to run rose up inside him again, but his sense of duty prevailed. He had to tell Talon. Surely the man would completely snap upon seeing his second in command carved to bits and left for the animals to feed on. Perhaps Talon would snap so completely that Sherald's half-baked plans would be irrelevant and Talon would do something stupid and do himself in. He could only hope.

Feeling somewhat hopeful, a curious feeling given the two bodies he'd just stumbled across, Sherald mounted up and rode for the meeting point. He would have to work himself into a state of panic by the time he got there. Couldn't let Talon see the pleasure. Couldn't take the chance. Not when he was this close to freedom.

#

The gang met back up not long after dark. No one had found a trace of Lon and Drak. Talon was a swirl of emotion, at times annoyed that two of his best men had gotten themselves lost, and at others fearful that they had met their end. Yet he tried to remain calm. It would do no good for his men to see him panicked.

205

Cord kept an eye on the wagon camp. They had already made one nighttime move, Talon wasn't about to risk that they would make another. The rest of the men lounged about, speculating on what kind of loot the travelers might have and the quality of the girls. Talon could enjoy dreaming of neither.

Cord whistled sharply. Talon dropped all thoughts of Lon and Drak and rushed to his side. "What is it?"

Cord pointed across the way. In a gap between two wagons, a group of four had huddled around a campfire, separate from the rest. He did not recognize two of the men, but he did recognize the man he had identified as the scout, and he recognized the girl.

Talon's heart fluttered when he saw her. She was just coming into womanhood, with the chestnut hair and the pale complexion that he loved most of all. She seemed to be directing the meeting, and they all hunched over a journal of some kind. He could almost see her, naked and chained in his tent, fighting for survival. He could smell her fear on the air.

"Talon," Cord said sharply. Talon snapped himself out of the daydream to find Cord scowling at him. "What do you think?"

"I think that they're plotting their next move. "

"Should we hit 'em now?"

Talon thought it over and looked back over his shoulder at the rest of the crew. Sherald hadn't reported back yet, meaning that they were down to six men. "No. Not yet." He looked back over at the caravan, forcing himself to focus on the task at hand and not get distracted by the beautiful girl in the dancing firelight. "That's a lot of wagons. They'll have to spread their guards out. We wait until they move and we hit the back. We won't have enough men to hit them all at once."

"Sounds like a plan," Cord said.

"Keep an eye on them; I'll tell the others." Talon pushed up off the ground and slinked away. He quickly briefed the others and ordered them to get some sleep. He was anticipating that they would move at first light. Then he settled in himself and soon drifted off to sleep, dreaming of the girl and all the things he would do to her.

It seemed to be just a fleeting moment before one of his men was waking him, but Talon knew from the fog that circled his head that he had been asleep for a while. Gibbons was shaking him awake, his gun in his right hand, ready to fire.

"Rider comin', boss. Get up."

The fog lifted and Talon was on his feet and moving. The rest of the group had all sought some sort of cover and drawn their weapons. There was no reason to believe that they were in danger, but his men never took chances. Talon drew his own gun and walked toward the edge of the wood to meet the coming rider.

Sherald exploded into the clearing a moment later, breathless and wild eyed. "I found Lon and Drak, boss. It ain't good."

"They're hurt?" Talon's heart felt like it was in his throat. Drak…his number one guy.

"Dead, sir. Brutalized. He left them by our camp. Animals have been feeding on them."

Talon's worry turned to anger in a flash. Not only had the mystery man killed his best man, he'd butchered them and left them to be eaten. He had left them at the camp as a sign. He stormed over to his own steed. "Show me." To the others he barked out. "Stay here, stay out of sight. No one moves until I get back." To Sherald, he barked, "Go!"

They raced through the woods, using what little moonlight they had to expertly weave through the trees. They had all ridden through this forest so many times that they knew the way by heart. Akil was disappearing into the southern horizon and the eastern sky just beginning to light when they made it back to camp.

Talon's eyes immediately went to the slumped figures of his fallen gang members. "No," he growled, jumping off his steed and racing to Drak's body. He lifted Drak's face with his hand and stared into the empty sockets where his eyes used to be. The body was a torn and bloodied mess of tissue by then, the face gone now.

Talon let go and the body fell over on its side. "He'll die for this. Whoever that man is. I will tear him apart with my bare hands." Enraged, he turned to Sherald. "Don't just sit there like an idiot. Get down here and bury them. Bury them deep. How dare you leave your mates out here to be desecrated like this?"

"I…I thought you'd want to see…." Sherald stammered.

"And now I want them buried. Get to work." Talon stormed away, wanting no part of the grizzly chore that was at hand. He stalked off to his tent and ducked in. There was a bottle of fine liquor he had stashed and he needed it now.

Talon was greeted by the sight of his belongings strewn across the floor. His wardrobe had been toppled and smashed, his clothes all shredded, as was his mattress. His mirror had been shattered. Worse than all of it, the stranger had taken an axe to the tree stump and removed the chain where he kept his prizes locked up. Talon screamed out in anger. He wanted to smash something, but there was nothing left to smash.

He came steaming out of the tent. Talon could feel nothing but blind, empty rage. He was completely impotent and hated the feeling. It was that feeling of utter helplessness that had driven him into the streets as a youth. The helplessness that drove him to a life of crime, that fed his need for pain and violence. It was a helplessness he swore he'd never feel again. Now, some stranger had plunged him right back into it.

Talon found Drak's tent, rifled through his belongings, and

found what he was looking for, an intricately decorated sword with a sleek, tempered blade and a bejeweled hilt with matching sheath. Drak claimed that he had taken it off the body of a dead Iridian major, though Talon had always believed that Drak himself was that allegedly deceased soldier.

Talon attached the sword and sheath onto his belt, on the left side opposite his gun, and ducked out again. Shooting the man would not suffice. He would carve the man up like the man had done to his men. He would take his time. He would enjoy himself.

Talon stormed past Sherald without a word, mounted his steed, and rode off quickly. He no longer thought about the girl. He only thought of the mystery man.

And of revenge.

CHAPTER 20

Ridge followed the creek on his way out. He had taken the time to thoroughly destroy Talon Volpe's belongings. He made sure that it was done right and nothing was spared, including his little torture area in the corner. Ridge only wished that he could be there when Volpe returned to find it. The mere thought of the legendary Talon Volpe reduced to impotent rage excited Ridge.

He had no idea where the expedition was and he didn't care. He was here now with a vast territory to explore. Among the many wild rumors that had floated around about Aranwa for decades was one that suggested the area was ripe with precious metals. If he could find one of those deposits, Ridge could return home a wealthy man.

So instead of making his way back to the convoy, he walked northwest, using the creek as a guide. Ridge did not consider himself an explorer, but he was vaguely excited by the prospect of seeing lands no one else had ever laid eyes upon.

He did not look back or fear pursuit by Volpe and his gang. If they found him, then good luck taking him alive. Ridge doubted that they could even do that. Aranwa was a big land and Ridge was an expert at getting lost. They would never find him.

Not until Ridge wanted to be found.

#

Aribeth was too excited by the prospect of what lay in front of them to sleep. Instead, she lay by the campfire and tried to picture the future in the flickering flames. She could now feel the fire that used to take over her father when he was on the verge of something new and exciting. She felt the drive to keep going, to push forward.

Aribeth took a deep breath and closed her eyes, letting her mind wander. It wouldn't be Bretonville, this new settlement of hers. It would be better. It would be a perfect little community of peace and prosperity. It would be a place where people would raise their children, far from the greedy hands of the Ministry. A truly new world. She would not let the politicians interfere. She would fight to the end to keep Aranwa free.

Content, she opened her eyes again. On the other side of the fire Leland slept peacefully, his face turned to her. Aribeth watched him sleep. He had been everything she could have hoped for: wise and brave and inventive. The thought of Leland returning to Cadoa and his family brought a ping of sadness to her reverie. Maybe she could convince him to stay.

As Akil began to finish her nightly jaunt across the sky and the stars began to disappear, Aribeth got up. She couldn't wait any longer. They had already wasted a full day of travel. Full of excitement for the new day, she padded quickly over to Leland and roused him from his sleep.

"Come on. Get up. Let's get moving."

Leland stirred, groaned, and rolled over. "It's still dark."

"Not for long," Aribeth answered. "Come on. Let's get up. Let's go."

Leland groaned again and sat up. "We don't need to leave so fast. People are tired. They need the break."

Aribeth sat down next to him. "They've had all day. We're so close now. I don't want to waste any more time."

"We're nowhere near close," Leland responded. "It's a longer haul than your daddy's map makes it look. I need you to temper your enthusiasm."

"Still, the faster we start moving the faster we get there. Sitting around here isn't getting anything done."

Leland finally gave up. "Fine." He stood and stretched and smirked at Aribeth.

"What?"

"You're just like your father. He acted like a little kid. Every day he was up before the sunrise, always ready to see what was next, what was beyond the next hill. I think he might have been happy to wander around this place forever."

"I'm sure he would have," she answered. Aribeth thought of her father, happily traipsing around the countryside, giddy at each new discovery, and it brought tears to her eyes. She turned away from Leland, hoping to hide her sudden sadness. "I'll start waking people," she struggled to say.

Leland gently took her arm, turned her, and wiped the tears from her cheeks. "It's okay," he said softly. "I cried when my daddy died too."

"You were a kid."

"So are you," Leland said with a chuckle. "He'd be proud of you, Aribeth. You've gotten them this far."

Aribeth dropped her eyes to the ground. "I guess. I just wish he was here. He should be leading this mission, not me."

"Would you rather be back in school, or out here under the moons, living life? Personally, I'd rather be out here than in some classroom."

"Yeah," she said with a sigh. "I would too. Thank you."

"Don't mention it," Leland answered. He stood there, holding her arms, their eyes locked on each other, neither saying a word. She thought, for just a moment, about kissing him, but at her feet, Colonel Holt began to stir and the moment was lost.

"Well, let's get them up," she said. She wasn't sure if she should be thankful for the interruption or not.

#

As Talon was discovering his fallen friends, the wagon train moved out, meandering their way southwest to avoid the brunt of the dark woods that stood between them and their goal. They would skirt the edge of the forest and then turn due north, gradually bending their route to the northwest before they reached Breton Fuller's designated landing spot.

As they had done when the convoy first pulled out, the guards were deployed along the line, each responsible for guarding five families, each riding on an alternating side of the line. Now though, with the very real possibility that someone was out there, they all kept a sharper vigil and their hands closer to their weapons.

At the front of the line, Aribeth and Leland rode side by side, neither mentioning their shared moment from earlier in the morning. They had been riding for over an hour when Aribeth began to look around, twisting and turning in her seat as she looked every which way.

"What are you doing?"

"Ridge never came back?" she said.

Leland took one casual glance over his shoulder. "No, he never did come back." He saw the worry on Aribeth's face and moved quickly to temper it. "He probably just wandered off. There's a lot of land to explore out there. He was never really a part of the group."

Aribeth felt sick. "We've got to go find him." She started to peel away from the group, but Leland reached over and grabbed her reins.

"It's been days, Aribeth. If he's not back by now he's not coming back, good or bad."

213

"He could be lost, or hurt. He may be laying out there somewhere right now, wondering why no one has come to find him yet." Her voice was rising with her panic.

"We can't spare the men to go look for him. Besides, you were just complaining about the time we've wasted. You want to stop now?"

"I'll go alone," she said determinedly. "I know my way around. I will find him."

"You're the leader. You can't go. I can't go because I'm the scout and I'm the only one who knows the land. We can't spare any of Colonel Holt's men because they need to watch for bandits. There's no one to go."

"We can send one of the men," she answered. "We don't really know that there are bandits out there. We haven't found any proof of that."

"It's still a bad idea. Trust me on this."

Holt, who had been riding behind them at the head of the line of wagons, noticed the animated discussion and sped up, sidling up between the two of them. "Is there a problem, Ms. Fuller?"

"Yes," she started. "Ridge…Mr. Secova, is missing. He went into the woods a few days ago and he hasn't been back. We need to go look for him."

Holt shook his head sadly. "He's gone, ma'am. Going to look for him now is just a waste of time. Either the bandits got him, or the critters. Or…." He let the word hang in the air.

"Or what?" Aribeth asked.

"Or he chose to go his own way. He was probably just using us to get him over the river, and once he got over here he took off. If he's been gone for days, then he's got a huge head start. We wouldn't even know where to begin to look, ma'am. I'm sorry, but he's gone."

Leland nodded in agreement. "Listen to him, Aribeth. I

know that you didn't want to lose anybody, but he was always a wildcard. He probably never had any intention of staying with us. For all we know, he could be a part of Volpe's gang and he's been spying on us all along."

"I can't believe that," Aribeth said, trying her best to hide a shudder. She didn't want to believe it, but it suddenly seemed plausible. "I just don't think—"

"Of course you don't," Holt said. "You see the best in everybody. But Secova is a lowlife. He's a charming lowlife, but he's still a lowlife. Don't worry your pretty little head about him."

Aribeth turned her attention back to the road ahead. Had she delivered the entire expedition into the hands of Talon Volpe by taking Ridge on? In her heart she didn't think so, but she had to admit that there was a possibility. "Colonel Holt," she said, still staring straight ahead. "Best warn the rest of your men, just in case."

"Will do," he said, and dropped back.

"Do you think he's a spy?" she asked Leland once Holt was gone.

Leland wouldn't look at her. "Probably not. I think he just signed on to get out of Cadoa. The timing is so convenient. I think he just took off." Leland looked to his right and the imposing woods. "He's out there somewhere."

#

Talon rode hard back to the settler's camp, making no attempt to disguise his approach. He got there to find his men sitting around in a circle making small talk, and Cord was nowhere to be found.

Gibbons, hat in hand, stood up and approached. "They pulled out, just before sunup. Cordie is following after them, staying back and up in the woods. He told the rest of us to sit tight and wait for you."

Talon's anger had reduced from a flaming passion to a slow, steady burn. He kept his expression tight. "Good. But I'm not interested in the settlers anymore. Forget them."

A ripple of shock ran through the group. "Are you sure?" Gibbons asked.

"Yes, I'm sure," he snapped. "Drak and Lon are dead. Massacred. The mystery man, the tough guy, he did it. I want him and I want him alive. I want to take him apart, piece by piece, and make him watch as I roast and eat his flesh." The four of them all exchanged uncomfortable glances. Talon was in no mood for hesitation. "What's the matter with you? This man killed your brothers. He has to pay."

Finally, Betsch, a rail thin man who was considered the best steedman of the bunch, stood up. "You heard him, boys. We got a killer to catch. Let's get out there and find him." Betsch walked confidently to his steed, mounted up, and started off. "I'll start at the camp and work north. I'll ride all the way to the mountains if I have to." He spurred his steed and was off.

Roeth, a bronze-skinned, dark haired man with crystal blue eyes, jumped up next. "I'll go west."

Sidor, a short, stubby man with flaming red hair, volunteered, "I'll go east, as far as I've gotta go."

That just left Gibbons. "Lotta ground to cover boss," he said. "I'll split the difference between Betsch and Sidor. But you gotta know that finding one man in a land this big…"

"Don't give me excuses," Talon snarled. "Just find him."

#

The land was largely flat, with occasional rises and falls, an easy walk for a man in Ridge's shape. He crested a rise and in the distance the land rose sharply with tall, dark hills taking shape. Below him, the land dropped off sharply to make a massive valley. Off to the west and beyond the highlands, towering white

216

clouds dotted the sky, casting deep shadows over the land.

Even for a man of Ridge Secova's background, the view was breathtaking.

He looked carefully over the land, trying to decide which way he wanted to go. He decided to keep heading due west, straight at the highlands. He would have to keep an eye on the clouds; could be trouble there.

Ridge eyed the distant highlands and thought to himself that surely those hills held untold wealth. His future, his destiny, must lie in those hills. Clear of mind and purpose, Ridge started off again.

#

Burying the dead had been hard work, and Sherald was spent. The spring rains hadn't started yet and the ground was still hardened from a lengthy winter, so the digging process was time consuming. His muscles still burned from the exertion.

That had been the easy part, though. Dragging the desecrated corpses of the two men Sherald had spent so much time with was much harder. Sherald's experiences with death had been sudden and fleeting. You rode in, you did some shooting, you moved on. He had never lingered over a dead body, much less one that had been torn to shreds. He puked several times before it was all done.

By late morning he was done and shuffled off to his tent. He needed a bath, fresh clothes, and some sleep. After that, he would pack his belongings and take off. If there was one good thing that had stemmed from the whole event, it was that Sherald now had clarity.

Talon Volpe's days were numbered, one way or another. He was coming completely unhinged, losing men, and the settlers would drive him out eventually. There was no future with Talon any longer, and Sherald was in no way ready to go out in a blaze

217

of glory with him.

The decision came easy. Clean up, rest, then pack up the money he had stored away, and what he could steal from the others while camp was empty, and head off. He was a man who could live modestly in some small community. He didn't crave luxury like Talon. He had stashed away enough to do that, far away from Aranwa.

Sherald emerged from his tent with a roll of fresh clothes and a bottle of cheap liquor. It was a good day for liberation, he thought.

Until Betsch rode into camp.

Betsch was a hardcore follower of Talon's, one of his oldest and most trusted hands, and an excellent steedman. He sat on his steed and stared daggers down at Sherald. "Are we taking a little personal time there, Sherry?" Sherald hated it when people called him that.

"Yeah I am. I just spent hours burying Lon and Drak. I'm hot and sweaty and dirty and smell like a corpse. So yes, Betsch, I am taking some personal time."

"Put it up. Boss wants the killer found. Wants him bad. Mount up and come with me. We got a lot of ground to cover."

"Come on, man. I smell like death."

"I ain't sleepin' with ya so I don't care how you smell. You didn't see the boss. He's hot and he wants this guy now. Everybody looks."

"I was here when he saw the bodies, so I know exactly how he was," Sherald shot back. "He went freaking nuts." The look on Betsch's face told Sherald that no excuses would be tolerated. "Fine. I'll go out and look. I just want a few minutes to clean up."

Betsch was having none of it. "You clean up when we're done. Put your crap up and come on." Betsch turned his steed around, stopped, and turned back around. "Unless you don't want him found."

Sherald tried as best he could to act offended. "What do you mean by that?"

Betsch brought his steed closer. "I mean, you're here all alone. We all got money stashed around. Nobody's watching. Maybe you're thinking about retiring."

Sherald's stomach dropped, but he kept a stone face. "You're so full of it, Betsch. I haven't had the time or the energy to start going through people's stuff. You want me to show you the graves? You want to dig them up and verify? Let's go."

"Put your stuff down. Shake it out. Let me see it."

"Betsch—"

"Do it boy," Betsch snarled down at him. "Now."

"Fine." Sherald put down the bottle, took each piece of clothing he had gathered, and shook them out one by one, showing that there was nothing hidden inside. He then turned out the pockets of his current clothes, even going so far as to take off his boots and pull down his pants to prove that he hadn't stashed anything. "Satisfied?"

Betsch was still eyeing him suspiciously. "Put your crap up and come on. We got a murderer to catch." Sherald started to protest. "Don't give me no lip, just do it. Plenty of time to clean up later."

Disappointed, Sherald did as instructed. Another half hour, hour at the most, and he would have been gone. Then again, had Betsch shown up ten minutes later, he would have caught Sherald red handed, and then he would have been lying in a grave instead of digging one.

Trying to look on the bright side of things, Sherald jumped on his steed to join the hunt. He still might be able to make a break for it, he thought. And if it required him to take Betsch out in the process he wouldn't hesitate to do it.

Sometimes you have to do what you have to do.

CHAPTER 21

It was a full day's ride around the forest. On the second day, the trees disappeared, the land flattened out, and everyone breathed a sigh of relief. There had been no sign of man-eating predators or blood-thirsty bandits.

Once clear of the woods, the land was dotted with a series of small creeks. The frequent sources of water were a godsend as the group had begun to run low. The further they travelled, the more saturated and spongy the ground became. They gradually descended into a valley, and once they reached the floor, Leland called for a stop.

As everyone made camp for the night, Leland took Aribeth aside. He pointed out an area to the northwest of their position where the ground rose again. "Those hills are where we're going. From here it looks really high, but it's not. We're just very low right now. The problem is between here and there. All this land," he said, sweeping his hand in front of them to indicate the ruddy, soggy land they had yet to cross, "It's like a minefield. When your father and I came, we had three other guys with us. We crossed this point, turned around, and one of them was just gone. He wandered off to look at something and the ground just swallowed him up."

"So how do we know where to go?"

Leland swallowed and looked away. "I'll go out there and

check it out. I'll mark the safe passages along the way. It's going to take some time though. We'll have to move everyone forward in small increments."

"Okay, let's go," Aribeth said.

"I'll go," Leland stressed. "You'll stay here. I'm more expendable than you are."

"Don't say something like that," Aribeth responded. "You are not expendable. Without you I'd be completely lost out here. We are in this together."

"And if we get swallowed up, what about these people?" They both looked back at the camp. "They'll have no scout and no leader. You'll have stranded them in the middle of a swamp."

"We're Cadoans. We always find a way. Two people are going to get this done a lot quicker than one will."

Leland had learned along the way that Aribeth was as stubborn as they came and that arguing with her was a lost cause. "Fine. Wait here." He walked over to Gregg's wagon, where they made small talk for a minute, then pulled two long tree limbs that he'd picked up along the way and came back. He pushed one over to Aribeth.

She smiled up at him. "You knew I was going to insist on going, didn't you?"

"Yes, I did. Now, you're going to use this like a big walking stick. Never take a step without checking the ground in front of you. When you do take a step, feel all around. We're looking for soft spots, unseen ponds, all sorts of thing. If your stick sinks more than ankle deep, you don't want to step there."

Leland then pulled a shoulder bag off his steed, opened it, and pulled out some shorter, sharper sticks. Aribeth recognized them as homemade versions of the type of survey markers professional builders used. He held one up.

"Once we charter a safe path through, we mark it. If we move a little at a time, we should make it out of here in a few days."

Aribeth stood and surveyed the landscape, biting her lip as she tried to calculate the distance they had to travel. "What if...," she asked while keeping her gaze on the hills that were the ultimate destination, "We go all the way through? We let the people camp and rest, and we chart the whole passageway through. Then we move. If we know where we're going, we could cross that distance in one day."

Leland followed her gaze and thought it over himself. "We could do that. It would be faster, but we would be separating ourselves from the herd. If something happened, we couldn't get back and no one could get to us. Plus, once we find the way we have to come all the way back here to get everybody else started."

"Not if we had a signal. We could fire a shot in the air. When they hear the shot, then they know it's time to move. I think it would be much more efficient this way."

Leland shrugged. "If you think. You're the leader."

Aribeth didn't hesitate. "All right. Let's go talk to Colonel Holt and Mr. Gregg and let them know what's going on. Then I want to get started."

#

Two days of searching had resulted in nothing, and the members of Volpe's gang slowly filtered back into camp. They were weary and frustrated. Even Talon had lost the anger that had driven him in the beginning. He had never felt as defeated as he did in that moment.

Roeth had started a fire and brought down a javelina, which was roasting on a spit by the time Talon rode in. They all sat by the fire and ate in silence, not saying a word.

Talon looked around at what was left of his gang. Cord was missing, supposedly still following the settlers, though no one had seen or heard from him. Lon and Drak were dead. His gang of eight was down to five.

Worse, as he looked into the faces of his remaining members, he could see the doubt and the fear in their eyes. Such was life on the wrong side of the law. Every man knew that their clock was ticking.

He was losing them. He needed something to turn the tide and bring the men back into line. As badly as he hated to admit it, he needed to move past his desire for vengeance and refocus on what they did best.

Yet, Talon had lost the passion for the chase. The settlers were long gone now, having headed off into Aranwa's interior. With only five men at his disposal, any sort of direct assault would be suicide. He had to wonder if it was even worth the risk. There was so much more to gain by hitting the established settlements on the east side of the river.

Later that night, Talon was awakened by the sound of voices outside the tent. He rolled over, pulled his gun out of the holster on the ground beside him, and levelled it at the door. Moments later, a figure appeared in the opening.

"Talon?"

Talon relaxed and dropped the gun. "Cordie? That you?"

Cord came fully into the tent. "Yeah boss. I been followin' the settlers, thought you might want a report."

"You hear about Drak?"

"Yeah," Cord answered. "Hate to hear that." They both went silent for a moment in tribute, then Cord went on. "Listen boss. If you want to get 'em, now might be the time. They've stalled at the marshlands. A couple of people have separated from the group. We could trap 'em."

"I don't know that we have enough men." Yet even as he said it, he began to plot it out in his mind. If they could move in close enough to take out the lookouts, catch the others while they were sleeping....

"We could do it. We're the Talon Volpe gang. Most of those men will freeze up as soon as they see us. If we hit them hard and fast...."

Maybe he was right. Hitting the settlers might be just the tonic to get the men back on their game. And if things went sideways, there were worse things than to go down shooting. "I'll think about it. Get some rest, Cordie. We'll look at them tomorrow. See what I think."

Cord started to leave when Talon called out to him. "You didn't see any sign of a tough looking guy out there. A loner?"

"No boss," he answered. "Didn't see any such thing out there. But we'll find him sooner or later. He'll catch back up to his friends."

Yes, he would, Talon thought, suddenly aware of an entirely different reason to hit the settlers.

#

The camp was barely visible on the horizon now. Aribeth and Leland had worked their way well out into the marshlands, marking a zig-zagging trail along the way. Things had gone smoothly. They had managed to locate two very large pits and several smaller ones that were capable of sucking a fully-grown man in completely. There were dozens of other soft spots where the ground would grab ahold of a leg, but not deep enough to cause any real danger.

Working non-stop, they were more than halfway through the maze already. The once distant hills were drawing ever closer, still looking ominous with the towering white clouds that never seemed to move.

The work was tedious and slow. Along the way, Aribeth and Leland exchanged stories of their childhood. Leland told of the hardships of being forced into the role of provider at an early age.

Aribeth told of the constant moving that came with being the child of a professional settler.

It took them two days to mark a clear path through the fields that would be wide enough for the caravan to follow. When they finally reached solid ground on the other side, they were too exhausted to do anything but sleep. While Aribeth started a fire, Leland fired a single shot in the air, alerting the others that it was now safe to follow.

The wagon train began the journey almost immediately after. Gregg and Holt went to every family, advising them to take care, follow the markers carefully, and to be deliberate. With everyone clued in, they began to cross the wetlands in single file. No one thought about bandits anymore.

#

On a bluff overlooking the wetlands, Talon watched the crossing with interest. Cord, who had stepped into Drak's role as his number two, sat beside him, waiting. "What do you think boss? Hit 'em now?"

"No." Talon looked back out. "We can't go charging in down there. We go around the marsh, stay in striking distance, and wait. I want to see where they go once they get up into the hills."

"You want me to stay on them?"

"Yes. Stay on them. I'll go back to camp and get the others ready. There might be some good places for an ambush up in those hills."

"I could go ahead, scout for some places. It's gonna take them some time to get across there."

Talon closed his looking glass and handed it to Cord. "You do that. Don't lose them though. Find us a good spot. And if you see the mystery man, don't try to take him."

Without another word, Cord took the glass and slipped away. Talon continued to stare down into the valley. He didn't feel the familiar bloodlust that he normally built up before a job. Instead, he felt a cold, hard focus creeping over him.

CHAPTER 22

They all camped together again once the caravan made it to the other side. Aribeth felt the pressure lifting. On her father's map, they were right there. The journey was almost complete. She was going to make it.

The next morning, Leland briefed everyone on what lay ahead. The landscape now became one of rolling hills crisscrossed with frequent creeks and plenty of short grass and bushes for the animals to feed on. It was important to keep each other in sight, because if someone strayed off course now, they would be harder to find.

At daybreak they started off again, Aribeth and Leland at the front. The struggles at the river seemed long forgotten at this point, the promise of a better life in Aranwa waiting just over the next rise. The wait was excruciating. It took every bit of restraint that Aribeth possessed to not go galloping ahead. She couldn't wait to see what was next.

The first indication of trouble came late in the afternoon, when the wind began to pick up out of the west. Beside her, Leland kept a careful watch on the western skies, occasionally making disgruntled sounds.

"What?"

"Nothing."

Aribeth didn't believe him, but she kept quiet and they kept riding. After several minutes of silence, he grunted again. She looked to the west and saw the billowing white clouds were turning dark. There was a noticeable chill in the air.

"What?" she asked again. "And don't tell me nothing."

Leland stared off into the distance and grunted again. "Storm brewing out there. Probably need to find a place to shut down for the day."

"Now?"

"Soon," Leland answered. "From the look and feel of it, could be a bad one. I don't like that cold snap in the air."

"We've still got at least a couple of hours of daylight. I'd hate to shut down now and waste that time. Maybe we can get out of the way."

Leland stopped his steed and waited for Aribeth to do the same. "Look out there. Do you see that? You see those dark clouds? From there…." Leland pointed to the spot where the dark clouds began. "All the way over there. You think we can outrun that? I know that you're in a hurry, but I need you to be smart here, Aribeth."

"I get it," she said. Aribeth was embarrassed. In her life, her father had only scolded her on a few occasions, and it had felt the same way she felt now. "Can we at least push on a little further? It looks like the storm is still a way out. We could find a place to camp."

"Now you're thinking," Leland said with satisfaction. "Find a good place to pull up for the night. Then we wait out the storm. The storms over here—"

"You know, we have storms back home," Aribeth said, intentionally putting a mocking tone in her voice.

"At home, where you know where everything is and there are settlements everywhere and you can walk in any direction and stumble across someone in a day or two. It's a little different out here. A family gets lost, wanders off the path in the dark, you may never find them, and they may never find you. We don't have any idea what may be out there. Your father and I only explored a small part of Aranwa. Somebody could wander off the side of a cliff, or into the arms of savages."

"I get it," Aribeth said, annoyed. "Everything is worse here." They rode in silence for a few more minutes as they negotiated a particularly hilly stretch. "I find it funny," she said after a little bit.

"What's funny?"

"That this place scares you so much," Aribeth answered. "So far, I don't really see that this place is any scarier than back home."

That didn't sit well and Leland sat and pouted as they rode. She waited patiently as he burned. After another minute, he finally started talking. "I'm not scared," he said, sounding almost sheepish. "I just...it's the unknown. Like that creature we ran into in the woods. I didn't know what to do, how to kill it. Everybody thinks that I knew, but I didn't. I was just taking a chance, hoping that I could at least distract it."

"So why did you shoot it where you did? I've heard that you're a dead eye shot, so don't tell me you didn't hit him where you wanted to hit him."

Leland shrugged. "I shot him where I shoot all of my prey, right where the head meets the neck. Every animal I know of is vulnerable there."

"So even though you didn't know this particular animal, you had a good idea of where to hit it? So it wasn't really unknown at all, it was just a little different. I think Aranwa is the same way. It's not unknown. We have creeks and rivers and predators and storms at home. It's just different over here. Once you look at it that way, maybe it's not so scary."

229

"It's scary when you're the first one there and you don't know what's different until you're in the middle of it. When you're suddenly faced with a desperate situation and you have no idea what to do, and peoples' lives hang in the balance. Or when you've got a hundred and fifty people counting on you and one screw up means somebody dies." Leland finally looked over at her and looked her hard in the eye. "I can take whatever comes to me. I have no fear of dying."

"That makes sense," she answered. "You know that I wasn't questioning your courage, right?"

"Sounded that way," he said as he spurred his steed and pulled ahead of her. She let him go ahead, giving him space to work through whatever he was working through.

As they began to climb another hill, the wind began to whip with increased velocity and the temperature dropped rapidly. Aribeth called out to Leland, but he either couldn't hear her or ignored her and kept riding. She sped up, but he topped the next hill before she could catch him.

Heavy drops of cold rain began to fall. The drops hit hard, an icy, stinging impact that took Aribeth's breath away. Ahead, Leland turned and shouted something, but the wind had picked up and there was no chance she could hear him. She spurred her steed but it resisted, not wanting to continue in the face of the quickening storm.

The rain quickly intensified and brought with it wicked flashes of red lightning and the sharp peel of thunder. With her steed still refusing to continue, Aribeth slipped out of the saddle and tried to encourage the animal to move. She managed to pull it forward a few steps before the animal dug in and refused to move any further. Ahead, Leland had disappeared over a hill. Worse, behind her, the rest of the expedition was nowhere to be seen. They'd strayed too far in front for everyone else to keep up.

Aribeth found herself alone, in a strange land, with visibility quickly approaching zero. She pushed down the wave of panic that tried to wash over her. She knew that Leland was straight ahead. Again, she tried to pull the steed forward.

A shrill whistle pierced the air, so high and loud that she let go of the reins and covered her ears. She had just enough time to process what was happening before a bolt of lightning struck just a few feet from where she was standing. The impact and the immediate clap of thunder that followed knocked her to the ground and sent her steed running. She hit the ground, rolled away from the flash, and when she looked back up, the steed was gone and she was completely alone. To the side, the ground was blackened and scorched from the strike, but luckily there was no fire.

Now Aribeth really struggled to hold herself together. The rain beat at her face and the cold reached through her clothes, chilling her to the bone. She struggled forward, trying to walk straight against the raging cross winds and blinding rain. Another lightning strike hit off to her right, but it was further away and no threat.

She started up the hill, feeling like she was walking in wet sand the entire way. The lightning was getting more intense; the red bolts of electricity made it look like the sky was on fire, and it was so bright that Aribeth had a hard time seeing. She was essentially walking blind, taking it on faith that Leland was just ahead of her and that neither one of them had been blown off course.

She climbed the hill, hoping to see Leland, to see something, once she got there. Instead she got more of the same: black clouds, heavy rain, and red flashes in the sky. Aribeth twisted to look behind her, hoping against hope that someone had caught up. When she did, the wind caught her and she went tumbling down the hill, her head bouncing off the ground while rocks battered her. She rolled for what seemed like forever, losing all track of where she was. Finally, the hill levelled out and she rolled to a stop.

Aribeth ached all over and her head pounded. She didn't bother to stand up or look around. Instead, she lay there, face down in the wet grass, and let the rain pound on her. She began to understand the latent fear that always lived just below the surface in Leland. In a moment, Aranwa had reached out and swatted her.

The rain continued to pound as time lost all meaning. At a certain point, Aribeth began to pray, feeling certain that she would soon meet her end. She passed into an odd state of peace that was somewhere between being asleep and being in a trance, her consciousness desperate for an escape.

Then she felt herself being lifted off the ground. Aribeth struggled to open her eyes as someone slung her over their shoulder and carted her off, stomping over the rugged landscape and bouncing her around some more. Aribeth could see nothing but darkness. Night had fallen but the moons were nowhere in sight, blocked out by intense cloud cover. In the distance, the red flashes of lightning still danced across the sky, now far away from her.

She tried hard to stay awake and alert, but the motion was too much and soon she drifted off to sleep.

#

Cord had picked out the perfect spot for an ambush. It was in a small valley, one of the few places on the trail the expedition was travelling that would accommodate the entire group. There would be steep hills on either side. Talon's men could wait just beyond the crest of the hill and be completely invisible. Then they would swoop down, using surprise, speed, and darkness to overtake their prey.

Talon laid out the plan. The settlers consistently alternated their security personnel on opposite sides of the convoy, meaning three per side. Roeth, Sidor, and Cord would attack the west flank while Gibbons, Betsch, and Sherald hit the east. Talon would come in from the north, hitting the scout and the girl, who always rode out front. They anticipated that the group would hit the narrow pass by twilight, allowing them to use the shadows to their advantage.

They took their positions and waited. In his position, ahead and to the right of the approaching caravan, Talon felt like himself for the first time since Drak had disappeared. His heart beat faster, his body filled with adrenaline as he prepared himself for action. He longed for the gunfire, the panicked cries of women and children, the sight of blood on the dirty ground. He lived for it.

He would take what he wanted, from whomever he wanted, at any time. He would kill the scout, take the girl, and wait for the mystery man to come for her. And while he waited, he would have plenty of time to have fun with his newest toy. Talon knew he would have to be careful, though. He wanted to keep her alive until the man came. He wanted the man to see her die.

The first problem came well before they got to the pass. The scout and the girl kept riding further and further out front of the rest of the group. They seemed completely oblivious to the fact that they were leaving everyone else behind.

The scout and the girl rode into the pass well in advance. Talon cursed the luck. If he took them now, it would alert the rest. If they waited, the scout would be past the ambush spot, meaning that Talon would have to decide between challenging them out in the open, two on one, or forgetting about them in order to join the attack on the rest of the expedition. Talon desperately wanted the girl, but his men needed him to join the attack. Then the scout began to leave the girl behind, starting up out of the pass ahead of her. Worse news.

Then the storm hit. He hadn't been paying attention to the weather. Talon had given no heed to the shifting winds or the darkening skies. Almost at once, a heavy sheet of rain closed in around them. The scout disappeared, over the hill and into the storm. He lost sight of the girl a moment later.

Talon almost went after her right then, willing to sacrifice the mission to get the girl. He pulled his weapon, fixed his eyes on her last known position, and prepared to charge when lightning struck nearby. It blinded Talon, knocking him off his feet. His startled steed darted away. He struggled to his feet, then immediately had to duck again as another steed came barreling over the hill, jumping right over him.

Muttering a fine assortment of curses, Talon readied himself for another run. He felt the hair on the back of his neck stand up and heard the high-pitched whine in the air, and instinctively ducked as another lightning bolt struck, far too close this time. The clap of thunder was deafening. It felt like the bolt must have hit right next to him, the smell of burning ozone was so strong. When he finally regained his senses, he realized that it wasn't quite that close, but close enough.

Talon got to his feet, struggled back to the top of the hill, and looked over, but it was no use. The rain was coming right at him in sheets so thick that visibility was impossible. Realizing it was hopeless, Talon ducked back behind the hill, thankful for whatever protection it offered him, and settled in to wait out the storm.

Further down the line, the storm had hit his boys with equal force. It had only taken a few minutes and one close lightning strike to send them all scattering. Most of them headed back to camp, while a few just took off, running for the sake of running.

#

Alvarez Proffitt considered himself an excellent soldier, one in the prime of his career. He had left behind his old life in Cadoa because his superiors didn't see him the same way. He was stuck in a rut, wasting away as a mid-level officer in a military that was essentially nothing but a national police force. Aranwa was an opportunity to kick start his career.

Therefore, he took the assignment seriously. He took every opportunity to get close to Aribeth Fuller, who would ultimately be responsible for assigning permanent positions once their new town was up and running. He also made friends with Colonel Holt, the old man whom he figured was his strongest competition.

So far, the trip had been boring. The exciting things all seemed to be happening to others, while he wound up sitting on the sidelines watching. Proffitt was itching for action, desperate for a chance to prove himself.

That chance seemed lost to him now. They had moved far from the wild river and the dark woods, and were closing in on their destination. The Talon Volpe gang had shown no sign of making a move on them, causing Proffitt to question if they had ever really been there at all. It was beginning to look like Aranwa would be more of what he thought he had left behind.

These were the thoughts that ran through Proffitt's mind as he rode along the left side of the convoy, the cloud cover overhead perfectly capturing his mood. Proffitt knew he'd have to make some hard decisions soon. It was looking likely that his military service was reaching an end.

In midafternoon, the cloud cover broke, and it brought with it a chance for redemption. Proffitt was busy scanning the landscape off to his left, looking for any sign of trouble, when the clouds broke and the sun poured through, and glinted off something metal up on the next hill.

In an instant, Alvarez Proffitt sharpened up. Whatever the sun had hit upon quickly moved with a flittering movement. It didn't take much imagination to guess what it was. Someone was watching them.

Proffitt's senses went into high gear. His visual scans became sharper, more focused. He had to make sure of what he was seeing. The last thing he needed was to get people riled up for nothing. He kept watching as they rode, up one hill and back down into another small valley.

There it was again. Only this time, Proffitt caught sight of a dark figure crouched on the next rise, trying to stay out of sight, watching through a looking glass. It was only for a moment, and then the figure ducked out of view. No doubt now.

Proffitt let out a short, soft whistle. Colonel Holt, riding ahead and to the right of the wagons, immediately looked over his shoulder. Aware that they were being watched, Proffitt rolled his eyes and tilted his head in the direction of their watcher. Holt understood well and slowed his ride, falling back while Proffitt sped up so that they could ride side by side.

"What are you seeing, Alvarez?" Holt whispered.

"We got a watcher. He's staying up on the hills and peeks out every so often. I've seen him twice now."

"You're certain?"

"Absolutely certain," Proffitt answered calmly.

"Very well," Holt said, and spurred his steed to move back up in the line. Proffitt fell back but kept watching ahead to make sure he saw no sign of their spy. When he was confident the watcher had moved ahead, he directed his steed out of line, patted the animal twice on the hind quarters, and quickly ducked back into formation. That was the sign they had all worked out. Proffitt looked over his shoulder as Bethel, riding behind him at some distance, who tipped the bill of his cap in recognition.

Ahead, Holt had casually drawn alongside Gregg's wagon, which wasn't unusual since they often spoke during the long ride. Only now, Proffitt knew that they would be discussing strategy. Proffitt kept switching his watch from the hills to watching Holt and Gregg talking. It became quickly apparent that the Gregg was slowing down.

Holt dropped back again. "See anything?"

"Not recently," Proffitt said, his steely eyes still focused on the land ahead. "What's the plan?"

"Gregg's slowing everybody down. We're going to stop at the base of that next hill and take up defensive positions. We'll arm everybody we can, get the women and children in the middle, as protected as possible, and wait for them to make their move."

Proffitt risked a quick glance over at Holt. "What about Fuller and Jax? Don't we need to let them know?"

"Hell," Holt said, a tinge of disgust in his voice. "They rode on ahead without us hours ago. We can't risk trying to catch up to them now, we'll give it away. They should have stayed closer but they weren't paying any attention."

"Fine by me," Proffitt said. He felt no remorse that Leland and Aribeth had separated and were out there alone. They were supposed to stay close and didn't. Now they would be on their own if Volpe's gang did attack.

"What's going on?" a man named Hoch asked him. Proffitt was riding alongside his wagon and Hoch had been watching the goings on. Hoch, a widower, was accompanied by his teen daughter, who sat next to him on the wagon. Proffitt knew that she would be a prize for Volpe's gang.

"I spotted a watcher. We're going to stop and take up positions. You got any guns?"

"Sure enough," Hoch said. "Daisy and I, we'll both join the

fight."

Proffitt risked looking away from the impending hills for a moment. "Mr. Hoch, are you aware that the Volpe gang likes to take prisoners? Especially female prisoners? I don't know if your daughter should be —"

"I'm a better shot than he is," Daisy Hoch said. "I'd stand a better chance with a gun in my hand than just sitting around waiting on them to grab me. I'd rather die fighting."

Proffitt smiled at her warmly. "A girl after my own heart. Fine. We're going to stop at the base of that hill, circle up, and wait."

Hoch cleared his throat, then said, "Are you sure this is a good idea? Aren't we inviting them to attack?"

"Yep," Proffitt said, his eyes back to scanning the hills. "If they come at us, we'll be ready and we know where they are. They probably don't know we're onto them. We figure this is as good a chance as any to choose the battle. So, yeah, we're baiting them."

Proffitt edged his steed away from the wagon but caught young Daisy Hoch staring and gave her a playful little wink. The wind began to pick up and the temperature dropped rapidly. Seemingly out of nowhere a storm was barreling in towards them.

Ahead, Gregg reached the base of the hill and turned his wagon, starting the circle. The other families recognized the movement and followed suit without knowing why. They moved quickly now, each of Holt's men moving down the line, informing the families. Surprisingly, all went smoothly. Everyone who could fight grabbed a gun, while the others huddled together behind the wagon at the top of the circle. The fighters locked, loaded, and took positions of cover either inside or below the wagons, spreading out along the whole of the circle. The security detail brought their steeds inside the circle and took positions along the way to coordinate.

With that all done quickly, the settlers all settled in to wait for the attack that was sure to come.

#

Sherald was going insane.

Since Betsch had come across him in the camp, the older man hadn't let Sherald out of his sight. He seemed to know what Sherald was planning, somehow sensing the betrayal.

Every time Sherald caught Betsch looking, it made him even more paranoid. He needed to get away, to escape the continuous scrutiny. He needed to get far away from Volpe, from Betsch, from Aranwa.

Yet he found himself on steedback, hiding, waiting, ready to unleash death on the unsuspecting travelers, Gibbons on one side, Betsch on the other. He wondered if Betsch had shared his suspicions, because it seemed that when Betsch wasn't watching, Gibbons was.

He even wondered if they would use the attack to take him out as well. When it came to Volpe's gang, the only person who was irreplaceable was Volpe himself. It would be easy; so easy that Sherald had planned on doing the same to Betsch. He still might, if he got the chance.

Sherald didn't want to attack the settlers…they had nothing that he wanted. He prayed all afternoon for something to happen, to divert the coming bloodshed. As the winds picked up, he wondered if someone, somewhere, had gotten that message.

"Stay focused," Betsch snarled. "They're coming. Be ready." Bestch's cold blue eyes bore into Sherald's. Their steeds all twitched and whinnied and bucked.

"Must be a bad storm coming," he said conversationally as he patted his steed on the side. "Not like them to be so antsy."

"Don't care about no storm," Betsch growled. "Money and girls, that's all that matters. Kill whoever you gotta. Keep 'em from puttin' up too much of a fight."

Sherald gave up the attempt at conversation and turned his thoughts inward. He wouldn't kill. He would shoot, but he would shoot to miss and hang around the edges. With any luck, an opportunity would present itself.

Opportunity knocked in the form of a raging thunderstorm, which seemed to rise out of nowhere. The wind churned and the rain fell in thick, hurtful drops, and then the lightning started and all hell broke loose, with the steeds bucking and charging and every man for himself.

Gibbons took off, barking at them to return to camp as he did. The others, Roeth, Sidor, and Cord, came scrambling over the hill moments later, each heading in a different direction.

Sherald took it as his cue to run, only to find Betsch staring at him, gun in hand. "Don't even think about runnin', boy. I know what you been thinkin'. I seen it in your eyes." Betsch cocked the gun and pointed it right between Sherald's eyes. "Nobody runs out on Talon Volpe, boy. Nobody."

Sherald braced for the end, waiting for the sound of the shot. Before Betsch could pull the trigger there was a huge lighting strike nearby and a big clap of thunder. It gave Sherald the chance he needed.

He pulled his own gun and took off, firing a glancing shot as he went. Betsch, who was stunned by the lightning, fired too late to hit the moving target, and cried out as Sherald's hurried shot tore into the meaty part of his upper left arm. Enraged, he turned to pursue.

Sherald rode hard and crouched low, constantly changing direction to avoid giving Betsch a clean shot. With the constant thunder, he couldn't tell what was gunfire and what was thunder.

He just kept riding.

Once he risked a look over his shoulder to see Betsch still bearing down, trying to line up a shot. Sherald turned his steed hard right, cutting across his path, changing the angle.

Betsch fired too late again, Sherald's sudden move throwing off his aim. Only this time, instead of trying to repeat Sherald's moves, he let his own steed swing out in a wide curve to the left while Sherald looked right. When Sherald inevitably moved back to the left, he brought himself right into the line of fire.

There was another loud clap, but this one wasn't thunder, it was a gunshot for certain. Sherald felt the bullet explode through his knee a fraction of a second before his steed bucked and sputtered, and threw Sherald forward and out of the saddle. The animal crumpled to the ground as Sherald went flying.

Sherald hit, barrel rolled, and came up with his gun in his hand. His knee was on fire, his brain screamed in pain. He knew by instinct that he had only seconds to live. Betsch would be coming, gun ready to finish the job.

Betsch was closing in, ready to do just that, but he was riding too fast. Sherald's fall had thrown everything off. With a grunt, Betsch pulled on the reins, trying to turn hard, but the ground was too wet and he was going too fast. The steed skidded and stalled before Betsch could get the animal turned. When he finally did bring the skidding animal under control he found Sherald on one knee, gun in his hand. Betsch had just enough to time to see what was coming, for his eyes to lock on the gaping black hole at the end of Sherald's gun, before Sherald pulled the trigger and blew Betsch clear out of the saddle and into oblivion.

CHAPTER 23

Leland was not a man given to verbalizing his feelings. Whatever parental guidance he had received in his young life had taught him to be strong, silent, and self-reliant. Leland had learned to lead by example and to never count on anyone other than himself.

Then this girl had entered his life and everything had changed. She forced him to look inside of himself, to question. She brought out the fears that he had spent his life trying so hard to bury. Aribeth saw right through him, and Leland found it unnerving.

Just when Leland started to feel that she was right, that there was nothing to be scared about, Aranwa reached out and swatted them both. Never had Leland seen a storm pick up so much speed or hit so fast. They should have had another hour, half hour at the least, to find a place to camp. Instead, it broadsided them.

In a moment, he knew that he needed to find them a place to take shelter. He turned to see Aribeth rocking in the saddle, trying to spur her steed forward. He yelled at her to get down. She did as he asked and Leland trooped on over the next hill, looking for something, or somewhere, to go.

He managed to climb the next hill and then another, but there was no use. The rain was too intense. Unless Leland just happened to stumble over someplace, he wasn't going to see anything out here.

Leland turned back, expecting to find Aribeth right behind him. Only she wasn't there. Leland felt a new kind of fear beginning to crawl up his spine. He retraced his steps as quickly as he could, fighting hard against the heavy rain and the swirling winds. She was gone.

Leland realized in an instant that there was no hope in running around looking for Aribeth. The visibility was too poor and he was likely to get himself lost. Instead, he circled a hill, using it as a windbreak. It didn't help much with the rain, but it did keep the wind off. He pulled his coat up over his face, made himself small, and waited. Leland never went to sleep, never let his mind drift. He was keenly aware of every lightning strike, and when the hail started he was aware of that too.

Leland had plenty of time during the raging storm to think about the settlers and of Aribeth, all separated from him, stranded out here and taking a pounding. The settlers had each other, but Aribeth was completely alone, and he had only a basic idea of where she was. If she had kept going, kept wandering, he might never see her again.

As soon as the storm began to subside, Leland was up and moving. Leland's coat had kept him dry for the most part, though the bottom of his pants legs had been exposed and he was soaked and cold from mid-calf down.

He didn't have time to worry about that. Darkness was rapidly approaching and the thick cloud cover would keep the moons at bay. He had to find Aribeth before he lost the light completely.

Leland circled back around the hill to get his bearings, then started retracing his steps. He called out for her, but she never answered. He kept looking, scanning the landscape, certain that she had strayed from the path. His mind filled with visions of her stumbling into the path of some vicious animal, being torn to shreds while he was wandering around like a fool, looking for her.

In the dying light, he almost missed her. In fact, he almost stepped on her. He found her face down at the base of a hill. She had wandered slightly off course, but she hadn't made it far. He quickly knelt and checked for a pulse, and finding it put him somewhat at ease.

Still, Aribeth was far from out of danger. She was unconscious, bleeding from her temple, and shivering, her clothes soaked through. Quickly he scooped Aribeth up, threw her over his shoulder, and started off. He needed someplace to go, someplace where he could start a fire and get them warm.

He walked in a straight line, thinking of nothing other than finding some sort of oasis. Leland knew full well the dangers that could lurk in the dark of a rare, moonless night. Yet he knew that he couldn't think about that. He had to stay focused on the job at hand.

Finally, the cloud cover began to break and the light from the twin moons began to reach the ground in fractured beams. The light was intermittent, but welcome. After what seemed like an eternity, he spotted a copse of trees off to his right.

Leland lugged Aribeth's still prone body there as quickly as he could and found, thankfully, that the ground was dry thanks to the thick canopy provided by the trees. Leland worked quickly, gathering what wood he could to start a small fire. With that done, he stripped Aribeth, laying her clothes out to dry. Finally, he lay next to her, pulled her in tight to his body, and covered them both with his coat.

He tried not to think about how her skin felt under his hands. He tried not to focus on how hard she shivered. He tried not to image a scenario where she would stop shivering and die there in his arms.

Eventually, he fell asleep.

#

"Lee?"

Aribeth's voice felt tiny and distant in her ears. She awoke to find herself naked, pressed up against Leland, and covered with his coat. She had no recollection of how she had gotten there, and only vaguely remembered the feeling of being lifted and carried, but at the time she had thought it was a dream.

Now she was pulled tight against Leland, the light from a fire at her back casting dancing shadows on the trees. She was both cold and hot at the same time, an odd sensation. Leland's hands were rough on her back, contrasting with the smooth warmth of his coat.

Leland was sleeping, yet his face was twisted in a look of concentration. It was as if he had to focus to sleep. She gently pushed on his chest.

"Lee?"

Leland grumbled, then forced his eyes open. A tender sliver of a smile crossed his weathered face. "You're awake."

"I guess," she said sheepishly. "Unless this is heaven."

"I would like to think that heaven is a little more than laying on the hard ground in the arms of a hillbilly."

"I could think of worse things," Aribeth said, trying to make it sound like a joke. She didn't want him to know how right it felt to be laying there with him at that moment. She shouldn't be thinking that. She didn't even know how old Leland was. Aribeth decided to change the subject. "What happened?"

"I found you passed out after the storm." He touched his finger gently to her right temple. "I think you hit a rock right here, knocked you silly. You were covered in grass burrs. You're probably going to itch like the dickens for a little bit. The main thing I was worried about was you getting sick. You were cold and wet. I knew I had to heat you up. I promise, I haven't taken advantage at all."

"I wouldn't think that you would," Aribeth answered. A cold shiver ran up her spine and she pulled herself in tighter to Leland. "Thank you for coming for me. I know you were mad at me. I couldn't blame you if you had left me out there."

"I wasn't mad at you," Leland interrupted. "What you said hit a little close to home, that's all. I never considered myself scared of anything, but this place...."

"I see that now," Aribeth answered. "I've never seen a storm that ferocious hit that suddenly."

Leland seemed to take a small bit of satisfaction from her admission. "Now you see. This place always seems to have something up its sleeve. The first time you start getting comfortable, it gets you. I learned that when I was here with your father."

"What was it like?" Aribeth asked. "He made plenty of notes about what he saw, but I can't get a sense of what it was actually like."

"Like this, but harder. We walked everywhere. When we started out, we had four people: the two of us, a map maker, and a plant expert. The map maker is the one who fell into the river on our crossing. The plant maker, he cracked up. He started saying that he could hear the savages, the lost tribe, calling out to him. He said he could hear their war drums. He ran away. When we were leaving, we found some of his stuff in the marshlands. We figured that he got swallowed up."

They both fell into silence, listening to nothing but the crackling fire and the soft sounds of insects going about their business in the night. After a lengthy silence, Leland finally spoke again. "Your father, he got sick while we were here. Another storm, not near as bad as the one we just went through, but we both got soaked. He wouldn't change his clothes and got sick. He was laid up in Norales for weeks after we got back. I don't guess he ever recovered. I never thought of it like this, but I guess I lost my whole group."

"Don't blame yourself. I see it now, how this place does." Leland made a funny face and Aribeth stifled a giggle. "I'm not hearing tribal drums or anything like that. I'm not going crazy."

"We're here. We must be crazy."

"No," Aribeth said defiantly. "We're going to conquer this place. We're going to make Aranwa a place where people can live free from the corruption of the Ministry. When we do that, my father will have his dream realized and you will not have failed."

Leland breathed slowly and deeply, chewing over her words. "I wish I had your faith."

Aribeth, possessed by a feeling she never took the time to understand, leaned up and kissed him lightly on the lips. "You will." His pale blue eyes flickered in the firelight, something passing behind them, and he leaned down and returned the kiss tentatively.

Aribeth found it attractive, almost humorous, that this big strapping man seemed so unsure of himself. She took control, freeing her arms and wrapping them around his neck to pull him in again, kissing him much more deeply. She let go, letting the moment and the passion consume her.

Leland followed her lead.

#

Aribeth's clothes were still damp, but bearable, as she stood in the early morning light. She breathed deeply and was fully aware that it was a new day in more ways than one. Leland was still asleep by the fire, which was now nothing more than smoldering sticks.

Aribeth took a long look around, trying to familiarize herself with her surroundings. This place, this oasis in a sea of short grass and rolling hills, was completely unfamiliar to her. She took her father's journal out of the bag and thumbed through it, but again, there was no mention of such a place.

She wandered around, keeping their makeshift camp in sight, until she heard gently running water nearby. Aribeth began to get excited. She followed the sound deeper into the trees, and soon she emerged from the trees to find a creek running, the water spilling over a milky white rock ledge and forming a pool at the base, which then fed another creek that snaked away into the trees. Just beyond the sandy banks of the spring and in front of the tall trees, thick bushes with beautiful yellow flowers stood, swaying easily in the morning breeze.

She was at the bottom of a set of falls. She turned and watched, as if in a trance, as the water ran and fell, starting much higher than where she stood now, crashing down to the next ledge and then the next until it wound its way to her.

Again, Aribeth pulled out her father's journal and there it was. He had named the place Breton's Falls. This was the place he had set aside for his settlement. She ran out onto the rock shelf, splashing around in the ankle-deep water, feeling like a kid again. She felt a huge smile breaking across her face as she turned a full circle and she surveyed the landscape. She had made it. She was home.

Aribeth took it all in, looked skyward, and called out. "I did it, Father. I made it. You were right." She lowered her head and again took in the breathtaking view.

She committed the vision to memory, then went racing back to tell Leland. He was just beginning to stir as Aribeth went sliding in next to him. "We made it," she said excitedly. "We're here. Come on." She took Leland's hand and dragged him to his feet, not even giving him a chance to get dressed.

Aribeth pulled him out onto the rock and waved her hands all around. "Isn't this the most beautiful place? I think you were wrong. This *is* heaven."

"I didn't realize we were this close. If it wasn't dark, I would have known. Your father fell in love with this spot."

"I can't blame him." Aribeth hooked both of her hands around Leland's bicep. "We've got to get the others and bring them here. We've got a lot of work to do."

There was a sudden snap of tree limbs from behind them. Leland moved quickly, pushing Aribeth behind him as he moved toward the source of the sound. Aribeth feared another of the vicious creatures they had met in the woods. She was about to run back to camp to retrieve Leland's gun when a man stepped out of the tree line.

He was a tall man, dressed in blood red and black, and he stepped out of the trees with a pistol already in his hand. Leland began edging back, pushing Aribeth along, positioning himself to take the shot if the stranger fired.

"Isn't this a pretty sight?" he asked with a menacing grin. "From the looks of it, I would say someone had a pleasant enough night."

"We don't want any trouble," Leland said, still backing up.

"But I do. You see, your little group is trespassing. This is our land. All of it. And no one trespasses on Talon Volpe's land."

"You don't own this land," Aribeth called over Leland's shoulder, sounding much braver than she felt. "This is free land."

Talon Volpe cocked his pistol. "Are you going to back up that claim, missy? You kill me and it's all yours." He kept stalking them, edging closer with each step. "I don't give up my possessions all that easily. However, I might consider a trade."

"What kind of a trade?" Leland asked.

"There is a member of your party, a fancy man, but he looks like he's seen his share of trouble. He butchered two of my men. I want his head. You tell me where he is, and I might kill you quick as opposed to taking my time with it."

"Ridge?" Aribeth said, thinking out loud. "Is he talking about Ridge?"

"Ah, he has a name," Talon said with delight. "Ridge. Yes, your friend Ridge. Where is he?"

Leland started to answer but Aribeth beat him to it. "We don't know. He went off into the woods and we haven't seen him since. We all figured that he went off on his own. We didn't know anything about him killing your men."

"That's a shame," Talon said. To Leland he said, "I hope you don't mind, but I'll be taking your young friend here. Gonna pick up where you clearly left off. We're going to have ourselves a fine old time."

"Like hell you will," Leland said through gritted teeth.

Talon was not threatened at all. "Exactly. I'm glad we see eye to eye."

Leland pushed hard into Aribeth as Talon fired. Aribeth screamed as blood and bone flew up into her face from where Talon's shot had slammed into Leland's collarbone. He called out in pain, shoved her, then fell face down in the shallow water. "Run," he screamed.

Talon was closing in on Leland, lining up a kill shot, and Aribeth could do nothing to stop it. She was stuck in her tracks, frozen by fear. Leland began to roll and Talon's second shot ricocheted off the rocks, and then Leland was at the edge and falling over. Aribeth heard the sound of solid impact and Leland grunting, followed by a splash. Talon's gun danced toward Aribeth as he gingerly stepped to the edge and peeked over.

She saw it, the opportunity to get away. Volpe standing on

the slippery rocks, inches from the edge, looking away. Aribeth gathered her strength, set her feet, and prepared to run at him as hard and fast as she could.

She took two hard steps and then Talon's head snapped around and the gun bucked, and Aribeth felt fire reaching into her thigh as she fell. "Dumb move," he said. "Brave, but dumb. Gonna be an awful long walk back to camp with a wound like that. Get up."

Aribeth glared up at him, both hands pressed firmly over the wound in her leg. "I'm not going anywhere with you. You'll have to kill me."

Talon sauntered over to her, eyeing her like a piece of meat still on the hoof. When he stood over her, he holstered the gun and grinned down at her. "I plan on it. But first, you're gonna scream for me."

"Go to hell," she muttered.

Talon held his head back and laughed. "Sweetie," he said. "They're always brave, at first." With that, he lifted his left foot, put the toe right on her wound, and pushed down hard, driving the point of the boot into the bullet hole. Aribeth screamed out in pain, and the more she screamed, the harder he pushed. When he finally let up, she fell back and tried to cradle her burning leg to her chest. "See? I told you that you would scream. Now, look what you did." He held up the boot up to her face. "You got blood on my boot." He kicked her in the face and Aribeth felt her nose crack and blood begin spilling down the front of her face. She fell backwards, and a moment later, he latched on to her hair, just above the scalp, and began to pull her, dragging her over the rocks. She began screaming, both in pain and anger, while clawing at his hands, but he wouldn't let go. He was laughing as he carried her away to her fate.

.

CHAPTER 24

Bethel fell asleep to the sound of thunder booming all around him. He had taken up a defensive position under Dr. Grant's wagon, a rifle in his hand, watching anxiously for attacking bandits. It became clear that the attack wouldn't come as the storm raged, so he let down his guard and eventually drifted away.

He woke to Colonel Holt shaking him awake. Bethel came awake quickly when he saw the old man's face. The sun had not yet risen, and he could now see stars in the sky.

"Get up. Hurry," Holt whispered.

Bethel pushed the rifle aside and scrambled out from under the wagon. Proffitt, Reeder, and Bertrand were already there, checking weapons by the light of Echonos. In the east, the sky was just beginning to lighten.

"Sir, what are we doing?"

"Search and rescue," Proffitt said as he holstered one of his pistols. "Jax and Fuller got themselves lost. We're going to find them and bring them back."

"And, with any luck, find those bandits," Reeder added with a smile. He was already on his steed and ready to go.

"Mount up, Hough," Holt barked. "Let's get out there."

Bethel beamed at the opportunity. Quickly he grabbed the rifle, checked his pistol, and ran for his steed. As he stepped over to retrieve it from where it had been tied to the rail of another wagon, Parrie stirred. She had been asleep against the wheel of the wagon, her hat tilted down over her eyes and her rifle cradled in her arms. She looked up, saw Bethel getting his steed, and shot up.

"Are we pulling out?"

Bethel looked down at her. "We're going looking for Fuller and Jax."

"I'm coming," Parrie said eagerly, already headed for her own steed. Bertrand beat her to it, untying the animal and slapping it on the hindquarters, which sent it scampering away.

"Go fetch."

Holt took Parrie by the arm and turned her. "You stay here and guard the camp. We'll be back. Do not let anyone leave until we get back." Then to Bethel, he said, "Mount up, Hough. Let's go."

"Colonel," she protested as Holt mounted his own steed. "I can help. Just—"

"Are you questioning the direct orders of a superior officer? Stay here and guard the camp," he barked.

Parrie blushed and dropped her head. Bethel could tell by looking that she was both embarrassed and hopping mad. He could relate.

Bethel did as he was told. Once up on his mount, Parrie looked up at him with pleading eyes. He felt bad for her. She had come to his rescue in the forest.

Still, Bethel had worked his way into the good graces of Colonel Holt, and now, for the first time, he saw possibility in Aranwa. He saw rapid advancement and a nice, easy military post. If he stuck with it long enough, he might even make general.

Parrie, meanwhile, despite her intelligence and hard work and courage, was still a woman. She would never be able to escape that fact, and women simply weren't officers, not in a proper military unit. He wasn't about to sacrifice the gains he had made out of a misplaced loyalty for an old school mate.

This was the real world, after all. Academy was just a memory. Bethel gave Parrie a sheepish grin and a shrug and started off.

#

Ridge had been kicking around in the hills for days, looking for treasure. He'd dug though creek beds with his bare hands, looking for precious metal. He investigated every unusual rock formation, poked around in every cave. Yet he found nothing but more land.

When the storm hit, he had been sifting through the rich soil of a large creek, almost due north of Breton Fuller's falls. He had beat a quick retreat when he saw the lightning begin flashing in the western sky, and had taken refuge in a cave that was little more than an indentation in a rock wall under a sandstone shelf. Still, it worked to keep him out of the brunt of the storm, and allowed him a somewhat comfortable night of sleep.

It was the gun shot that woke him up. Ridge was up and out of the cave in a heartbeat, his preferred blade in his hand, ready to strike. He looked eagerly for a challenger, but found himself alone on the rocky outcropping.

Ridge had convinced himself that the gunshot was just a dream until the second shot rang out, followed shortly by a third. There was no mistake. The shots had come from somewhere nearby, but below his current position.

A woman screamed out in agony, and then it all came into focus. Aribeth. He had led Talon Volpe and his men right to them. They had kept going without him, and Volpe's men had tracked them here.

Ridge grabbed his gun belt and strapped it on as he made his way quickly down the hill. Ridge couldn't remember a time he had ever felt guilt, yet he couldn't think of another name to give the feeling that stuck in his gut. He had seen Volpe's tent, the blood, the teeth, and he knew what kind of hell Aribeth was in for. He should have waited. Should have taken them all out and then the expedition, and Aribeth, would have been safe.

He worked his way down to a secondary rock outcropping. He spotted blood dotting the grass and rocks and heard splashing down below. Quickly he moved down further and found Leland, bleeding profusely from a wound in his left shoulder, dragging himself up out of the pool at the base of the falls.

Ridge moved to the water's edge, took Leland's good arm, and pulled him out. He stood and muttered a thank you. First Ridge noticed how Leland's left arm hung limply at his side, then he noticed that Leland was naked.

Leland at once started walking away, holding his damaged left arm tight against his side. Ridge fell in step with him. "What happened here?"

"Talon Volpe. He just…popped up." Leland seemed to be in shock. "He was just there. Shot me, took off with Aribeth." He took two more steps, then stopped and turned, quick as a cat, his right arm shooting out and locking around Ridge's throat before he could even think to move. Ridge slapped at Leland's hand with his own as he felt himself being lifted off the ground. Leland pulled Ridge close. "He was looking for you. Said you killed his men. You brought this on us."

Leland tossed Ridge away like so much trash. He landed on his back and skidded across the ground. Ridge sat up and rubbed at his neck as he caught his breath. Leland was much stronger than he looked. He gave Leland a nice head start before he started trailing again.

"I did kill two of his men, because they came after me. I was just exploring, minding my own business. It's not my fault his men were stupid." Ridge made sure to stay far enough back to avoid any more sudden attacks. "If it's any consolation, I kind of feel bad about the whole thing. Your arm and all. And Aribeth."

"You feel kind of bad?" Leland stopped and turned again, which sent Ridge scrambling out of the way. "You feel kind of bad? He's doing God knows what to Aribeth right now, and you feel kind of bad? You're a real humanitarian, Secova." Leland stomped off again.

Ridge followed him to a make shift camp in a grove of trees, where he immediately noticed Leland's clothes strung about and the impressions in the soft dirt around the campfire. "Wow, Lee. I see you have really gotten to know our fearless leader. I didn't think she'd go for your type. Congrats."

"Shut up, Secova," Leland growled. He stooped over and began gathering his clothes with his one good arm. Ridge stood and watched, feeling a tiny tinge of jealousy that Aribeth had chosen the hillbilly. Then again, Ridge had taken himself out of the game.

"What's your plan, big man?"

"I'm gonna find Volpe and cut his heart out," Leland said as he struggled to dress himself.

"I like the plan and all," Ridge smirked. "Problem is, he'll kill you where you stand. You can't fight Talon Volpe with one arm. Besides, how are you going to find him? You have no clue."

"I'm a tracker."

"By the time you track them down, Aribeth will be feeding the scavengers. Luckily for you —"

He never got to finish. Out of nowhere there was a gun at his temple. The soldiers who had been guarding the caravan appeared in the copse, led by the white-haired colonel. Ridge tilted his head ever so slightly to see the young man of the group was the one holding the pistol to his head.

"You're a brave man to hold a gun to my head, son."

Holt pulled a rusty but sharp saber from his belt and pointed it directly at Ridge's heart. "A man in your position would be best served to keep his mouth shut. Wouldn't take much for us to kill a no-good traitor like you."

"It's not him," Leland said through gritted teeth. Ridge was impressed. A lesser man would have succumbed to the pain by now. "It was Volpe. Secova just got here, helped me out of the water." Leland stopped dressing long enough to look Holt in the eyes. "We've got to go after her. Right now. The longer he's got her...."

"He's right," Ridge added. "I've been to their camp. If Volpe gets her back there, it will be a fate worse than death."

"Then we go," Holt said resolutely. He pointed at Leland, still struggling to get dressed. "You stay here. You're useless with one arm. When we're done, we'll come get you and lead you back to camp."

Leland, now dressed from the waist down, stood, gathered his gun, and started walking. "No way I sit this out."

Holt scrambled to catch up. "You're just going to put us all in danger, Jax. I'm ordering you to stand down."

Leland turned quickly on Holt, showing the same catlike quickness he had earlier. Ridge tried to hide a smile as Leland snarled at the colonel. "You don't order me to stand down. I'm not a part of your group and I don't take orders. Now I got Aribeth into this, and I'll get her out. You come if you want, but nothing is keeping me out of this. Got it?"

Surprisingly, the battle-hardened colonel backed down and backed away. Ridge moved past all of them, slapped Leland on the good shoulder, and took the lead. "Now that we've got that settled. As I was saying, I've been to their camp, so I know where he's going. If we move fast, maybe we beat him there. He doesn't have much of a head start."

"Or he could just slit her throat and leave her laying out on the plains, and we'd never know it." Leland groused. "We follow him and try to catch him before he gets to camp."

"He won't," Ridge said. "I've seen his place. He likes to torture his victims. He'll take his time. I'm telling you, we can go around and beat him there."

"And I'm telling you that we can't risk it," Leland fired back. "He may not go back to camp. If you're wrong…."

Holt stepped in between them. "We split the difference. Secova, you come with us. We've got steeds, we'll ride to camp and cut him off. Jax, you stay on his trail. Hough, you stay with Jax. Let's move."

Leland grabbed Holt's arm. "If he gets to camp before I can catch him, wait for me. I want him."

Holt jerked his arm away. "We'll save the girl. You're either there or you're not. I'm not going to risk her life for you to get revenge. You want in, you better be there." Then he turned to his men. "All right boys, let's ride. Secova has the lead."

As they started off, Holt called out to Ridge. "Secova, if you're jerking us around, I don't care how good you are with that knife of yours, I'll kill you myself."

"I'm sure you'd try," Ridge smirked.

#

It had been a lucky day for Talon. He had woken to the smell of wood burning and reasoned that his prey was nearby. Then, he had found his steed munching on grass in a field not far from where he had taken shelter. In fact, there were three riderless steeds grazing in sight of each other. One, he thought, looked like Betsch's steed, and he wondered briefly if something had happened to him.

Talon took his steed and quickly followed the burning smell

to Leland's camp. By that time, they had moved on to the falls. Talon could hear them talking from a distance.

He had crept up on them, listened to their conversation, and waited for the right time to spring. The scout, a much bigger man than he had appeared to be from a distance, was stark naked and, Talon had to admit, impressive. Not that it mattered.

Talon shot him down but the man was quick. What should have been a fatal shot hit him in the shoulder, and the coward had rolled himself off the edge of the rock face rather than meet his fate. That had left the girl defenseless.

She kicked and screamed and clawed at him all the way to his steed. Her struggling would ordinarily be fun, but Talon was in no mood to play. Not yet anyway. He knocked her out with the butt end of his pistol and tossed her over his steed like a limp rug, and was gone. As he rode, he passed the other steeds lingering in the field and thought about driving them off or shooting them, but he passed. The two had become separated from the rest, the man was badly injured and on foot, and no one else was anywhere around. There was nothing to fear. He would retreat to camp and have his fun while he waited for the tough man to come looking for her.

Talon rode off into the misty morning, confident in his victory.

CHAPTER 25

"I screwed up."

Leland was crouched over the muddy hoof prints of a steed not far from where the impromptu posse had split up. He pointed out to Bethel where the animal had been tethered, the hoof prints coming in and the ones going out.

"You see how these are deeper, more pronounced? The steed was heavier than over there," he said, pointing to where Talon had brought the steed in. "That's because he's carrying Aribeth." Leland stood and looked off to the east, shaking his head. "He's gone. No way we can catch him now."

"But the others might, if he goes back to the camp like Ridge thinks he will. Maybe we can catch up yet. If we hurry, we can get back to the camp and get some more steeds."

"Do you know where camp is from here?" Leland asked skeptically.

Bethel looked around, furrowed his brow, and looked some more. "Somewhere back that direction," pointing to the southeast.

"Somewhere in that direction," Leland repeated. He was in no mood to tolerate foolishness, and Bethel struck him as a fool. "Fine. We know he went this way. I'll follow him, you work your way back to camp and see if you can get some more help."

"And take them where?" Bethel asked. "I don't have the slightest clue where this guy's base is. And if you're moving I won't know where you are."

Leland, in excruciating pain and filled with dread for Aribeth, struggled on. "Listen, you either come with me or you go back to camp. I don't have time to sit here and piddle around with you."

Bethel stuck close to Leland. "Colonel Holt assigned me to protect you, so I stick with you."

Leland walked on, tracking in the direction of the heavier footprints, Bethel yipping at his heels the entire time. Bethel tried to engage him in small talk as they walked, but Leland was in no mood. All he could think about was Aribeth; about the beauty of the night before, the shock of Volpe emerging from the trees, the terror that awaited her.

Leland felt a deep, burning hate like nothing he had ever felt before. A hate that was far beyond what he felt for the farmers who kept encroaching on his family lands or the Ministry and their corrupt practices. He couldn't wipe the image of Volpe and his unholy smile from his mind. He couldn't stop hearing Aribeth's pained screams.

He picked up the pace, ignoring the pain in his arm. Leland had tunnel vision, and the only think he could focus on was Talon Volpe.

"Hey, hey," Bethel started slapping Leland's good arm, snapping him out of his madness.

"What?" Leland had no idea how far they had travelled, but he was aware that they were back in the rolling hills and had left the falls far behind.

"Look," Bethel said, pointing off to their left where a pair of steeds, complete with saddles, grazed in a field.

Leland felt the weight temporarily lift off his shoulders. "That one is Aribeth's," he said, pointing to a light brown with black spots on its hind quarters. "I don't recognize the other one."

"Who cares?" Bethel said with enthusiasm. "Let's get 'em

and get to riding. We're back on the hunt."

They wrangled the steeds without incident. Bethel helped Leland into the saddle of Aribeth's steed before taking the strange one for himself, and they continued their search. After just a few minutes, they stumbled across a confusing mix of tracks along the ground. Leland gingerly slid out of the saddle to get a closer look.

"Looks almost like a chase," he said. "I wonder if the others already caught up to him." He walked some more, his eyes trained on the ground in front of him. "No. It's not right." He looked to the sky and saw numerous large black birds circling overhead. "Bad news."

They worked their way quickly to the focus of the bird's attention and found the remains of a man and a second steed, though the scavengers had been doing a quick job of claiming the bodies. Bethel turned away from the sight and vomited.

"I don't believe he's one of ours," Leland said coldly. "Maybe one of Volpes'?"

Bethel wiped his mouth with the back of his hand and forced himself to look at the corpse. "Nobody I know. Proffitt saw a guy watching us yesterday, so we know they were out here. We were ready for them, but they never attacked and then the storm hit. Maybe they got confused and shot each other."

Leland grunted, looking from the steed to the man and back, and then on to the ground for more tracks. "The other guy," he mumbled. He scrambled past the bodies and picked up a second trail. "The other guy hobbled off this way." He stuck his fingers into a rounded hole alongside some footprints. "He's using a cane of some kind." Leland looked back at Bethel, who was keeping his distance. "It's not Volpe, but he may be part of the gang. We can catch him, maybe ransom him."

"From what I hear, Volpe isn't the type to bargain."

"It's worth a shot. I don't think this guy is getting far. Let's move."

#

Sherald just couldn't catch a break. After gunning down Betsch, he thought he was home free. The rest of the gang had scattered in the ferocity of the storm, and Talon was nowhere to be found. If he could have gotten Betsch's steed, he was home free.

Except that the dumb animal had run off and Sherald had lost him in the rain. Having no desire to try and track down the animal on one good leg in the rain and the dark, Sherald had hobbled over to the corpse of his own steed, taken a shotgun off the saddle, and used it as a crutch. The gun was ruined now, the barrel clogged with grass and mud and bent from supporting Sherald's weight.

He hobbled his way through the night, just walking in a direction that would take him to the river and eventual escape. He no longer cared about anything else. He just wanted out and away from Volpe and his band.

So of course, Cord found him. Talon's newly appointed right hand man had taken it upon himself to go back out looking for the stragglers after the rest of the group made it back to camp. He found Sherald right away and gave him a ride back to camp. There he was debriefed by Cord while Sidor did the best he could to bandage up Sherald's ruined knee. Put on the spot, Sherald quickly made up a story, laying the blame for his knee and Betsch's disappearance on the settlers.

No one seemed to question the report, though the fact that the settlers had taken out another one of their brothers got the rest of the group riled up. No one, he found out, had seen or heard from Talon.

Sidor, the resident nurse of the group, finished the bandage job and gave Sherald a bottle of liquor for the pain. He took it, eager to kill the agony of the wound. While he self-medicated, he wondered how he was going to get away now. He had no steed, one leg, and couldn't get his money without raising suspicion. He had to find a way to get the others to leave the camp and give him time to make a move.

Cord took the others aside to discuss the next course of action. Gibbons and Roeth favored going after the settlers for yet another killing. Sidor and Cord both favored waiting until they could find Talon first, especially since they were now outgunned. They came to Sherald to cast the deciding vote, and he saw his chance.

"We gotta go after Talon first," he said, summoning up as much sincerity as he could muster. "We can't leave a man behind." He put the bottle aside and struggled to his feet. "He's out there now. We gotta go."

Sidor put a gentle hand on Sherald's shoulder and pushed him back down. "You aren't going anywhere, brother. You'd just slow us down." He turned to the others. "He's right. We gotta bring Talon back, then we hit 'em."

They were all in agreement and ready to ride. There was enough daylight left that they could make a decent sweep of the area before nightfall. As the gang started making preparations to ride out, Talon came riding hard into camp with a young brunette draped across his saddle, kicking and screaming for all she was worth. Sherald's heart sank. It was too late, and now he would have no choice but to sit here and listen to the girl scream as Talon tore her apart.

The rest of the gang met him with excitement. Gibbons yanked the screaming girl off the steed, tossed her on the ground, and put his boot to her throat. "Looks like we got ourselves a new toy." The others cheered.

Talon exchanged hugs with the four. Cord pointed over to Sherald. "The settlers," he said. "They took out Betsch, wounded Sherald. Yet, he was still going to ride out to find you. We wouldn't let him."

"Really?" Talon peered across the camp at Sherald, who was sitting on the ground, back against a tree. He walked over. "So, you tangled with the settlers?"

"Yes sir," Sherald answered. He feared that Talon was going to look inside of him and see the lie. "We got turned around in the storm and rode right up on them. Everybody started shooting. I don't know if we hit anybody. We turned to get out of there and then he cried out and I saw him slumped over, his steed running wild. I knew I couldn't do anything to help. They woulda killed me too."

Talon listened to his story and stroked his chin. "Well, just another reason to take them out." He started to turn away, then stopped and turned back around. "You sure Betsch is dead?"

"Not absolutely," he said. "I didn't stick around."

Talon mulled it over. "I saw his steed running around, but I never saw him. Guess they got him." He walked away and Sherald breathed a heavy sigh of relief.

Talon approached Gibbons and gently pushed him off the girl. "You know that's not how we treat out guests. Show some manners."

The girl coughed and gagged, working her way up to her knees. Even from a distance, Sherald could see the terror in the girl's eyes. She tried hard to hide it. "My friends will come for me," she said hoarsely. "They'll kill you."

The group laughed. The girl kept gathering herself, and Sherald saw what she was thinking. She was getting her feet under her, preparing to make a break for it. What she didn't see was Roeth, slipping around behind her. He had seen it too.

"Darling," Talon purred. "I'm counting on your friends coming for you. We'll kill them. Then we'll kill you. Then we'll go kill the rest of your little group. That's what we do. There is a reason no one comes to Aranwa." Talon crouched in front of her. "It's not because of some stupid lost tribe or man-eating animals. It's because of me. I'm the monster in the woods. I'm the man-eating killer. The second you crossed that river, you killed yourself and everyone you brought with you."

The words made her angry, and she began to breathe heavily. Sherald wanted to call out to her, to warn her, but he didn't dare. It would do no good anyway. As he watched, the girl scooped up a handful of dirt and tossed it in Talon's face, jumped to her feet, turned, took two quick running steps away....

And Roeth punched her full in the face. The impact sent her crashing backwards, rolling head over heels. Talon stood and wiped the dirt from his face, laughing the entire time. "This one's got some fight," he called out. The men cheered in response. "Boys, stand her up and strip her down."

Four sets of hands reached out for the girl, pulling her up and tearing away her clothes. She screamed and fought as much as she could, but there was nothing she could do. When they had her completely bare, Gibbons held her in front of Talon, both hands gripped around her arms.

"Now dear, we're going to play a game. You want to escape and I want you to try. I'm going to take you back to my tent. It's the big one over there, the one your friend destroyed for me. I'm going to give you a chance to run. If you can get by me and get out of the tent, you can go. You hear me boys? If she gets by me and gets out, you let her go." He walked up to the girl and traced the line of her jaw with a finger. "It's that simple. Are you ready to play?"

Sherald turned his head away as Talon gripped her by the

back of the neck and led her away to the tent. He knew how this game would end. It was fixed from the start. And even if she did manage to get by—and no one ever had—the boys would track her down and bring her back.

No one got away from Talon Volpe.

#

Ridge, Holt, Bertrand, Proffitt, and Reeder made it to the outskirts of Volpe's camp just after nightfall. To Ridge's heartbreak, he was too late. They could hear Aribeth's tortured screams guiding them in. "Listen to that," Holt said. "That poor girl. What are they doing to her?"

"Nothing you'd want to know," Ridge said solemnly. His blood ran like ice water in his veins. No one deserved to go through what Aribeth was going through, and every man down there would pay for their transgressions. "We're not waiting for Jax," he said. "When we get there, we go in, guns blazing."

They made it to within sight of camp. Aribeth's screams had finally stopped, but they could hear the men laughing, telling jokes and making small talk. Ridge pulled his knife and his gun and prepared to charge in.

Holt pulled him back.

"What are you doing, old man?" Ridge snarled. "Now is no time for cowardice. We're going."

"Think for a second, Secova," Holt whispered. "I don't like what's happening down there any more than you do," he said. "But we don't know how many people are down there, what kind of weapons they've got. They could be sitting down there waiting on us. This could all be an ambush. We've got no light at all back here, no moon, nothing. Five guys against who knows? He could have twenty men down there."

"He doesn't have twenty men," Ridge answered. "I don't think there was more than nine or ten tents."

"Okay, fine. Ten men. That's still two-to-one in their favor. And they could have a second camp nearby we don't know about. We go charging in there, they could tear us apart, and then what happens to Aribeth?"

"If we don't move now, she's dead."

Proffitt put a hand on Ridge's shoulder. "She's not screaming any more, she may already be dead. Whatever has happened, there's no changing it now. We've got to think that this isn't a rescue attempt any more. It's revenge. Let's be smart about it. We wait till dawn; that way, even if they are waiting for us, we can see what we're running into. Maybe they let down their guard."

Despite Ridge's bloodlust, he saw their point. "Fine," he grumbled. "We wait until dawn. Then we go down there and we slaughter them all like the animals they are."

CHAPTER 26

They waited, anxious but not nervous. Except for Reeder, Holt and his men were experienced in the ways of war, and the possibility of impending death did not faze them. Ridge had spent his entire life on the edge. He didn't fear death. He considered it his ally.

They camped out on a slight rise overlooking the camp, where they could see the flickering light from a campfire and heard the mutter of voices. The wait seemed endless, like the night was protecting Volpe, keeping him from their wrath.

Ridge had slipped into an almost trancelike state when he heard the gentle approach of feet through the woods, coming towards them. Whoever was coming was trying hard not to be heard. Ridge silently nudged the rest of the men awake and they readied their weapons. If Volpe had a man stalking through the woods, he was about to make a grave mistake.

Instead, Leland poked his head of the woods, leading with the barrel of his long rifle, He was still shirtless, but had patched his wound with tightly packed leaves. He didn't show the slightest indication of being cold. Bethel emerged just behind him.

The others relaxed and lowered their weapons as Leland and Bethel joined the huddle. "I thought that you weren't waiting," Leland said, an edge of anger in his voice.

Ridge jerked his head in Holt's direction. "They think it's too dangerous to attack them in the dark. They're afraid that he's got a small army down there. I think ten men at the most."

"We've got seven, that makes us even," Leland said. "I say we take them now. The longer Aribeth is down there—"

"It's probably too late for her," Proffitt said sadly. "She quit yelling hours ago. We've got to expect the worst."

That was the wrong thing to say. Leland snatched Proffitt by the shirt and jerked him forward. "Hours? You let her sit down there and scream for hours? Do you have any idea what the beast could have been doing to her?"

Beside them, Ridge smirked. "They were more interested in their own lives than hers. Like I said, I was ready to move when we got here."

Holt and Bertrand stepped in, trying to pry Leland's hands off Proffitt. "You cowardly pieces of trash," Leland snarled. "You let her sit down there and suffer."

"It wasn't prudent…," Holt said, struggling against Leland's iron grip.

"This isn't war, you damn fool, it's a rescue. You don't let someone sit and be tortured." Leland tossed Proffitt aside, still steaming. "I'm not waiting for daylight. I'm going now. You can all sit around here and watch."

Ridge scrambled to his feet. "I'm coming with you. I figure I'm worth five guys. If you can take the other five, then we meet at Volpe."

"He's mine," Leland muttered.

"No need to be like that," Ridge grinned. "We can take turns. No reason he should get off light. Let's make him suffer before we kill him. Take our time. He took his time with Aribeth."

Leland grunted an acknowledgement. Ridge smiled bigger. He liked this Leland. He respected a man who wasn't afraid to do serious, yet righteous, violence.

"If you're gonna go, at least be smart about it," Holt

interrupted. "Let's all spread out around the camp and surround them. We can catch them in a cross fire." Without being told, his men began to silently deploy, moving quickly around the perimeter of Volpe's camp. "Don't bunch up," he said, more to Leland and Ridge than his own men.

"Tell your men to shoot carefully," Leland said, staring ahead intently.

"Yeah, we don't want them shooting us by mistake." Ridge said as he readied himself to move.

Holt sounded insulted. "My men know what they're doing. We won't shoot you. But do me a favor, don't get them killed."

Ridge nodded, exchanged a quick look with Leland, and then they began to move, Leland edging left, away from Ridge. Holt moved down the rise to Ridge's right while Bertrand, Proffitt, and Reeder moved around the back of the camp.

The tiny glow of the campfire grew as they got closer, but there were no men to be seen. It appeared that they were going to be able to walk right into camp.

Until Talon Volpe emerged from his tent. He was naked, smiling, covered in blood. He stood tall and proud in the night, stretched, and yawned. Ridge holstered his pistol, switched his knife in to his right hand, and was about to charge when all hell broke loose.

Something caught Talon's attention. His head snapped around, he moved subtly, and then Leland opened up with his gun, but the last second movement spoiled the shot and sent Volpe scurrying back into his tent. Almost instantly gunfire began erupting from the camp, with Holt and his men returning the fire. Ridge scrambled behind a tree for cover, waiting for another opportunity to strike.

#

Talon felt better now, having blown off some steam. He

271

stepped out of his tent, enjoying the cool night air. Talon stretched out strained muscles and yawned. His thoughts drifted to the settlers, and the mystery man. Talon wondered how long it would take them to come. He was ready for another fight, for more blood. It got his heart pumping.

He stretched again when something in his brain began to fire. Not so much a sound or sight, but a feeling that something was not right. From somewhere behind and to his left, he thought he heard the rustle of leaves and he turned quickly.

Then the world exploded.

A massive gun fired from somewhere, the projectile exploding into the trunk of a tree nearby. It would have shattered him had he not moved. Instantly he was moving, ducking back into the tent. "They're here, they're here."

He didn't need to worry. His men had all fallen asleep with guns at the ready, just in case the search party arrived earlier than expected. They were also ready for the fight, and eager to avenge their fallen comrades.

The night air came alive with gunfire, bullets whizzing through the air. Volpe grabbed a pistol out of his holster, stuck it out the tent flap, and emptied it in a wide arc. He wasn't trying to hit anyone, just buy some time. With the gun spent, he hurriedly put on his pants, grabbed two more pistols and the sword he had stolen from Drak's tent, and stepped out to join the fray.

#

The opening moments were chaos. Leland's hurried shot had caught everyone by surprise and everyone reacted by firing blindly. Now, Holt's men took cover in the trees, while Volpe's men hid by their tents. Ridge was ready to move again when he saw the barrel of a pistol sticking out of Volpe's tent. He ducked back for cover as Volpe fired into the night.

Ridge made cover behind a tree as one shot grazed by him to

the left and another glanced off the tree he was using for cover. He had to laugh. His good friend Death was looking out for him again. No half-assed bandit firing panicked shots into the night was going to take down Ridge Secova.

After Volpe's wild shots, everything settled down. No one wanted to be the first one to fire and give away their position. It was still dark, but sunrise was coming soon. Everyone settled in to wait. Ridge knew by experience that eventually, someone would lose their nerve.

That turned out to be Volpe. He came flying out of his tent, shirtless and barefoot, a gun in each hand and a saber fastened to his waist. He moved quickly to his right, firing a pair of shots before he entered the circle of tents that made up the camp and ducked into one for cover.

As soon as Volpe emerged, Holt's men opened fire. Leland let loose, his gun making the unmistakable boom as it went off, but his shot was high. From behind Volpe, Bertrand joined in with two quick shots that just missed. One of Volpe's men stood and fired back. Bertrand screamed out and then Leland fired again, and Volpe's man bucked and went down in a shower of blood.

With the attention focused on Volpe, Ridge began creeping out of the woods. His tent was now unprotected and Aribeth, or what was left of her, was still in there. As Ridge broke into the clearing, moving slowly, he caught sight of Reeder creeping out to his right. They acknowledged each other and Ridge moved forward as Reeder circled behind, keeping his gun trained on the camp.

He was almost to the tent when an aged black man from Volpe's camp yelled out and began firing. Reeder shoved Ridge down face first, returned fire, and danced away to his left. Leland's hand cannon roared to life again as Reeder made a run for the tree line. He was almost there when he took a shot in the leg and fell, crawling on hands and knees up the bank to cover.

Ridge went down and rolled, putting the tent between himself and the rest of the camp. The morning light was coming quickly now, a fine mist hanging in the air. Ridge used his knife to open a thin slit in Volpe's tent. He could see her, just a huddled mass of flesh in the corner. He couldn't tell if she was alive or dead, but she was there. Satisfied, he crept along the side of the tent, planning on ducking inside. Only when he turned the corner, he found himself face to face with Volpe himself, who was crawling along the ground on his belly, leading with his guns.

Volpe smiled and fired, forced Ridge to fall back again. Just as he gathered himself, Volpe flew around the corner and jumped at Ridge, slamming into him. Ridge dropped his knife, wrapped his arms around Volpe, and they rolled, locked together, neither able to get a shot in on the other.

#

Sidor was dead, having taken a shot to the back of the head. Cord was on the ground, clutching his arm to his chest. Gibbons and Roeth were flat on the ground, facing away from each other, only occasionally risking a shot. Sherald was still propped up against the tree, guns in his hands, but he hadn't fired.

He had been praying.

This, he knew, was their Judgment Day. He had wanted to run from the reckoning he knew was bearing down on them. Now, in the final moments, he knew that there was a reason his every attempt had been thwarted. He had been judged and now would face the consequences.

His only hope was to appeal to the attackers, to pray for mercy, but for the moment even that was out of the question. Sherald had no doubt that one of the others would kill him if he made any sort of effort to flee.

Instead, he closed his eyes and prayed for deliverance. He

begged forgiveness for his sins, and as he did, each one flooded back into his memories. Every victim, every death, every rape, as if they were all waiting on the other side to torment him, anxiously awaiting his arrival on their plane.

His guns were right there. They offered a quick end to the waiting and the fear. He couldn't do it, not if there was still a chance. He tossed the guns away, shifted onto his stomach, and began to crawl away from camp, out of cover. As soon as he knew he was exposed, Sherald began to yell out, "Don't shoot."

Behind him, Roeth and Gibbons yelled but they didn't dare move on him. Sherald crawled out of the camp and began up the bank. He'd just made it a few feet when a large, shirtless man with a wound stepped out from behind a tree and pointed a large gun at his head.

Sherald held up his hands and said again, "Don't shoot. I'm not—"

Leland shot him before he could finish.

#

Twice Leland had Talon Volpe in his sights, and twice he had gotten away. The first time, someone had distracted Volpe at the last moment and he had turned, and what would have been a fatal shot sailed high. On the second attempt, Volpe had been moving fast and was hunched over, and again Leland shot high.

However, one of his men had risen to provide cover fire. He had his back turned to Leland, shooting away, and Leland very calmly put a shot into the back of his head.

Leland waited, ready to take another shot and debating if he should storm the camp and take his chances. Volpe's men had not availed themselves well, firing wild shots into the darkness. Now, with the sky beginning to light, their lack of cover would be their undoing.

Leland had just started his advance when another man came

crawling out of the camp on his stomach, yelling for people not to shoot. Inside the camp, the other gang members were screaming at him, which elicited a fresh volley of fire from Holt's men.

The man kept crawling, and eventually crawled right up on Leland's boot. He had looked up at Leland with soft green eyes wet with tears and started to beg for his life.

In other times, Leland would have taken mercy on the man. But this man had thrown in with Talon Volpe, and was therefore as guilty as Volpe himself. Leland was no longer in a forgiving mood. He shot the man at point blank range, the bullet shattering the man's youthful face. Leland stepped over the body and continued his approach.

He felt nothing.

#

Talon Volpe and Ridge Secova were locked in a battle of survival. Volpe had lost his guns, Ridge had lost his knife, so they rolled and punched and kicked at each other, neither able to land a decisive blow. In the back of his mind, Ridge was impressed. Volpe was proving to be every bit as tough as advertised, and therefore, a worth adversary.

Volpe rolled Ridge onto his back, levered himself up, and loaded up a right cross, but Ridge kicked his legs out from under him and Volpe fell face first as Ridge rolled away. Looking up, he spotted his knife in the dirt and began to bear crawl over to it. Volpe grabbed at his feet, but Ridge kicked back and continued crawling.

When he was close, Ridge gave up the crawl and lunged for the knife. Volpe had stood and drawn the sword, which looked more decorative than functional, and had just missed slicing Ridge's legs off.

Ridge scooped up the knife, rolled to his knees, and prepared to strike.

Volpe was faster. He buried the sword deep into Ridge's upper chest, just below his collarbone. Ridge grunted with the pain as Volpe withdrew the sword and prepared another thrust. Anger surged through Ridge and he shot to his feet, side stepped Volpe's next jab, and caught his right arm with a glancing cut that drew a fine line of blood.

Volpe grabbed at the wound with his left hand as they circled each other. Volpe thrust with the sword but Ridge backed away, still circling, trying to get on Volpe's side. Yet, Volpe had clearly played this game before and kept Ridge in front of him, constantly reaching out with the sword.

Ridge knew he would never get close enough to strike like this. So, while continuing to dance away from Volpe's blade, he reached across with his left hand, drew his pistol, and fired a quick, short distance shot. Volpe jumped on the movement and stepped forward quickly,

Ridge's shot penetrated Volpe's abdomen low on the right side, causing him to lower his arm, and it was that tiny, last minute adjustment that ultimately saved Ridge's life. Instead of driving the point of the sword through Ridge's heart, Volpe's aim dropped and he instead drove it into his belly.

#

Leland had made it to the edge of camp, and he saw Ridge and Talon Volpe engaged in brutal hand to hand combat. He had a decision to make. There were three men left in Volpe's camp; he could see them, and none of them knew he was there. He could take them out, he could assist Ridge, or he could go for the Aribeth in the tent.

Aribeth was the most important thing. He would go for her. Holt and his men had the others pinned down and Volpe was occupied. He could at least get Aribeth out of harm's way.

Except that Ridge got his gun loose and fired a shot, which

drew the attention of the other three men in camp. Leland was in no man's land, exposed. He moved quickly, firing a reflex shot that hit the ground in front of a wounded black man, who recoiled from the shower of dirt that was kicked up. Leland continued moving right, going for cover, but away from his goal.

He kept shooting as he made for the trees on the other side of the camp. Holt and Proffitt provided cover fire as Volpe's men tried to track Leland.

Holt moved in, trying to take advantage of the fact that all three men were shooting at Leland. He ran right up to the camp, stepped between two tents, and the wounded black man was right there, sitting on the ground, cradling his left arm to his stomach and shooting with his right.

Holt levelled his weapon just as the wounded man swung his head back around. They fired instantaneously, the black man falling over dead as Holt took a shot to his midsection, stumbled backwards, and fell.

#

They both dropped to their knees in pain. Volpe still had a lax grip on the sword. Ridge lashed out with the knife, catching his right hand at the wrist and nearly lopping it off with one smooth, vicious stroke. Volpe shrieked and fell back, clutching at his wrist with his left hand. Ridge pulled the sword out of his stomach and tossed it aside. He tasted blood now, and it wasn't his. Volpe knew it was coming, and began pushing himself along the ground with his feet, trying to put distance between them.

Ridge was a wild animal, crawling along on the ground, bleeding profusely but feeling no pain. He caught up to Volpe and drove the knife into his thigh, and used it to pull himself up so that he was right on top of Volpe.

He pulled the knife free, poised to deliver the final blow, but Volpe grabbed Ridge's wrist with his one good hand. He tried to use his right as well but the hand was useless, hanging limply from his wrist. Yet Volpe proved to be surprisingly strong, holding off Ridge, stalemating his knife hand.

Tiring of the battle, Ridge used the fingers of his left hand and jabbed them into the stump where Volpe's right hand once was. He cried out in agony. Ridge brought the knife down into his chest, driving it into Volpe's left lung.

As Talon Volpe lay in the dirt, bleeding and gasping for air, Ridge leaned in close and whispered in his ear, "Ridge Secova." Volpe's eyes sought Ridge's out, a look of confusion etched across his face. Ridge sneered down at him. "I want my name on your ears as you die."

Ridge pulled the knife free and let Volpe see it there, covered in his own blood, before Ridge drew it across his throat.

#

Bethel, firing from a covered position in the woods, had hit the black man early in the battle, but since had simply been laying occasional cover fire. By his count, there were three of them left, but they were sticking close to the tents and staying low to the ground, firing and moving.

He had been trying to screw up the courage to charge the position when Leland had appeared in the space between the camp and Volpe's tent, on his way to get Aribeth. He'd almost made it when Ridge fired, and that had drawn attention and fire Leland's way.

Leland fired and scampered. With their attention drawn, Bethel realized the time was right to move. Holt beat him to it. The old man, though, was too slow and stiff, his footfalls too heavy. He had drawn the attention of the black man and they had fired at each other.

Bethel's heart sank as he saw his mentor drop his gun, stumble backward, and fall like a sack of rocks. With a surge of anger, Bethel ran across the distance. He had to get to Holt, pull him away from fire before one of Volpe's men finished him off. Bethel fired as he ran, not aiming, just hoping to keep the guns at bay.

They fired in response, but the shots blistered through the air past him. As he approached Holt's prone body, he tossed his gun to the ground and slid headfirst to the old man's side.

Colonel Holt looked up at Bethel with wavering eyes. "You damn fool," he said between coughs. "Why'd you drop your gun?"

"Don't need it," Bethel said. He crouched, took Holt under both arms, and began dragging him back into the safety of the woods as Proffitt kept Volpe's men pinned down. They had just made it out of the line of fire when they both heard Leland fire once, then again, and then, as quickly as it had all begun, the firefight was over.

#

Ridge rolled off Volpe's dead body and dragged himself across the ground to the tent. He was covered it blood, both his and Volpe's. He had never felt such excruciating pain, yet he did not fear. Death had ridden with him today, not against him. Death was still an ally.

There was a terrible firefight in progress in Volpe's camp, but Ridge cared nothing about it. He had full confidence that Leland and the others would win that battle. Weary from the fight and the blood loss, Ridge finally found his way into Volpe's tent and the lump of flesh in the corner that was once Aribeth Fuller.

Ridge knew in his heart that she was gone, but he had to be sure. He crawled over to her, touching her gently on the back.

She shrieked, coming to life in an instant and flying across the small space, slapping at air, skittering like a wounded animal. "Get away, get away."

"Aribeth, it's me," Ridge called out. "It's me, calm down. You're safe."

Aribeth was feral, slapping at the air in front of her, hiding her face, repeating over and over, "Get away get away get away."

Ridge drew closer, noticed Volpe's long coat lying on the floor, and picked it up. She was still frantic, fighting away invisible monsters, when he got back to her. He forced himself up on his knees and tossed the coat over her shoulders before wrapping her up tight and holding on as she bucked underneath him.

"Let go let go let go."

"Aribeth, stop it," he snapped. "You're safe. He's dead. Volpe is dead."

His words finally seeped through and she looked at him. He saw in that moment a deep pain that time would never be able to wipe away. The idealistic girl he had last seen was indeed dead. She looked at him for just a moment before she noticed the coat, and then she writhed away again.

"It's his. Get it off me. Get it off. Get it off."

He held tight and started to shake her. "Aribeth, wake up. Don't be stupid. Hey!" He shook her as violently as he could, which sent fresh waves of pain soaring through him. "Calm down. It's over, Aribeth. It's over."

Aribeth stopped writhing and looked at him like he was a total stranger. "It's over?"

Leland poked his head into the tent moments later, and instant relief spread across his face when he saw her. "You're alive."

Aribeth jerked her head toward Leland, saw him, then buried her face in Ridge's chest. She began sobbing uncontrollably, refusing to look anywhere near Leland.

Leland tried to hide the heartbreak. "At least she's alive," he said, dropping his head and pulling away, leaving Ridge to comfort the shattered girl.

#

Bethel's run had drawn the attention of Roeth and Gibbons, the last of Talon Volpe's gang. They fired at him, missing badly, and then they ran out of bullets. They both ducked to reload, but when they looked up, Proffitt and Leland had them in their sights. Both men raised their hands in surrender, and Leland gunned them both down.

With the gunfight over, other sounds filled the air. Sounds of men crying out in pain. Four of Volpe's men lay scattered about the camp, one outside the camp where Leland had shot him, and Volpe was nowhere to be seen. "Let's go check on your boss," Leland said as he holstered his weapon.

"I'll go check him," Proffitt said. He was bleeding from the forehead thanks to a sliver of tree bark that had been blown in his face during the shootout. "You go check on Bertand; he got hit too."

Reeder came limping into camp, his weapon still drawn. "I'm fine guys, don't mind me."

Proffitt looked him over once. "You just got hit in the leg. Hell, that's nothing more than a scratch." Reeder scowled at him and Proffitt laughed. "Just kidding. You did good, Rook. Have a seat."

"Nah," Reeder said. "I'll go get Bertand. Jax, I think I heard your girl in there."

Leland's eyes lit up. "She's alive?"

"Unless Secova got castrated I would say she is."

Leland rushed past Reeder and to the tent. He heard her crying out and Ridge trying to calm her down. He ducked down and stuck his head in the tent. "You're alive."

Aribeth took one look at Leland and lost it. She buried herself in Ridge's arms and began crying. Leland understood. He had been responsible for looking out for her and had failed. It was his fault that she was in the condition she was in. Feeling completely worthless, Leland left the tent.

He stalked silently past the camp and the wounded soldiers. Holt was now sitting, coughing up blood but alive. Reeder was helping Bertrand out of the woods, both limping badly. He pushed past Bethel and Proffitt, who were standing around, coordinating their next move.

"Where are you going?" Bethel asked, putting some authority in his voice.

"To get help," Leland said without looking back. He took one of Volpe's steeds and rode off as fast and hard as he could, wondering if it was possible to outrun a broken heart.

CHAPTER 27

Leland returned to the caravan, where Parrie rode out to meet him. "Mr. Jax, thank goodness you're okay. Did the others find you? Holt and his men—"

Leland rode past her without acknowledging her, charging on into camp. Parrie rolled her eyes. "Now he's doing it," she muttered as she spurred her steed to catch up.

Leland made the camp, jumped off his steed, and went searching for Dr. Grant. Other settlers gathered around, asking questions and expressing their relief, but he ignored them all. Grant was sitting in the shade beside his wagon, talking quietly with his wife, when Leland approached. He looked up at Leland with questioning eyes.

"Something wrong, Mr. Jax?"

"Get in your wagon and follow me. Now."

Grant had been a doctor long enough to know that when you received an order like that, you didn't ask questions. Grant struggled to his feet and up into his wagon. Leland turned to look for Jamison Gregg, only to find him already standing there.

"I take it that you bring bad news," he said, his kindly face showing his despair. Leland put an arm around his shoulders and turned him around.

"You take the group straight that way. Maybe a day's ride, if that. You're going to come across a river, follow it to the northwest and you will come to a series of falls. That's Aribeth's Falls. That's where you're going."

"What about the others? We need protection."

"There's nothing to protect you from. I'll send the girl along, but you won't need her. Volpe and his gang are dead. All of them." He started to walk away, but stopped and stuck a finger in Gregg's face. "When you get there, I want you to tell these people that they'd best appreciate this place. A terrible price was paid for it. Aribeth paid a terrible price for it. You make them understand."

Gregg nodded in understanding and walked off to begin passing the word. Grant was pulling his wagon out of formation and Leland stormed back to his steed. Parrie was still on steedback, watching. "Where are we going?"

"You're going to escort these people to their destination. Grant and I are going back for the others."

"Damn it, would you stop?" Parrie growled. "I can help. I'm so tired of being left behind. I—"

"Are you a doctor?" Leland snapped. Parrie was taken aback and didn't answer. "What I need is a doctor, not a pouty little girl who wants to play soldier." He turned his steed and glared at her, eyes burning. "If you wanted to play soldier, you should have been there an hour ago. Do what I told you and see these people home." He rode away, leaving Parrie sitting there, embarrassed and angry.

#

By the time they made it back to Volpe's camp, Bethel and Proffitt had done what they could to make their patients comfortable, and then they started tearing down the camp. They had scavenged everything of value from the tents, and were in the process of building a funeral pyre. They would leave nothing, no reminders that Talon Volpe ever existed.

Grant immediately went to work. Leland stuck close to his side, doing whatever was needed of him. The wounds to Reeder and Bertrand were painful but superficial, and they would be fine in time. Holt's wound was more serious. Luckily for him, the bullet had passed clean through, so they needed only to manage the wound and watch for infection, though Grant warned that Holt would likely suffer from the effects for the rest of his life.

Grant did not know how Ridge was alive, much less walking around. Ridge laughed as Grant treated him, and regaled the doctor with what they were all sure was an exaggerated version of his battle with Volpe. He assured Grant that death was a long way off for him. Leland thought he had completely lost his mind.

Aribeth's physical wounds were easily treated. Volpe had inflicted a lot of pain, but no permanent damage. The psychological wounds were a different matter. Grant pulled Leland aside. "That girl is shattered," he whispered. "I'm not sure she'll ever come back. What he did to her must have been awful."

"I don't want to think about it," Leland said. "She'll live?"

Grant looked back at Aribeth, who had slipped into a catatonic state. "If you can call that living. If that man were merciful, he would have killed her."

"Volpe wasn't a man. He was something far worse."

With the wounded stabilized, they made room in Grant's wagon for Holt, Ridge, and Aribeth to ride and sent him on his way. Proffitt went with them. Bethel and Leland stayed behind to finish taking down the camp. Leland himself did the honors of throwing Volpe's corpse on the fire and lighting the pyre. Bethel was ready to ride out, but Leland stayed behind, sitting and watching it burn. Even then, Leland couldn't shake the anger that continued to burn deep in his soul. He felt impotent.

He felt like a failure.

#

286

Summer

The settlers had set to work making Breton's Falls their home almost immediately. The land was divided into lots and parceled off to the settlers, who had purchased their lots through Mr. Behrens prior to leaving. Holt and his men were given their own lots as part of their pay, with the wounded receiving additional land as compensation.

Ridge refused to take any land. While the settlers set about building homes and planting crops and turning Breton's Falls into a real town, Ridge recuperated under the watchful eye of Dr. Grant.

Leland offered what assistance he could, hunting to bring in food and offering an extra pair of hands where needed. He knew he needed to return to Cadoa and his siblings, but he was waiting, hoping that Aribeth would snap out of her trance.

Yet as summer hit with full force, bringing with it unbearably hot temperatures and frequent storms, Leland knew that his time was up. He had lingered too long and his family needed him. Aribeth showed no signs of getting better.

On a beautiful morning that held the promise of a blistering hot day ahead, Leland loaded up his steed for the ride back to Cadoa. A thorough search of the area around Volpe's camp had revealed a series of underground caverns that Volpe's gang had been using to cross the raging river undetected. With that discovery, crossing into Aranwa had become easier, and Jamison Gregg was supervising the construction of a bridge that would make the journey even easier.

Leland finished packing and said goodbye to the friends he had made during his stay. There was just one thing left to do. With a heavy heart, he started for Aribeth's cabin.

As soon as the settlers had seen Aribeth's condition, they

had set about building her a fine home. They set it above the falls, where she could look out on the falls and the town she had founded. Aribeth now lived as a shut-in, interacting with people as infrequently as possible.

Leland knocked on her door timidly. Aribeth answered with a weak, "Yes?" Leland swallowed and entered.

Aribeth was just a shell of the bright-eyed girl who had sought him out months earlier. She was pale and emaciated. Her hair was a tangled mess and her clothes were dirty and worn. She sat on an unmade bed and stared at the door with dead eyes.

"I'm leaving, Aribeth," Leland said softly. "I didn't want to go until I talked to you." She looked through him. Leland turned to leave, then stopped. Instead, he went to her and sat beside her on the bed. She immediately scooted away from him.

Leland put his elbows on his knees and dropped his head. "I'm sorry. I told you that I would protect you and I failed. If I could do anything…." He looked over to find her staring at him. She seemed to focus. "Anything at all, I would. Tell me what you want me to do, Aribeth. You want me to kill myself?"

For a fleeting moment, her eyes seemed to ignite. "Leave."

The last, faint hope of forgiveness died with that single word. Leland stood. "Whatever you want. I am sorry, Aribeth. I will never forgive myself for what happened to you."

Yet Aribeth didn't hear him. Her momentary focus was gone as quickly as it had come, and she had drifted away again. Completely defeated, Leland left her there. He would never forgive himself, but there were other things to consider, other people who needed him. He started the long walk back down the hill, trying as best he could to focus on home and the people who were waiting for him to return.

#

Ridge was also ready to move on. His midsection was still

tender and his breathing wasn't quite as good as it once was, but he was healthy enough to move and there was a big country to explore. He bid goodbye to the Grants and prepared to set off.

As he crossed the town square, he spotted Leland forlornly mounting his steed. "Hey, Jax. Wait up," he called out. Breaking into a light jog, Ridge crossed over and caught Leland. "You're really leaving huh? Doc's been saying that you were going to."

Leland cast a furtive glance back at Aribeth's. "No reason to stay. I've got family waiting on me."

Ridge nodded knowingly. "Still a basket case, huh? That's too bad. She seemed like a great girl from the little bit of time I spent with her."

"She is a great girl," Leland snapped. "She'll get better. She just needs time." He started to ride away.

"You coming back?"

"Doubt it," Leland called over his shoulder. "Take care of her, Secova."

Ridge watched Leland ride away, glanced up at Aribeth's cabin, and scoffed. Time was the last thing she needed. She'd had time.

Ridge started for Aribeth's. On the way, he bumped into a petite young lady with white-blonde hair, who was crossing the street with a satchel in her hand. "Excuse me, ma'am," he said, then did a double take. "Burrows?"

Parrie shrugged. "In the flesh. Haven't seen you around much."

"Recovery. Dr. Grant's a stickler for bed rest. You're looking good. Took off the uniform, grew out your hair. I like the look."

A sadness passed across her face. "I have no use for an army that had no place for me." She held up the satchel she was carrying. "I'm doing Aribeth's job. I survey the lands, write out the deeds, things like that. I'm fairly good at it."

"Not much to it," Ridged said dismissively. "I'm sure it's much easier when you actually have the land to write the deed to and no Ministry to look over your shoulder. Forgery, that's where the fun is." Ridge stepped past her. "Have a good life, Burrows."

Ridge worked his way up the hill to Aribeth's cabin, but he didn't knock. He barged in. A startled Aribeth skittered into the corner, cowering at the sudden movement.

"What is this? What are you doing?"

Aribeth relaxed just a bit. "Go away."

"I'm going to. But first you're going to get your butt out of here and you're going to get back to your life. Come on." Ridge held his hand out to her, but she refused to take it.

"I have no life. I have nothing."

Ridge reached down, gripped her wrist, and yanked Aribeth up off the bed and onto her feet. Aribeth panicked, kicking and screaming for him to let go, but Ridge kept pulling, dragging her out of the cabin and into the day. Aribeth squealed when he pulled her out into the light, squinting from the brightness.

She continued writhing, but Ridge was too strong. He maneuvered her around in front of him, put both hands on the side of her head, and forced her to look down into the village that had sprung up while she'd lived as a hermit.

"Look at that," Ridge said between gritted teeth. "Look at it," he snapped again, more forcefully this time. "You did that. You led those people here, and you didn't lose a man. Not one person. You did that. Look at it."

Aribeth stopped struggling and stared down into the town. "It doesn't mean anything."

Ridge spun her around. "To them it does. It means everything to them. And it meant something to your father. They named this place Breton's Falls after him."

"They did?"

"Yes," Ridge growled. "They look at you as their leader. It's high time you started acting like it."

The anger flared up in Aribeth again. She quickly bowed up at Ridge. "Do you know what they did to me? Do you have any idea?"

"No. But I do know that every day you hide away in that cabin, you let him do it to you all over again. You keep letting him beat you, day after day. Talon Volpe is nothing but a pile of ash, but he's still torturing you because you let him."

Aribeth's anger wavered. She stepped back away from him and Ridge saw in that moment a fleeting change get through.

"You are stronger than this, Aribeth. You just need to fight. If you can jump into a freezing, raging river and swim across it just to save my miserable life, then you can beat this. Quit letting that miserable piece of trash dominate you."

"I'm not the same girl," she muttered.

"No, you're not," Ridge agreed. She looked up at him quizzically. "You're a woman now, not a girl. You've suffered. You've learned and you'll grow. Sometimes life kicks you in the teeth. Survivors kick back. I know you're a survivor." He let go of her and backed away. "You just need to realize it."

Ridge stepped past her and started down the hill.

"Where are you going?" Aribeth called out.

"Don't know," Ridge said with a smile. "Just gonna see what kind of trouble I can fall into. Survive, Aribeth. You deserve it."

Aribeth fought back the tears that threatened to fall. As her eyes tracked him, they swept across the little town. For the first time she saw what this land had become. She watched the people going about their daily lives. She watched the morning breeze ripple through the growing crops. She laughed as children played in the fields.

Finally, she quit fighting back the tears and let them fall. After a long, heavy crying jag, she wiped the tears off of her cheeks and looked skyward. "We made it, Father," she whispered. "We really made it."

EPILOGUE
FALL.

The summer crops were coming in and preparations were being made for winter. No one knew what to expect from an Aranwa winter, so they were preparing for everything.

Breton's Falls was a burgeoning town now. Settlers trickled in almost daily, each looking for a new start in this wild land. In Cadoa, land barons like Thom Behrens advertised Aranwa as a paradise; a land of freedom and opportunity. People came in droves.

They didn't all come to Breton's Falls, however. Other agents had begun starting their own communities. Civilization was spreading like wildfire through the Aranwa wilderness.

Aribeth found her strength and emerged to claim her role in the town, though she chose to keep Parrie on as her assistant. Her days were busy. She acted as mayor, judge, and arbitrator. Keeping the families happy and resolving petty disputes took up much of her time.

Alvarez Proffitt was named the town marshall. He took on Reeder and Bertrand as deputies, while Bethel found himself out, forced to carve out a new niche. He no longer dreamed of returning home. Aranwa was his home, for better or worse.

On a windy, partly cloudy day just before harvest, Aribeth was busy arbitrating a dispute between two farmers regarding water usage when an olive-skinned, tow-headed boy ran into her office, calling her name. "Ms. Fuller. Come quick. Come quick."

Aribeth looked from the men in front of her to the boy and back. "Sounds urgent." She stood and bent over her desk. "Maybe if you two would talk to each other instead of arguing, you could work this out yourself." She pushed away from the desk and addressed the boy. "What is it? Show me."

"This way," the boy said as he burst out of the door. Aribeth followed, walking quickly. The boy led her to the main street through town and pointed west.

Rising from the ground was a large dust cloud, kicked up by the approach of a large column of men on steedback. The sun glinted off highly polished metal. "I wonder what all of this is about."

She stood patiently, waiting until the head of the column reached her. These men were clearly military. They wore uniforms of green and gold with black trim, and rode in a tight precise formation. The head of the column was a middle-aged man, deeply tanned, with perfect golden blond hair and deep green eyes. He looked down from his magnificent steed at Aribeth and gave her a polite but dismissive smile.

"I wish to speak to the leader of this community."

Aribeth shielded her eyes from the sun as she looked up at him. "You're looking at her. Can I help you?"

"You are the leader?" The man asked incredulously.

"Yes," Aribeth answered defiantly. "Can I help you?" She was aware that a crowd was beginning to form behind her. She felt a nudge and found Parrie standing at her side.

The man dismounted his steed, squared up to her, and bowed deeply. "My name is General Jere Vinnings, Supreme Commander of the People's Army of Iridia. I am here to inform you, on behalf of His Regency, Chancellor T'agp De Santis, that you are trespassing on Iridian lands. Everyone here has thirty days to leave Aranwa or suffer the strictest penalties."

Parrie bristled at the threat. "What do you mean by strictest penalties?"

General Vinnings turned ever so slightly to face her. "I mean, strictest penalties. Use your imagination."

Aribeth stepped in front of him. "I don't have to use my imagination. And you can tell Chanchellor Whatever His Name Is that we have no intention of leaving. We travelled to this land when there was nothing. We've suffered and struggled and sacrificed too much to leave it all behind, simply because a bunch of buffoons in fancy uniforms comes riding into town."

Vinnings appraised Aribeth for a moment before the slightest hint of a smile touched the corner of his lips. "Interesting. Perhaps you would like to deliver that message personally?"

Aribeth met his stare without backing down. "I would be pleased to do so."

Aribeth and Vinnings continued to hold each other's gaze. "Colonel Rayburn," Vinnings snapped without breaking eye contact with Aribeth. "Your battalion is to remain here. Begin constructing works. Iridian law is to be obeyed at all times. Ignorance is no defense."

"Sir," called Colonel Rayburn, and promptly a division of troops left formation and moved into town.

"Madame, I will give you ten minutes to make your arrangements, and then I will see you back to the capital and His Regency."

"Fine," Aribeth whispered. She finally broke the stare down, turning to Parrie. "Find Mr. Gregg. Tell him that he is in charge until I get back."

"Why him? I can take your place."

"Because," Aribeth started, her patience strained. "Mr.

Gregg is level-headed and diplomatic. You are implusive and quick tempered. I need someone who will keep the peace." Aribeth started to walk away, but stopped and turned back to her assistant. "And Parrie, nothing changes until I return and say otherwise. Got it?"

Parrie nodded. Aribeth repeated herself. "Nothing changes until I return." She glared at Vinnings, who grinned back at her.

"Be careful," said Parrie.

"I will," Aribeth assured. "It's going to take more than this to scare me."

Behind them, Vinnings laughed. "You have nothing to fear, I assure you. His Regency will be a most gracious host. I'm sure he'll find your spirit...entertaining."

Aribeth spun to face Vinnings with fire in her eyes. "I'm no one's entertainment, sir. I assure you, if you think that you're taking this land without a fight, you've got another think coming."

"Oh, please, madame," Vinnings said. "There's no need for threats. Let's go discuss the matter with His Regency. He is, above all things, a man of great wisdom and generosity. You should not fear losing your precious lands." He leaned in close until their noses were almost touching. "Because, dear, this land was never yours to lose."

Donny Hunt is a writer, daydreamer, sports nut, music lover and proud Texan who masquerades as a customer service professional in his spare time. He lives in Amarillo with his family and four dogs. The Quest for Aranwa is his second novel.

www.ingramcontent.com/pod-product-compliance
Lightning Source LLC
Chambersburg PA
CBHW020257200626
46816CB00001BA/340